Conclusive All-Inclusive Confusion

ABSOLUTELY AMAZING eBOOKS

Habent Sua Fata Libelli

ABSOLUTELY AMAZING eBOOKS

Manhanset House
Shelter Island Hts., New York 11965-0342

bricktower@aol.com • tech@absolutelyamazingebooks.com
• absolutelyamazingebooks.com

All rights reserved under the International and Pan-American Copyright Conventions. No part of this publication may be reproduced, stored in a retrieval system, or transmitted in any form or by any means, electronic, or otherwise, without the prior written permission of the copyright holder.
The Absolutely Amazing eBooks colophon is a trademark of
J. T. Colby & Company, Inc.

Library of Congress Cataloging-in-Publication Data
Beckwith, David
Conclusive, All-Inclusive Confusion
p. cm.

1. FICTION / Mystery & Detective / Cozy / General. 2. FICTION / Mystery & Detective / Amateur Sleuth.
3. FICTION / Mystery & Detective / International Crime & Mystery.
Fiction, I. Title.
ISBN: 978-1-955036-78-8, Trade Paper

Copyright © 2024 by David Beckwith
Electronic compilation/ paperback edition
Copyright © 2024 by Absolutely Amazing eBooks

November 2024

Conclusive All-Inclusive Confusion

DAVID BECKWITH

ABSOLUTELY AMAZING eBOOKS

Will and Betsy Black Books
by David and Nancy Beckwith

A Hurricane Conpiracy (Book 1)
A Calculated Conspiracy (Book 2)
A Narcotic Conspiracy (Book 3)
A Cosmetic Conspiracy (Book 4)
A Jamaican Conspiracy (Book 5)
A Ransom Conspiracy (Book 6)
A Cover-Up Conspiracy (Book 7)
A Demonic Conspiracy (Book 8)
A Treasure Conspiracy (Book 9)
A Cruising Conspiracy (Book 10)
A Nautical Conspiracy (Book 11)

Available at fine booksellers

AbsolutelyAmazingEbooks.com

Jamaican Sine Paiting

CHAPTER 1

Beauregard Montgomery "Monte" Connors would've been more excited if he hadn't been dragging. He had been up since three to catch the 7:36 flight from Detroit to Miami. He was nervous anyway since he was a neophyte traveler, and the events of the morning thus far had not been totally reassuring. He silently thanked the good Lord that he had his family with him and didn't have to face this unknown alone. After all, Detroit Metropolitan Airport was the busiest airport in Michigan with over 1,100 flights a day that went to four continents.

He had been gotten up at three to make sure he didn't oversleep and miss the airport shuttle bus. His daughter, Eve, had assured him that riding the shuttle would be no big deal, and normally it wouldn't have been. He had bundled up, and it had been a good thing that he had, since the bus's heater wasn't working properly. But now he somewhat regretted having that bulky jacket and wool fedora to haul around on the plane and then having to keep up with in the Atlanta airport as they waited for their connecting flight to Miami. He'd been glad they changed planes in Atlanta since a grandmother and her two disruptive grandchildren had sat behind him on the packed Boeing 787. The whole way, all he heard was her repeatedly telling them to stop this and to stop that as they bumped the back of his seat and did other irritating things. He was a naturally nonconfrontational person who didn't want to make a scene if it was at all possible. He just gritted his teeth and told himself that it was only for a couple of hours. He reminded himself that maybe irritations like this were the reason he had seldom travelled out of Highland Park, but he knew the real reason was that until now he couldn't afford to do so.

Monte would celebrate his fiftieth birthday on this trip. This milestone was one of the reasons he had decided to go. He had spent his entire life in Highland Park. He was not by nature an adventurous person. He was a confirmed bachelor and only child who had always lived at home taking care of his divorced mother, Nevaeh, until the Lord had taken her to heaven. He had never even had a girlfriend. After Nevaeh's death, he continued to live there in the house where he was born and raised despite the radically worsening neighborhood. After all, the house had been Monte's only asset and would bring very little if he sold it. It was probably not worth more than the five or ten thousand dollars other houses around him had sold for.

Monte was one of those nondescript people who you would never remember if you met him on the street. Each day for seemingly forever, he had waited for the same fried egg and bacon sandwich to be called out by the same cashier at the same deli near the church, but she still had to ask his name every day to put on his ticket. He had no qualities that made him special other than if you noticed that he walked in recent years with a tad of a clunky, heavy gait, looking mildly uncomfortable, since both his usual tucked-in, permanent-press, white shirt and his well-worn but dark, high-rise, single-pleated worsted-wool pants had become a bit tighter, making his stomach protrude slightly under his belt. He still wore the same model of black Bostonian wingtips that his father did. After all, if it ain't broke, why fix it.

Monte's was a gait that didn't exude confidence, making people believe that he really believed in himself. He rarely looked people square in the eye or smiled. It was like he wasn't present but instead was caught up in his own head.

Monte was average height and his only defining feature was the same thin glasses he'd worn since high school. The rest of his wholly colorless, pasty face was like droopy Play-Doh and didn't play memorably to a camera.

His same-length brown hair was perfectly round on top. Of course, it was the same hairstyle he'd had in high school. Monte took special pains to maintain his softly doughy appearance every morning, making sure his hair was neat and clean and that his face was eternally clean-shaven as well. He was forgettable — bland, plain bread on a platter of French toast.

Conclusive, All-Inclusive Confusion

So, the risk averse, conservative Monte had never ventured far from home but continued to work for the Saint Benedict Catholic Church on Church Street, the church he was raised in, as their sometimes fill-in organist and piano player. He also helped in the church's food kitchen and thrift shop. It wasn't exciting, but it was a comfortable, familiar place.

Highland Park was once a vibrant community with a rich history. It is here that Henry Ford began the mass production of automobiles on a moving assembly line. Mass production expanded from here and soon affected all phases of American industry as it set the pattern for twentieth century living. This was no longer the case in the twenty-first century, however. This three-square-mile city nestled in the heart of Detroit had evolved into one of the most economically depressed places in the United States as it faced a list of long and dire difficulties. It had shrunk from a peak population of over fifty thousand residents to one of barely ten thousand. Ford departed as did Chrysler afterwards. Even Highland Park's high school shut down, and the city found itself having the distinction of being the municipality that had been placed under emergency financial management for longest period of time in Michigan history. Highland Park residents endured inconveniences like water shutoffs and even had 1,400 residential streetlights repossessed and ripped out of the ground because the city of Highland Park couldn't pay their electric bills.

Crime, blight, and poverty were all entangled in this mess, both cause and consequence of a gutted school system and failing tax base and infrastructure. With the absence of streetlights and Highland Park's inability to provide anything beyond the most basic services, crime and gangs flourished. Despite this, the solitary Monte lived a quiet, ordered life with his main priority being avoiding trouble.

But Monte had not been totally alone after Neveah's death. In a move that was daring for him, he convinced Saint Benedict's priest to persuade authorities to allow him to adopt three girls, whose Highland Park single, drug addicted, homeless mothers had died, in lieu of having the girls thrown into the overburdened state welfare system. They were various ages when he adopted them. He had then raised them and helped them overcome the scars resulting from their former lives. Viv was now a customer service agent at the Lake Trust Credit Union. Eve worked at Highland Park's Powerhouse Gym. Viv and Eve had recently married;

Nan was a still-single librarian who lived with Monte at home. She also taught classes in creative writing.

Now the six of them were all on their way to Miami. The ripple effect of an act of kindness had led to Monte and his new family being on this trip. It began when Monte gave an overcoat that had been donated to the church thrift shop to a Highland Park wino amputee and Viet Nam veteran to keep him from freezing to death. A few weeks later, the wino showed back up at the soup kitchen with a lottery ticket in his hand. He gave it to Monte as a thank you. The lottery ticket turned out to be a winner, and Monte was suddenly worth a hundred million dollars. Half of the proceeds went for taxes, but he was still a very wealthy man when all was said and done. Monte just knew that this was Nevaeh's manna sent from heaven. After all, she had always looked out for him and told him that if he did good for others, it would come back to him in unexpected ways. Soon after, he visited the cemetery to thank her and took some flowers to honor her memory.

Monte was overwhelmed by his windfall and didn't know where to turn. Fortunately for him, one of the priests told him that he was a lucky man. He had a financial planner available to him right there as part of Saint Benedict's congregation as well as a daughter who was in the financial services industry. He suggested to Monte that he bring these two resources together. This made sense to Monte.

Once again all mighty God has provided the resources that I need.

✍

Banks Bridges operated a marginal, one-man, independent investment firm in Highland Park. Most of his business was selling low-minimum mutual fund periodic payment plans. The broker-dealer that he was affiliated with did have a cash management account called the Golden Rewards Cash Management Service that came with checks and a debit card, but Banks' clients rarely had enough money to meet its minimums.

At the priest's suggestion, Monte made an appointment for Viv to meet Banks. He didn't accompany her since he trusted her and thought he wouldn't understand what they were talking about anyway.

Conclusive, All-Inclusive Confusion

Banks salivated at the thought of meeting with Viv. Word had gotten out around the church about Monte's good fortune. Rumors ranged from a few million to many millions. Either way, this would be a windfall for him if he could land the account. Even if it was only one million, it would become his largest account.

Banks and Viv met. Banks insisted that he take Viv to lunch, and when she confided in him the amount of money that her dad had won, he took her out to dinner as well. An intense courtship commenced, complete with candy and flowers. The wallflower Viv was thrilled that a handsome, virile young man was so taken with her. Banks became relentless in his pursuit of Viv and his efforts to close the deal. After gaining Viv's trust, he worked on her to convince her that his firm offered customized services and personal attention superior to any conventional banking institution.

"My dear Viv, banking institutions are hard, cold entities. They are marketing organizations like any other business. You shop at Glory Supermarket, don't you? How many brands of bottled salad dressing do they carry?"

"I don't really know. Lots, I guess."

"That's right, lots. Does anyone in there advise you about which brand might be not only be superior but would be a bargain as well? Do they tell you which brands taste horrible and might ruin your salad?"

"Uh. ... No."

"That's right. And if left on your own, you're likely to choose poorly. Why? Because you're not an expert on salad dressings. Do you know what that store really cares about? I'll tell you. All they care about is that you spend your money and leave the store with a bottle of salad dressing in your shopping cart ... and that you don't sue them later because what they sold you was garbage."

"I guess maybe you're right."

"There's no maybe to it. You know I'm right. But what if while you were in that store, an expert on salad dressings chose the store's best product for you? You'd go home with the good stuff. Well, I'm that person. Financial institutions offer a wide array of products. Some are good; some are not. But do you know the difference? I do. I'm that guy who will stand in front of the shelf and choose the correct 'salad dressing' for you. Why? Because I'm a highly trained fiduciary who has your best interests at heart and who will cause your father to prosper rather than fail and be disappointed like too many other people. ... Does this make sense to you? I'm the guy on your side, not the side of the big, cold corporation."

What Banks said made sense. Viv was sold. Not only had Banks sold his services, but he sold himself as well ... and became Viv's husband.

My scraping by days are over. With a big fish like this, I don't need the rest of the minnows anymore.

Banks' actual birth name was Khoury Haddad, but he had changed it to Banks Nathanial Bridges. Banks N. Bridges had a much better ring to it, considering his profession and since he now called himself a financial planner. After all, it sounded so American. He was careful not to include the word "certified" in his title since he had only taken one CFP exam. He had flunked it twice before dropping out of the program all together. With Viv's help, he easily convinced Monte to trust him with his windfall. After Banks and Viv were married, Banks suspended his mutual fund business, gave away his accounts, and became Monte's excusive investment advisor.

Banks wasn't the only person who saw opportunity due to Monte. One of the few Golden Rewards Cash Management accounts he had on the books belonged to Jax Magnus, an insurance agent in the parish. Jax used it for his agency's checking account and also as an escrow account to deposit his clients' insurance premiums into.

Jax, an independent insurance agent, was also a member of the Saint Benedict parish. Jax was a marginal agent who was scraping by selling debit life insurance to the low income residents of Highland Park. He would collect the premiums on either a weekly, bi-weekly, or monthly basis depending on the frequency that coincided with when the policy holders had the money to pay. He lived in constant fear of being cut because of his low production. When Jax heard about Monte's good fortune, he hoped this might lead to an opportunity to make some real money for a change instead of just nickels and dimes. He wasn't used to elephant hunting but now went all out to land this one since maybe God had finally put a bonified elephant within his reach.

It all hinged on whether Jax could convince Monte that he had a future tax problem, and that Jax had the solution. Despite not knowing how much Monte had won or being a tax expert, Jax guesstimated Monte's

Conclusive, All-Inclusive Confusion

estimated estate tax liability based on the rumored amount of Monte's winnings. Jax made sure he padded the number in his favor to maximize his commission.

I'll even tell him that to arrive at a figure I assumed that the assets failed to grow. This will show him how conservative I am.

Jax still beamed at the final number he was now looking at.

Yes! That looks salable — and profitable for me — very profitable.

A fifteen million dollar paid up single premium life policy. That was the answer. A two million dollar investment would buy Monte a policy that would cover this estimated tax liability. And best of all, Jax would get paid fifty percent of Monte's expenditure as a commission.

Oh, how sweet it's gonna be!

But after thinking about it overnight, Jax got an even better idea. Why not quote Monte three million? Monte would still think he was getting a bargain. He'd be spending three million to get fifteen million. And Monte would never know he was being overcharged. He'd write the three million dollar check to Jax's agency, and Jax would send two million on to the insurance company and pocket the difference.

Yessiree Bob, together with the million dollar commission plus another million from the overcharge, I'll be on easy street. And a member of the company's million dollar roundtable instead of living in constant fear of having the rug pulled out from under me because of my low production numbers. Then I can hold my head up at conferences and be a big dog for a change.

Now, all Jax had to do was get to Monte before some other shark did.

Monte's daughter, Eve! She's my answer.

He had met Eve before at Saint Benedict's but hadn't paid her much mind. This needed to change. … And was about to. … He knew Eve worked for the Powerhouse Gym. He had seen her there when he went to collect premiums for some debit policies he had sold to some of its other personal trainers.

I'm overdue for some self-improvement. I think I'll join the Powerhouse Gym.

Jax hired Eve to set up a workout program for him. He invited her to lunch. He took her to mass at Saint Benedict's. This led to a dinner and a movie date. He began to pick her up at Monte's several times a week, making sure that he bonded with Monte as well as Eve. Before long he proposed, and Eve became Mrs. Jax Magnus.

Once this happened, selling Monte on single premium life became a forgone conclusion, and Jax graduated from being a debit policy peddler to being a real insurance professional with a substantial balance for a change is his Golden Rewards account. This sudden phenomenon did not go unnoticed by Banks.

The family convinced Monte that he deserved a vacation. He agreed to the trip since he had multiple reasons to celebrate since within six months of Monte receiving his windfall, both Viv and Eve had met nice young men.

Yes, once again, God had worked his magic in a mysterious but wondrous fashion since Banks and Jax, their suitors, had seemed to come out of nowhere to court and marry them.

Monte prayed for guidance.

The good Lord has smiled on my family once again. Thank you God and Jesus. I guess it's true. Sometimes the best things happen unexpectedly and come from the most unexpected places and begin with 'all of a sudden.' If it's your will for us to take a vacation together as well, I shouldn't question your divine judgement. You haven't steered us wrong yet.

After all, Monte rationalized that a trip would have a dual purpose. It would be a delayed honeymoon trip of sorts for two of his daughters as well as a vacation for him. Like him, none of the girls had ever been out of the state of Michigan. Besides that, none of them had ever flown.

What excitement! They voted unanimously on a trip to the tropics and after some research decided to visit the Seascape All-Inclusive Resort in romantic Runaway Bay, Jamaica.

Now they were enroute for the adventure of a lifetime.

There had been a little excitement at the Detroit airport, but it'd been overcome. Nan had worn a cute, blue-flowered pullover with sequins outlining the flowers. None of them knew that the sequins would trick the X-ray machine into thinking she was wearing a bomb. After going through the machine, several TSA agents had come running over and asked her for permission to pat down the area with the offending decoration. She had experienced pat-downs before from the Highland

Conclusive, All-Inclusive Confusion

Park police, but never one this extensive. The woman grabbed the front of Nan's blouse and firmly felt it in and around her breasts. Nan stood there speechless. Then the woman let go without so much as howdy-do. Shaken, Nan retrieved her shoes and belongings from the conveyor belt and shakily made her way over to a bench to put her shoes back on.

They changed planes in Atlanta with no incidents. The plane they reboarded was thinner than most, with two seats, the aisle, and then two more seats. It seemed as long as their original plane, but it was long and skinny. Monte heard the flight attendant tell a man that it was originally designed to be a commuter plane.

When they arrived at Miami International, Monte felt culture shock. Miami seemed to be a mosaic of cultures and diversities. It was an unfamiliar climate, with people speaking unfamiliar languages, eating unfamiliar foods, and wearing tropical clothing and footwear. He felt even more out of place in his wool fedora, flannel shirt, dark long pants, and clunky black shoes, lugging a heavy jacket. He saw Hispanics, Jews, Haitians, and people from seemingly every island in the Caribbean. He wasn't prone to be prejudiced, but he was a taken aback by the throng of people of all sorts. The airport seemed to be overflowing with them all, creating an almost smoggy atmosphere. He felt like he needed to find a COVD mask and put it on.

The long walk to their gate was an uncomfortable experience with people bumping and shoving them along the way. There were no seats available at the gate, so they resorted to plopping down on the floor like some other people to wait for their plane to Montego Bay to board and take off. The hour-long wait seemed interminable. Relief would wash over them when they finally boarded.

As they sat on the floor waiting for their plane to Montego Bay, Monte's two sons-in-law were comparing notes. Jax Magnus had married Eve, while Banks Bridges was Viv's recent spouse. When four seats were vacated, Monte and the girls quickly snapped them up, leaving only Jax and Banks on the floor.

"This damned floor is killing my back," Jax complained. "And who knows how many germs it has."

"Don't complain," Banks replied. "When we get to Seascape, we'll be living the life of Riley. You'll be able to get whatever you want on an unlimited basis whenever you want it."

"I can't believe we're going to be in a five-star resort in Jamaica," Jax said. "This will be the first time I've ever been outside the country. Have you ever been abroad?"

"Nope," replied Banks, "but this should be the first of a lot of trips to come now that Daddy-in-law Warbucks's motherlode has come in."

"Do you know how much he got?"

"Guess."

"I dunno. Five mill."

Banks smiled and turned his palms upward and wiggled his fingers at the ceiling. Then he motioned upwards with his thumbs."

"Ten?"

Banks smiled again.

"Twenty?"

"You're getting warmer."

"Surely not thirty."

"You still ain't close, but you're closer."

"You're shittin' me!"

"Since I'm his investment advisor and a fiduciary, I can't give you a number, but let me say this. If we play *our* cards right, none of us are gonna miss any meals ... ever again."

Clayton "Potsy" Potter was sitting close enough to overhear Jax's and Bank's exchange. His ears perked up, and a grin spread across his face.

Hark! A mark! Do I hear a mark?

He began to hum to himself the chorus to a Steve Miller song he had always liked.

> *Go on, take the money and run.*
> *Go on, take the money and run.*
> *Go on, take the money and run.*

Potter was a career flimflam artist. ... A first-class bunko man, heading to Jamaica for a little r-and-r and to get his head back on straight. His last scam had backfired on him and ended up costing him money, making him wonder if he was losing his touch. Now he knew where he was going to spend the week — Seascape Luxury Resort in Runaway Bay, Jamaica. The infinite hour-long wait suddenly seemed finite, and he couldn't wait to board the plane.

Conclusive, All-Inclusive Confusion

As if the airline had read his mind, the announcement came over the PA that boarding would begin. He heard Jax grumble, "About damned time, my back couldn't take much more of this floor."

After everyone boarded and got settled into their seats, the attractive head flight attendant gave her welcoming speech. She had a pleasant island lilt.

"Hello and welcome to American Airlines flight AA1502 to Sangster International Airport. For my fellow countrymen I say, 'Gud day. Wah gwaan? Mi, mi deh yah. **(Good morning. How are you all? Me, I'm going well.)**' If you're going to Montego Bay, you're in the right place. If you're not going to Montego Bay, you're about to have a really long day."

This brought a giggle from some of the passengers. Potsy thought to himself, *If the amount of that honeybun that I just heard about in the gate is even close to accurate, I'm definitely in the right place, and it's only going to get righter over the next few days. And if I'm right, this is a family tree with an enormous crop of nuts, and they're about to meet one squirrel who likes to get his share.*

The flight attendant continued.

"We'd like to now tell you about some important safety features of this aircraft. The most important safety feature we have aboard is .... The flight attendants. Please look at one now. May I say with all modesty that American Airlines has some of best flight attendants in the airline industry. Unfortunately, none of them are on this flight."

Some zoned out veteran travelers zoned back in. A few chuckled. Monte looked at Nan uncertainly. She just smiled.

"There may be fifty ways to leave your lover, but there are only four ways out of this plane."

The flight attendant went on to tell where all the exits were, told people to look around, identify the one closest to them, and count how many rows they were away from it in case the lights went out.

"If you are traveling with a small child and if we must use oxygen masks, … that's that margarine cup that'll descend from the ceiling … do us all a favor. Stop screaming and then put yours on first. After that, you can decide which child is your favorite and help him or her mask-up next.

"Remember, your seat cushions are designed to be used for flotation. In the event of an emergency water landing, please paddle to shore and keep them with our compliments."

This brought on a few sniggers. The flight attendant continued her well-rehearsed speech.

"In the seat pocket in front of you is a safety feature pamphlet. It makes a very good fan and one I use when I am having my private summer. It also has pretty pictures. You have my permission to play with it now. One last thing. Your seat belt. It's a pulley thing, not a pushy thing like in your car because you are ... on an airplane."

After takeoff, the flight attendant came back on.

"Just to remind you, this is a nonsmoking flight. ... For both cigarettes or anything else that will take you higher than our planned cruising altitude ... And that includes in the lavatory. If we see smoke coming from one of the lavatories, we will assume you're on fire and put you out. This is a free service we provide.

"We do have two smoking sections, one outside each wing exit. Oh, and I'm about to forget, we do have a movie. Let's see, ... hold on, until I can check and see what it is. Here we go. ... Today's move is 'Gone with the Wind.'

"Now, have an irie flight."

> # Please Pay Your Parking Fee Before Existing

CHAPTER 2

"Ladies and gentlemen. We have arrived at Sangster International Airport. For those of you who have visited us before, 'Welcome home.' For you who are first time visitors, I say, 'One love. May your stay with us be an irie one.

"Local time is two thirty-five. The temperature is thirty-one degrees Celsius or eighty-eight degrees Fahrenheit. As you may have noticed, there are some broken clouds in the sky today. We will try to have them fixed. We ask that you please remain seated as Captain Kangaroo bounces us to the terminal. Thank you for flying American Airlines. We have enjoyed giving you the business as much as we enjoyed taking you for a ride."

This brought a smile to some faces. To other people, it just went over their heads.

"This captain will soon announce when you will be free to depart. As you exit the plane, make sure you gather up all your belongings. Anything left behind will be evenly distributed among the flight attendants. Please do not leave any children or spouses. If you insist on leaving something behind, please make sure it's something we'd like to have. And remember the last one off the plane must clean it.

"We'd like to thank you folks for flying with us today. And the next time you get the insane urge to go rocketing through the skies in a pressurized metal tube, we hope you'll think of us at American Airlines. And remember, no one loves you, or your money, more than we at American Airlines do."

Sangster did not have air bridges. Passengers boarded and deplaned with a movable stairway and then walked across the tarmac into the terminal.

To the overdressed Jax, the warm felt like a blast furnace.

"Damn, it's hot here. I'm roasting. Do you think it'll be this hot the whole time we're here?"

Eve looked at him and said, "Am I going to have to listen to you bitch the whole time we're in Jamaica?"

"Hot gives me a rash."

"Bro, you're giving me one," Banks said under his breath.

His wife, Viv, gave him a reproachful, annoyed look that said, *Leave it alone. Not your fight. Let's not get this week started on the wrong foot before we even get out of the airport.*

Potsy deplaned and made sure he kept Monte and his family in sight as the robotically obedient passengers entered the terminal and filed ant-like down the bridges and corridors to get to immigration and then on to the baggage carousel. He wasn't sure just what his plans were. He'd just see what opportunities arose and improvise. He might have to wait until they got to Seascape before an idea came. He was a pro. He knew an idea would emerge. It always did. He was confident that the mark would tell him what to do next. He just had to be observant enough to recognize the clues.

To the relief of Monte and his family, the flight had been a smooth one and had gone better than they had anticipated. This changed when they entered the baggage claim area.

When the passengers entered the baggage claim area, their character morphed from Dr. Jekyll into Mr. Hyde as they tried to identify which carousel number had been assigned to their flight. Grown adults rushed the conveyer even though it was not spinning yet. Some small children stuck their fingers into the belt's flaps as their oblivious parents craned their necks in the opposite direction. Irritable hordes began to jostle for space around the not-so-merry-go-round, wedging their baggage trolleys into a prime place. They elbowed other people out of the way and cantilevered their bodies over the machinery, thoroughly blocking the view of others.

You'd think that the carousel had been about to deliver the King Tut exhibit or the Hope Diamond. And indeed, while one's luggage was often

Conclusive, All-Inclusive Confusion

more precious than valuable, and there was an urgency that comes with this penultimate hurdle. Everyone still had Customs to navigate before they would be allowed to leave the airport and enter Jamaica. They were seemingly oblivious to the fact that causing a fracas around the baggage carousel would never accelerate the delivery of their luggage and that the order their bags arrived would always be beyond their control.

Monte and his family couldn't help but get caught up in the confusion. They piled their carry-ons and heavy Detroit jackets onto a chair. Their items were of no great value. Monte had brought a small black weekender type of duffel bag with a nametag on it. It was no bigger than a laundry bag, which is what he planned to use it for when they got to Seascape. Since he had read that airlines sometimes lose luggage, he had packed a few essentials — an extra pair of underwear and socks, some toiletry items, some sneakers, and a couple of paperback books.

When Potsy saw all the Connors family's carry-ons stacked on the chair, he suddenly had his idea. He had not checked any baggage, so there was no reason to hang around any longer than he had to. If and when he got the chance in all this confusion, he'd snatch Monte's bag and take off for Customs. After all, he was an accomplished pickpocket. By the time, the Connors's luggage came down the carousel, he'd be long gone. He'd remove the nametag before he went through Customs and put it back on afterwards. He'd take a different customer service shuttle bus to the resort. Then when they all got to Seascape, he'd use returning the bag the next day as an excuse to introduce himself to Monte.

Luck was with Potsy. The snatch went off without a hitch. When Monte later missed his bag, he didn't make a big ruckus about it since there was nothing that he could do to probably recover it now that it was gone, and there was nothing especially valuable in it anyway. Live and learn. He was just glad there was nothing a great value in it.

THE BUILDING IS CLODES TO THE PUBLIC TO FURTHER NOTICES

CHAPTER 3

"Is that all of our luggage?" Monte asked.

"Yep," Banks said. "Let's get out of here. The sign says Customs is this way. Don't forget your coat."

"Sure as the dickens don't need that down here. I wish I hadn't brought it. Tired of lugging it around."

"Yes," Jax complained. "I don't think I've ever been so hot in my life as I was walking into the airport. I'd hate to have to live in this heat all year."

"Whine! Whine! Whine! My husband the whiner," Eve commented to Viv. "At home he whines about it being too cold."

Viv said nothing but gave her husband, Banks, a sideways look. He grinned knowingly as they made eye contact.

"Did one of you guys pick up my duffel?"

"Not me," they all said in unison.

"Well, it seems to be gone. It was right here under my coat."

They looked around to see if another passenger had picked it up by accident and saw nothing. Potsy was long gone.

"Did you have anything valuable in it, dad?" Nan asked.

"Not really. Just some personal items like underwear in case our luggage got lost."

"Then don't worry about it. Let's go through customs and get out of here. It's already the middle of the afternoon. Wow! Look at that line."

Conclusive, All-Inclusive Confusion

Customs went smoothly. The officer asked the usual questions. Why are you here? How long do you plan to stay? Where will you be staying while you're visiting our country? Do you have anything to declare?

When they cleared Customs, they saw a young man wearing a polo shirt with Seascape Luxury Resort embroidered on it. He was also wearing a Seascape baseball cap, his orderly dreadlocks protruding from under it.

"Sir," Banks asked. "Can you show us where the Seascape courtesy van is?"

"Yah, mon. I'll not only show you where it is, but I'll drive you as well. My name is Nakomis. Are you the Connors family? Welcome to Jamaica."

He loaded all of their luggage into the back of the silver Nissan twelve-seater commuter van. Seascape Resorts was printed in neat lettering on the door. Banks asked if he could ride shotgun, and Nakomis instantly agreed. Banks immediately noticed that the steering wheel was on the right-hand side.

When everyone was loaded, Nakomis said, "Everyone in? Yu good? Everything criss? Then, howdeedo. Welcome to Jamaica and Seascape Luxury Resorts. And if you were a local, you might respond, 'Very well, thank you or maybe everyting irie. Wah gwaan? Waa pree today?' Do you know what I just said?"

"No, mon," Nan said in a giggly voice. She then waited for everyone's approval for her two-word patois response.

"Very gud," Nakomis said as he tooted his horn at another commuter van. "Irie is another word for good or fine. The response wah gwaan asked the question 'what's going on,' and waa pree today was asking the speaker if he had any plans for the day."

"If you say so," Jax said in a somewhat pouty voice, and everyone laughed.

Then he added, "How far away are we from the hotel?"

"Luxury Resort not hotel. About forty-five minutes. But don't worry. Soon come."

"Can you turn the air conditioning up?"

"Why don't we leave the windows down so I can smell the salt air?" Monte suggested.

"Whatever," Jax said, "You're paying for the trip, but if my sinuses start acting up, it's your fault."

"I'll assume that risk."

They soon realized that driving in Jamaica was not for either the faint of heart or uninitiated driver. Just as they were beginning to learn that there was a wide overall cultural gap between the Third Word and the U.S., they began to appreciate that the art of driving was different as well. They soon recognized that the Jamaican drivers were both reckless and fearless. And the most reckless of all seemed to be the taxi drivers. Where was that laid back island attitude they had read so much about? Everyone seemed impatient and in a hurry. Monte didn't think he had ever, even in Detroit, seen cars driven at those speeds on such appalling roads. It seemed that Nakomis was blowing his horn constantly, and that close calls and near-death experiences occurred every five minutes. It was also disconcerting to see that even though Jamaicans drive on the left, many cars also had their steering wheel on the left as well since most had been imported from the U.S. Monte tried to imagine what it would be like to pass a car driving on the right when your own steering wheel was on the wrong side of the car.

They came out of a turnaround, and Nakomis pulled up behind another car and gave his horn a short toot. The driver slowed down and despite the fact that they were on a two-lane road, Nakomis pulled up beside him.

"Mawnin', Apple J," Nakomis called out through his open window.

"Mawnin' to yu too, Ruddy Puss. Yu gud?" Apple J called back.

"Ya, mon. Everyting criss."

"Arriving guests?"

"We love your country so far," Banks called out before Nakomis could answer. "This is the first time we've ever left the U.S."

"Well, welcome to Jamaica. Hope yu hab a irie visit."

Nakomis finished passing Apple J, who tooted again as they pulled away.

"Why did he call you Ruddy Puss?" Banks asked.

"Because that's mi street name. Everyone here has a pet name."

"Sounds like the same kind of stupid shit *those* people come up with in Detroit … You know who I mean, … the brothers, … but I guess chocolate jungle dumb-bunnies are chocolate jungle dumb-bunnies no matter where they live. … Exactly what you'd expect," Jax said in a low voice to his wife. "Anybody want a gummy bear?"

Conclusive, All-Inclusive Confusion

Nakomis overheard him and gave him a dirty look in the rearview mirror but said nothing. Everyone else in the car just looked embarrassed. Nakomis took a good look at Jax in his rearview mirror so he could make sure he remembered what this white jerk looked like.

To himself he thought, *I know you're a guest, you racist fatso, so I can't say anything. But I won't forget, and you better not give me a chance to pay you back.*

"Well, I guess I'll just have to adopt Banker Man for my street name," Banks said to change the subject. "And my brother-in-law back there — we'll just call him Tubby."

Jax frowned and gave Banks a three-finger salute.

"And my father-in-law back there. Just call him Moneybags. Afterall, he's paying for this trip with a once in a lifetime windfall he recently got."

Monte looked at Banks sternly like you need to learn when to keep your mouth shut. Nakomis said nothing but just made a mental note that he had just learned some useful information that would soon put a dollar or two in his pocket.

They headed out on Highway A1 towards Ocho Rios, home of the famous Dunn's River Falls. Since A1 was the main artery on the north coast, it was kept in much better condition than many of the side roads they passed. They saw resort after resort on both sides of the road sitting on large acreages. Many had their own private beaches. A1 would take them through three parishes before they would arrive at Runaway Bay. They skirted Falmouth, one of the best-preserved Georgian towns in the Caribbean, as well as Discovery Bay, where it is believed that Columbus first set foot in Jamaica, as they headed for Seascape in Runaway Bay. It had been named for the fleeing slaves who ran away from the sugar plantations as they escaped to Cuba.

There always seemed to be a car behind them attempting to get by. And every time they encountered a slow driver, a string of cars almost immediately lined up behind the guilty one and attempted to overtake him. And inevitably they would attempt to pass where it was either illegal or extremely dangerous, as on a blind curve. Speed limits seemed to mean nothing. A driver simply travelled at whatever speed he wished, obliviously putting the lives of everyone on the road at risk. It appeared that the primary rule they lived by was the adage that time is money.

And then there was the issue of tailgating. The apparent rule of the road was that it was mandatory for every driver to tailgate every other driver he came up behind. Monte wondered if Jamaican drivers studied the driving styles of Indy car racers. Like those drivers, maybe they were trying to take advantage of the draft of the car ahead of them to try to save gas.

Courtesy was not something Jamaican drivers possessed in heavy traffic. It was dog-eat-dog every time. Cars would inch along whenever traffic was heavy. Sometimes traffic came to a complete standstill. Whoever could maneuver their car between two others in the adjoining lane became the winner. It was often a hard-earned win since neither driver was willing to lose. Most of the time nothing was said between the two jockeying drivers unless there was a fender bender. If this occurred, both drivers would get out, survey the damage, and accuse the other of causing the accident, compounding the traffic jam behind them.

Still other bothersome customs were Jamaican drivers' habit of passing on the inside while making a righthand turn at a traffic light and also hearing the horn from the car behind them blow the moment a light turned green.

"What's with all this horn blowing?" Banks asked Nakomis.

"Different blows mean different things," Nakomis responded. "There's the 'Hello' blow, the 'thank-you' blow, the 'goodbye' blow, the 'I'm-sorry' blow, the 'watch-your-ass' blow, the 'the-light-has-changed' blow, the 'you're-a-damned-fool' blow, and the 'fuck-you' blow. You don't have all those in America? How do you ever drive if you can't communicate with other drivers?"

"As far as I know, we only have the 'reminder' blow and 'the fuck-you blow'," Banks said.

"And they call us the Third World."

Monte sat behind the driver and began to silently take in his new surroundings and compare them to Highland Park. The sight of the vivid, delicate hibiscus flowers reminded him that he was on vacation in a beautiful place and almost took his breath away. Even the birds were more colorful here in this landscape awash with pastels. With the van windows open, he could feel the ocean breeze and hear the waves crash on the shore. The smooth, velvety yet rocky looking sand beaches were maintained by mother nature not attendants with rakes. They seemed like they'd be perfect to him for walking on and exploring barefoot on as he took in the glistening gin blue and turquoise waters that seemed so warm

Conclusive, All-Inclusive Confusion

and inviting. Two leaning palm trees made him imagine himself swinging from an imaginary hammock he saw stretched between them, chilling out as he was being cooled by a wafting ocean breeze. They passed some grand and also some petite outcroppings that jutted out into the Caribbean and then a luxury villa sitting on a rocky tropical slope. The tide was going out, leaving an even more beautiful coastline. The whole scene looked low key and relaxed as the beaches seemed to swirl effortlessly with the turquoise Caribbean waters.

Then his mind reverted to the winter they had just left behind in Detroit where temps sometimes dropped to ten degrees or below, and it was cold from December to March. And not just cold but a bone chilling cold, thanks to the polar vortex that surrounded it. Even though it had been in the twenties when they went to the airport, the blowing winds had made it seem single digit. What might seem like a winter utopia to a newcomer was instead a winter dystopia to some veterans like himself. Highland Park's unallayed winter darkness had been made even more frightening by the proliferation of ethnic gangs.

Monte smiled, and Banks noticed.

"What are you smiling about, daddy-in-law," he asked.

"Oh, just thinking about the conversation that you and Nakomis just had on Jamaican driving habits. Did you know that a recent study concluded that Michigan is considered to be the worst states in the nation for winter driving?"

He kept his remaining happy thoughts to himself.

> NOW HIRING
> SMILING
> FECES

CHAPTER 4

"We've arrived," Nakomis announced. "Welcome to the Seascape Luxury Resort."

Sitting next to a long, well-manicured, elegant driveway that was flanked on both sides with a straight line of royal palms was a four-foot, poured concrete Greek Revival sign that said "Seascape Luxury Resort" on the top line and "Runaway Bay" beneath it in elegant Rafaella Bold lettering. A basketweave pink pastel background had been pressed into the stained concrete to emphasize the raised enameled black lettering. The sign was flanked on both ends by white Ionic posts. Beneath them gentle dusk-to-dawn lighting was encased in frosted glass globes. The sign was inset into a plain but gently arching, white concrete frame that ran around all four sides. Beneath it, sloping downward towards the curbed drive, was an immaculately kept Blue Star Creeper flower bed in full bloom. It was nestled between two silvery-green beds of Lamb's Ear that gently snaked in an s-pattern along the Creeper's borders and provided groundcover around two dwarf majesty palms.

"Wow!" Nan said. "That certainly gives a good first impression."

Her impression only got better as they drove into the resort's entrance along the curbed driveway made of grey pavers flanked on each side with a line of red ones the width of a sidewalk. The entrance to the resort's lobby was a massive Greek Revival building that had to be twenty to thirty feet high. It had a low-pitched roof with a triangular pediment and three oblong pediments over the entry. Along the front were six fiberglass-

Conclusive, All-Inclusive Confusion

reinforced polymer, fluted Doric columns. Each had to be at least twenty feet high and three feet wide. Each was seated on square bases that must have been at least two feet tall. Behind them supporting the other side of the roof were two square, fluted Doric columns that were the same size. A drive-through ran between the columns under a massive hanging chandelier. The whole structure was gleaming white.

"Oh, my God!" Nan gasped. "I've never been anywhere even remotely close to this."

She squeezed her dad's hand excitedly.

The main hotel towered above the lobby. It had an asymmetrical look. It was a seven story Victorian style structure. The seventh floor was the penthouse floor. The Connors family was booked into four of the penthouse suites. The exterior was constructed of spotless white-stucco with multiple high-pitched red clay-tiled roofs. Each of the hotel's 525 suites had a wraparound private porch, each with its own painted iron railing and bay window. The exterior of each wing was more minimalist rather than being decorative. On each corner of the building were high-peaked red Queen Anne style round turrets.

The spacious lobby had an tasteful beige marble floor. The interior was done in an elegant, yet old-fashioned cream-colored motif and decorated with generic artwork. A person could see all the way through it and see the ocean behind the building. They could hear soothing piano music coming from a piano bar not far away. While the lobby was busy with people, it still somehow conveyed a relaxing feeling. Within moments, a uniformed bellhop brought their luggage into the building on a brass rolling cart and stood patiently waiting for his forthcoming instructions.

"Welcome to Seascape Luxury Resort," said the smiling front desk receptionist. "My name is Queisha Hamilton."

"We're the Connors family."

"Yes, we've been expecting you. Your timing is perfect. Your penthouse suites have been cleaned and are ready for you to move into immediately. You will find that each has been individually decorated. You are 'Gold Club' guests and will therefore get our 'Gold Package.' This means that, among other privileges, room service will be available to you at no cost twenty-four hours a day. And since you are 'Gold Club' guests, your check-in has been mostly handled prior to your arrival. Just sign this form."

Nakomis stood by the front door and tipped his hat at Queisha. This was their prearranged signal that these guests could have megabucks. She nodded, acknowledging that she had gotten the message. Queisha pulled on her left earlobe, sending Nakomis' message to a slender, clean-cut Jamaican in a linen business suit. He stroked his chin, telling Queisha that he was on top of the situation.

It was all over in less than five minutes. Their excitement continued to mount in anticipation of their coming experiences. After Monte returned the form, the man in the conservative business suit walked over in a leisurely manner and introduced himself.

"My name is Mr. Christian Angel, and I am the hotel's Ambassador. Since I happen to be in the lobby, would you do me the honor of allowing me to escort you to your penthouse suites?"

Monte stammered, "Of … of course, Mr. Angel."

Angel snapped his fingers and motioned for the bellhop with their luggage to follow. He carried on a friendly conversation as he tried to size the Connors family up as they walked towards the penthouse floor's private elevator.

"This place is *really* elegant," Monte said. "It's got to be about the fanciest place I've ever stayed in."

"We like to think we're one of the premier luxury resorts in the Caribbean."

"What's the food like?" Jax asked as he munched on a gummy bear.

"I figured you'd ask about food right off the bat," Eve commented.

Jax frowned at his wife.

"Excellent. We have Las Olas, a Brazilian restaurant, The Knife specializing in grilled fare, Picasso for gourmands, and an Asian fusion and a Japanese restaurant, as well as an Italian and a French restaurant. And none of them cost extra but do require a reservation. Do you like sports? Have you guys ever played either beach or pool volleyball? Or done aqua aerobics? How about pickle ball or paddleboarding?"

"No, sir."

"What about partying?" Banks asked.

"We have activities every day by the pools. A steel band show, a pool foam party, even a chocolate party."

Conclusive, All-Inclusive Confusion

As he popped a gummy bear in his mouth, Jax said, "Yum."

"And a movie and popcorn night by the pool. And we also have a clothing optional beach if that's your thing. Something for everyone. Where's your home?"

"Detroit."

"And your first trip to the Caribbean?"

"Didn't have enough money to go before," Monte said.

"Yeh, 'till Daddy Warbucks here won the Lotto."

Monte frowned and said, "I wish you'd quite telling everyone that."

Chris Angel perked up. His mental cash register went "Ka-Ching."

To himself he thought, *Yes, this may be a good week for more than for just you.*

But aloud he said, "We're here to serve and make this the most memorable week of *your* life."

Monte suddenly felt like royalty and thought, *This is going to be one fantastic week. I'm beginning to like how the other half live.*

Jax was thinking that his feet hurt, and he needed to take a pee.

"Here we are," Angel said as he unlocked a door. "We have the first of four adjoining deluxe junior suites with a sea view. Mr. Connors, this has been assigned to you. I hope you approve."

Monte almost gasped as he saw his room for the first time.

We certainly ain't in Highland Park or Kansas anymore, Dorothy.

His suite had beige tile floors, cream wood furniture, orange bed runners and throw pillows on a four-poster canopied bed. It had nightstands with Lucite lamps, gilt-wood cushioned fauteuils, a desk with a phone, and more Lucite lamps — all accented by abstract artwork. The ten-foot barrel-vaulted ceiling was set off with crown molding and recessed lighting, and the walls were painted a darker beige that complimented the cream-colored furniture.

On the white bedspread a white terry-cloth beach towel had been folded lengthwise to make a standup abstract heart. Anchoring it was bottle of iced champagne on an elegant, gleaming carved blue mahoe tray with champagne flutes next to it, and surrounding the tray was a framework of alternating Hershey's Kisses and foil wrapped Nestle Dark Chocolate Mint Thins.

There was a sitting area with a round Charlotte Perriand coffee table, a circular couch, and Louis XVI-style padded chairs upholstered in a

Jasper fabric. The glass curtain walls gave their occupants a view of the outside. Monte almost squinted at the massive amount of light coming in through the floor-to-ceiling glass doors from his private balcony that also had a rooftop garden. Electronically operated cornice-boarded tan drapes gave the room privacy.

Angel interrupted Monte's reverie to speak. Monte tuned him back in about midsentence, "... Air conditioned with free liquor from your minibar. Your mini fridge is stocked with candy, sodas, water, and of course, Red Stripe beer. ... All compliments of Seascape. You will find a bathrobe and slippers in the closet. Here is your coffeemaker. Over there is your electronic mini safe ... instructions on how to set the combination are in it. Here is the remote for your flat-screen TV. Hit this button, and it arises from this dresser. Does this all seem acceptable?"

Monte looked where Angel was pointing and saw a cream-colored Queen Anne dresser. He attempted to answer Angel, but no words came out as he peeked into his bathroom. It was the dreamy sort seemingly crafted for kings and queens that he had only seen in magazines. He saw a green-marble double vanity with two sinks, a jetted jacuzzi bathtub big enough for two ... he imagined himself soaking for prolonged timespans as the jets caressed his body. ... With a separate shower plus an array of ritzy looking toiletries and a hairdryer! It was separated from the main suite with a peek-a-boo window, with privacy shades yet.

He finally stammered a response as he was drawn towards the view from the balcony, "I think this will do nicely."

Below him Monte had an aerial panoramic view of a series of meandering well-manicured paver pathways and three palm tree-flanked, lazy lake-style swimming pools that were interconnected with gently arching walking bridges and were surrounded by tropical gardens. Guests were hanging out around each pool as music played in the background. Others were in the pools, lounging by one of each pool's swim-up bars. The centerpiece of the largest pool was an in-pool swim-up Grecian gazebo with a giant Neptune sculpture in its middle that had water gently cascading down it.

"Will there be anything else, sir?"

Monte was in a daze and didn't answer as he stared.

Pinch me. I can't believe I'm here. I didn't know places like this were real.

"Sir? ... Sir? ... "

His mental haze lifted long enough for Monte finally become aware that he was again being addressed.

"Uh ... No ... I think I'm going to be extremely satisfied. In fact, I know so."

His voice squeaked as he spoke.

"Very well then. I will now take your family to their suites. Each has been designed to be unique. Welcome to Jamaica, and on behalf of our staff, have an irie week. Thank you for choosing Seascape Luxury Resort."

> GOATS
> PLEASE
> DRIVE
> SLOWLY

CHAPTER 5

Christian Angel returned to the hotel lobby curious to know more about the Connors family. He spoke briefly to both Queisha and Nakomis, only to find out that neither of them knew any more than he did about Monte Connors and his entourage.

"I just heard his son-in-law call him 'Mr. Moneybags' while I was bringing them in from the airport. The topic came up after they overheard me being called Ruddy Puss and wanted to know about Jamaican street names."

"That's more than I heard, Ruddy Puss. I was just following your signal," Queisha said.

"Is the computer up back there?" Angel asked, motioning to the employee-only room behind the check-in desk.

"Sure, and I'm logged in," Queisha said.

"Then give me a few minutes on it."

He came out about fifteen minutes later and whispered to Queisha, "Ruddy Puss was right. This guy recently won a whole lotta of money playing the American lottery. Until that happened, he was just a poor-ass church social worker. Ruddy Puss did good."

"This'll be good information for Neil," Queisha said.

"Don't give Neil the lead for nothing," Christian advised. "Make him pay for it."

Queisha gave Christian a look that said, *Do you think I'm a fool? I've played this game longer than you have.*

Conclusive, All-Inclusive Confusion

And indeed, she had.

Jamaican born Queisha Hamilton began her dubious criminal career in South Florida after emigrating there from Brown's Town, Jamaica. Then, she had been a young, single adult looking for adventure, and she found it. She initially became a drug runner for the Top 6 gang and eventually became their gang moll, servicing the entire gang, until one of their leaders, Dub Bootee, made her his exclusive personal hostess and assistant. Eventually the gang morphed into the popular rap group who also went by the name Top 6. Dub eventually became an associate pastor for the Green Rainbow Ministries in Key West, led by its leader, the effervescent multiracial shyster The Highly Exalted Reverend LeRoy Cho-Arturo. LeRoy, an ex-conman himself, was the church founder and not only ran the church ashram, but he also became a Monroe County Commissioner. After Dub got Queisha a job working for the ashram, she used the information she learned about Reverend LeRoy's operation to blackmail him for $50,000, causing her to flee back to Jamaica. She had threatened to expose a kickback scheme that the reverend had with the local businessmen and drug smugglers named the Blanchard brothers. They were paying Reverend LeRoy handsomely for his vote and influence in the awarding of county contracts. She then conned Key West Citizen reporter Michael Howell into thinking she would give him an exclusive on exposing the entire group, only to pull the rug out from under him.

Queisha was a perfect example of the turd not falling far from the bird. Her now deceased uncle, Neville Hamilton, and his now deceased son, Neville Junior, had been leading Brown's Town businessmen/investors and were also shyster politicians as well. Many of their businesses and investments had been fronts for Jamaica's notorious Shower Posse, the most powerful and possibly the most lethal posse, i.e. street gang, in Jamaica. With Neville Senior's help, Reverend LeRoy had been deposed and replaced by the newly Highly Exalted Reverend Dub Bootee, and Queisha had been promoted to be the ashram's treasurer even though she didn't know the difference between a debit and a credit.

The Hamiltons' downfall had come after their involvement in a massive plot to swindle Jamaica's Highway 2000 road building program had been exposed publicly, causing many of the members of Jamaica's People's National Party to be disgraced and jailed and forcing an election for a new Prime Minister. Both Hamiltons had been assassinated because they could possibly expose the remaining kingpins in the scheme. The central company involved in the swindle had been the Kingston and St. Andrews Corporation and their Incomparable Enterprises subsidiary. Queisha had been a token vice president of Incomparable Enterprises.

Queisha's fellow employees at the hotel didn't know it and Queisha would never let on, but her pedigree and credentials as a con artist far exceeded anyone on Seascape's staff. So, was she qualified to play a con game? You betcha!

The "Neil" they had referred to was Neil Hackinrider, a piano player who often contracted his services to the hotel. He normally entertained guests by playing in the piano bar as a singles act. At other times he played American songbook tunes and sang duets with Foxy-Roxy Sparrow, a female jazz torch singer who worked for the hotel in various capacities. The hotel also used the two of them to play for private guest affairs in the hotel like corporate conferences and wedding receptions. Their playlist normally consisted of classics from songwriters like Cole Porter and George Gershwin, but if called upon, they could play more modern songs from songwriters like Carole King and sing favorites like "Bad, Bad Leroy Brown" or "You Picked a Fine Time to Leave Me, Lucille." People in the know called him Neil-The-Heel for his other talents. What the hotel or the guests didn't know was that both Foxy-Roxy and Neil-The-Heel were accomplished con artists. They had found that working as entertainers was a perfect cover for their more lucrative activities. Both had in the past worked their craft in circuits as diverse as cruise ships and Las Vegas, Reno, and Atlantic City.

Neil had a select network of hotel employees that he would give cash finders' fees to if they identified guests who were potential marks. His network included maids, waiters, and bartenders as well as Queisha and Nakomis. A tip was normally worth $50 American, but Neil had been known to give a bonus if the tip worked out especially well. Christian was careful not to give Neil any more than he had to before Neil paid, even though to-date Neil had yet to ever stiff him. There was always the possibility of a first time.

As Christian turned to leave, Queisha called out to him, "I almost forgot to tell you something."

"What's that."

Conclusive, All-Inclusive Confusion

"I had just come on duty when the Connors family arrived, but Natalie, who worked the last shift, told me that just as she was getting off, a guest checked in and asked about the Connors family."

Christian's radar went up. "Do you know his name?"

"Said it was Clayton Potter."

"But he didn't say what he wanted."

"Nope." She pointed, "... Oh, there's Foxy-Roxy now. She'll know where Neil is."

Foxy-Roxy told Christian where to find Neil. He was smoking a cigarette at a beachside table behind the hotel. Christian gave him a synopsis of what he knew thus far about the Connors family without disclosing their identity. Neil gave him two one-hundred-dollar bills and told him to take care of Queisha and Ruddy Puss. Christian then gave him the name and the room numbers. He turned to leave.

"By the way, Queisha said there was another guest asking about them."

"But they just got here! Does she know who?"

"Said the man was alone and registered under the name of Clayton Potter."

"Whaaa! Are you sure about that name?"

Christian nodded.

"Son ... of ... a ... bitch!"

"You know him?"

"Hell yes, I know that snake. He's a bigger crook than I am. And, boy, can he play a role. If the boy was legit, he could win an Academy Award. And underhanded! He'd steal his widowed mama's social security check if he thought he could get away with it. I wonder what he's doing here. And also, how he found out about Connors' windfall. ... And I wonder how he plans to get his hands on Connors' money. ... Holy shit! ... Potsy Potter! Wowee! Wait'll Foxy-Roxy hears this."

> *Deanie's Seafood*
> *Fat Juicy Females*
> *By The Dozen*

CHAPTER 6

Potsy Potter put a Sticky-Note on Monte's door asking him to call at his convenience. He waited until late afternoon, but when he didn't hear from Monte, he returned to Monte's room intending to knock on the door and offer to return the stolen bag. He wanted Monte and his family to get unpacked before he descended on them. He kept a lookout since he wanted to make sure that he waited until he knew that Monte was in his room before he knocked again. As he was walking down the hall, Monte's door opened, and Monte began to walk down to the crowded elevator. Potsy followed and rode down to the lobby unobserved. Monte wanted a little alone time to grab something to eat in peace in the Orchid Buffet. Jax's whiny attitude and his gummy bear habit had already begun to grate on his nerves.

Monte thought to himself, *And this is only the first day.*

Potsy waited until he was sure where Monte was going before he approached him.

This is even better than meeting him at his room. .... And he's all alone. Thank you, lady luck.

"Are you Mister Connors?"

"Uh ... Yes ... Have we met? ... Do you work for the hotel?"

"No, sir. We haven't. And no, I don't. My name is Clay Potter, and I'm a guest just like you are. Sir, did you lose a bag at the airport today?"

"As a matter of fact, I did."

"Is this the one you lost?"

Conclusive, All-Inclusive Confusion

"Uh … Yeah, … Uh, Uh …I mean, yes, … it looks like it. How'd you get it?"

"I'm not sure myself. It was mixed in with my stuff, and I saw it had your name on it."

"Well, thank you for being so honest. How did you know who I am?"

"I heard someone call out your name. … I'm travelling by myself. Was hungry. And I came down to the lobby to get a bite."

"I was about to grab a bite alone as well. Would you like to join me?"

"Love to. Don't mind if I do. Thanks for asking."

They went through the Orchid's buffet line and found a table. Monte got a hot dog and fries. Potsy got a Caesar salad.

So, where are you from, Mr. Potter?"

"New York. I saw from the tag on the duffel bag that you're from Detroit. Is Mrs. Connors traveling with you?"

"No, just my three daughters and their husbands. A family vacation. Our first one together, actually. Do you travel much, Mr. Potter?"

"Please call me Clay. It's short for Clayton. Mr. Potter makes me feel so old. … Like my grandfather … even though I *am* a widower."

"We seem to be about the same age, and I don't feel old. By the way, I go by Monte."

Hot diggity damn. This is starting to work out better than I thought. Let's see how much bullshit I can load on him the first time out without overdoing it.

"I lost my wife to cancer," Potsy adlibbed. "What about yours?"

"Never had one to lose. My three daughters are all adopted. Did you have any children?"

"A son. We also called him Potsy. He was hit by a drunk driver and is now a brain-damaged epileptic quadriplegic."

Hmmm! Am I'm laying on the BS too thick? We'll find out.

"That's horrible. You poor fellow. You have had it rough."

"Yeah. That's why I took this vacation. Call it attitude adjustment. My doctor said I need it."

"Well, anything I can do to help, I'll be glad to. Actually, I'm kind of a social worker.

"Oh yeah! Do you work for an agency?"

"The biggest one of all — The Catholic Church."

"Would you mind if I ask for your advice from time to time? Sometimes I get depressed."

"I'd be honored. It's the least I can do."
"And now maybe I can stay off of the booze."
"Alcohol doesn't solve anything."
"That's what they taught us in AA, but sometimes that's all that seems to help."
"Let me try to help instead."

BINGO! That's just what I wanted to hear. Now I've got an excuse to keep coming back to him. Sooner or later, I'll find out what his hotspot is, and I can embellish my story accordingly. And then Potsy baby will be in like Flynn. OK, Potsy, take your time and don't screw this up by jumping the gun. You're a professional. Let the mark give you the opening you're looking for.

He began to sing to himself as he thought about all of Monte's money that hopefully would soon be his if he played his cards right with this chump.

We're in the money
The skies are sunny
Old man Depression, you're through
You've done us wrong
We'll be in the money
Come on, my honey
Let's spend it, lend it, send it rolling along

HAZARDOUS ROAD CONDITIONS DRIVE WITH CAKE

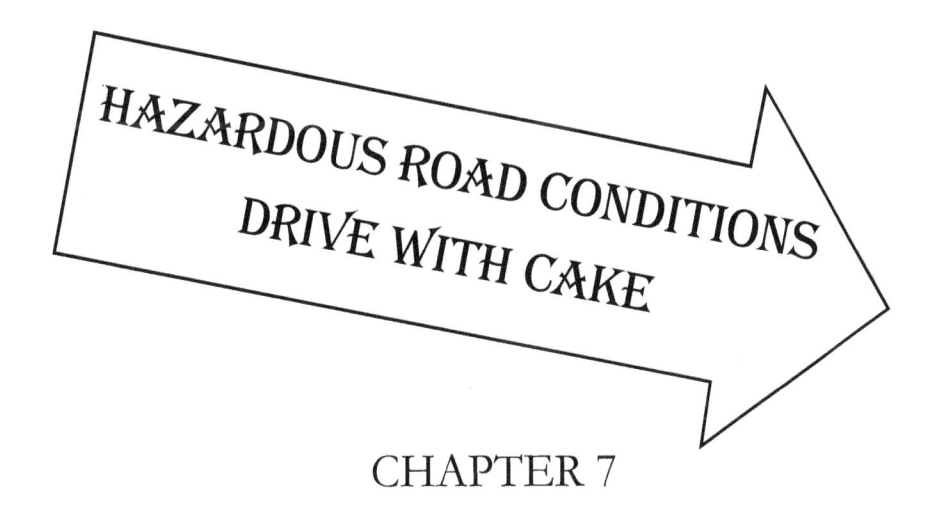

CHAPTER 7

Potsy's initial rendezvous with Monte had not gone unnoticed. When Neil Hackinrider saw them go into the Orchid, he knew that the Clayton Potter that Christian Angel had told him about was indeed Potsy Potter, his old competitor from his Vegas days. Before he knew that Neil was a fellow grifter, Potsy had once tried to swindle Neil only to end up getting swindled himself.

Holy mother of God! What in the holy hell is Potsy doing here? This isn't his usual territory. And how in the world did he get a line on this mark so soon? I just learned about Connors myself. And Potsy just checked into the hotel this afternoon. Damn, damn, damn! The boy's a fast worker.

He didn't hang around and risk Potsy seeing him.

Man, I'm glad I saw him before he saw me. I don't want to give away the element of surprise before I have to. I better go find Foxy-Roxy.

He dialed Foxy-Roxy Sparrow on his cell phone.

"Roxy, where are you? I need to talk to you."

"Out by the middle pool."

He found Foxy-Roxy at a shaded table reading a magazine. He briefly explained what he knew thus far about the Connors family.

"Ruddy Puss first picked up on them and told Queisha who told Christian. This mark appears to be a whale. But a potential problem has emerged. One of my old Vegas competitors is staying at the hotel — matter of fact just checked in today — and he's already trying to get his hooks into the father. Went to lunch with him at the Orchid already. He doesn't know that I saw them."

"Somebody I know?"

"I don't think so. Calls himself Potsy Potter. I beat him out of some money once."

"Figures. So, what do you want me to do?"

"If I get Queisha to send them a "Gold Club" invitation to have a special happy hour in Rum Runner's Cove, will you welcome them to the hotel and introduce me so I can assess them and come up with a plan to lighten their financial load? I'll cut you in on anything I ultimately get out of them. I don't want Potsy to get it."

✎

"We have a happy hour invitation tonight," Monte told Nan.

"But we don't know anyone here, Dad," Nan said suspiciously.

"It's from the hotel management to welcome us to the resort. After all, we are Gold Club members renting four deluxe suites. They're sending one of their management team to join us. I guess it's kind of like having the captain of a cruise ship welcome you aboard. I've heard about special people being invited to dine at the captain's table."

"All of us?"

"Yep. See what time would be good with Viv and Eve — and, of course, their husbands. And without being overt about it, try to make sure Jax doesn't look like a slob. And tell him to leave those damned gummy bears in the room. I'm sick of looking at the things."

Nan just nodded. She knew what Monte was talking about.

✎

When the Connors family arrived at six, Foxy-Roxy was waiting for them. Everyone introduced themselves. Foxy-Roxy had already pulled some tables together before they arrived to make sure she had adequate seating for the entire family.

Foxy-Roxy's birth name was Rosa Caputo. Her now deceased adopted stepfather, "Rocky" Caputo, had been an accomplished grifter who

Conclusive, All-Inclusive Confusion

specialized in sports memorabilia. He normally used the alias Tad Green and passed himself off as a former major league umpire who had gotten to know a wide variety of sports stars. He would wow potential marks with inside stories that sometimes he had heard or read but sometimes were made-up tales he fabricated about famous baseball legends, often on the spur of the moment to fit the occasion if he found out that the mark was a fan of a certain team. He would tell them about how the MLB was really a small universe and describe how the longtime players, managers, and umps would party together during the season when they were constantly on the road. He was a born storyteller who could regale a listener for hours with his "inside" stories, especially when he was inebriated. Which was often. His wife, Rosa senior, would throw just enough detail or correct his memory at just the right moment, to add credibility to Rocky's tall tales. She also innately knew just the right moment to mention that they still had remembrances from the "good old days" that they had considered selling to start education funds for their "children" and then go for the close. And, by golly, since the sales would be in cash and therefore nontaxable, they could sell these items below the market — a win/win for everyone except Uncle Sam.

Rocky was adept at most types of baseball cons. He was a very accomplished card trimmer and card doctor. Trimmers aim to cut a baseball card in a way that makes it closer to mint and then get a higher grade than it would normally get. They strived to keep the card's proportions relatively intact to trick a grader. Trimming takes advantage of the fact that card cuts, especially on vintage cards, can vary greatly. An expert trimmer can trim off a fraction of it to make the corners sharper and maybe raise the grade of a grade five card to maybe a grade that is eight or nine. When dealing with a rare card like a vintage Mickey Mantle card, this can mean a lot of money. He also billed himself as being a card doctor or expert in identifying under-graded cards. Rocky was good enough to fool most dealers and even fancy auction houses.

Rocky could also be an expert card autograph forger. He once even successfully pawned off a fake Honus Wagner on an unsuspecting wealthy collector. He never found out if the collector ever knew he'd been duped because after the transaction since Rocky had disappeared into thin air.

When he was able to get inventory, Rocky occasionally would sell vintage packs of baseball cards that he claimed were original and unopened. Before a transaction, Rocky would carefully open each pack, take out any cards that had value, replace them with worthless cards, and then reseal the packages.

Rocky and Rosa had a good life until Rosa's former husband, Alphonse, was killed in a robbery gone bad and she felt she then had to assume responsibility for Rosa Junior and Neko, her two children from her first marriage. Eventually Rocky stepped up to the plate and adopted both children. But then the unthinkable happened. Rosa died of lung cancer, and Rocky was left to raise the children alone. But Rocky, being the expert he was in dealing with bad situations, incorporated Rosa and Neko into his act. Both grew up to be accomplished grifters but parted ways with him when they were grown, each seeking their own pot of gold at the end of their own rainbow. Rosa, now Foxy-Roxy, hadn't seen her brother in years. She sometimes wondered where his life had taken him and how successful he was. There was no animosity when they parted . She wished Neko well and was sure he felt the same way about her.

> # NO SMOKING ALOUD

CHAPTER 8

After everyone had gotten settled at the tables Foxy-Roxy had previously pulled together in Rum Runner's Cove, she nodded towards the bar and a waitress came over.

"Welcome to Seascape," the waitress said in a friendly voice. "My name is Tennisha, and I'll be taking care of you tonight. Is this your first time to visit us?"

"Not only our first time to visit you, but also our first time to visit Jamaica as well," Banks commented.

"And we'll go out of our way to make sure it's not your last. On the table is our specialty drink menu. Have you had a chance to look at it?"

Jax reached across the table and grabbed it before anyone else could.

"I'll take one of each," he said and laughed.

Monte frowned at Jax's boorish behavior but said nothing. Everyone else just sat there since Jax was hogging the only menu.

Foxy-Roxy broke the silence by suggesting, "Jack — did I get your name right? …"

"Jax with an X," Jax interrupted.

"I think if the 'x' were followed by an 'a-s-s,' it would probably be more appropriate," Banks added under his breath.

"Jax …., with an 'x'," Foxy-Roxy continued, "has had an excellent idea. Why don't each of you order a different drink from the menu and familiarize yourself with some Jamaican specialties. I'll be glad to make some suggestions. You can pass the drinks around so everyone can sample them all."

"I think Ms. Sparrow has an excellent idea," Viv said.

"Please — Roxy — not Ms. Sparrow."

"And you can thank me for thinking of it," Jax said.

Eve rolled her eyes.

Foxy-Roxy then suggested six different drinks as a starter, explaining the ingredients that went in each one. She ordered some banana fritters, banana bread muffins, jerked sweet potato fries, fried plantains, and jerked chicken wings as well for the table. Tennisha brought their drinks, followed almost immediately with the appetizers. Jax's eyes lit up when Tennisha put the appetizers on the table and almost elbowed his wife, Eve, in the face in his haste to load up his own plate.

"Boarding house manners," Eve said apologetically.

Her comment went right over Jax's head.

"Drink as many drinks as you wish. You deserve it. After all, you're on vacation," Foxy-Roxy told them. "This is an all-inclusive hotel and drinks are covered in your daily charges. And no one has to drive home afterwards. Now, let me toast to my new American friends and hotel patrons."

Everyone held their glass aloft.

"May your anchor be tight,
Your cock be loose,
Your rum be spiced,
And your compass be true."

Jax added, "Fifteen men on a dead-man's chest. Yo-ho-ho and a bottle of rum."

Viv mouthed to her husband, Banks, "How original."

Instead of passing his drink around, Jax chugged his zombie down, burped, and held out his glass for Tennisha to bring him another one.

Soon they were sampling Foxy-Roxy's choices minus Jax's zombie — a Bob Marley cocktail, a dirty banana, a hummingbird, and of course, a Jamaican rum punch. With no fanfare, Foxy-Roxy discreetly ordered a non-alcoholic Ting, Jamaica's grapefruit flavored soft drink, for herself, of course on the rocks. The Connors family continued to pass their drinks around until each person had sampled them all. Within minutes their glasses were empty, and each reordered the drink they had liked the best.

Conclusive, All-Inclusive Confusion

Jax reloaded his plate with the items he had liked best after complaining about the spiciness of jerk seasoning. With no apologies, he cleaned out the remains of the platters of fried items — the fried banana fritters, fried dumplings, and fried plantains.

A third round of drinks was ordered and then a fourth. As the drinks made everyone relax, Foxy-Roxy gradually began to piece together the story of Monte's lottery win. Neil sat discreetly over at the bar waiting for Foxy-Roxy's signal to join them. When he got it, Neil came over, bussed Foxy-Roxy on the cheek like it was a chance meeting and made a comment about how glad he was to see her again. She commented about how great it was to have him back in the hotel. Monte suggested that Neil might want to join them. He readily agreed and soon made everyone at the table comfortable with his presence as he carried on a witty conversation. After all, Neil was a smooth and charming, gregarious people person who had a seemingly bottomless well of razzmatazz that hid his dark, ruthless side. He had perfected his effortless-seeming, low pressure, nonthreatening, outgoing persona over many years.

Neil was in the middle of one of his well-rehearsed stories, and everyone at the table except Jax seemed mesmerized by him. Jax's attention was on the order of jerk sliders before him that he appeared to have to himself. Even though he had complained about jerk seasoning earlier, after a few drinks he was beginning to acquire a taste for it.

Only Foxy-Roxy noticed the concerned look that momentarily caused Neil's brow to suddenly furrow. They made eye contact. He mouthed "Potter" and nodded to his left.

Once Foxy-Roxy saw who he was talking about, she almost dropped her glass.

Potsy Potter was Foxy-Roxy's estranged brother, Neko Caputo.

| CONSTRUESSHAIN ENTRANCE |

| RIGHT LANE MUST RIGHT LEFT |

CHAPTER 9

Foxy-Roxy did not sleep well that night after seeing Neko Caputo in Rum Runner's Cove. Memories began to crop up one after the other. Some were good; others were not so good. She recalled the day armed police had invaded the shabby rental apartment that big Rosa and Alphonse had called home, arrested him, and how she and Neko had been put in temporary state custody until her mother had stepped up to the plate and convinced the judge that she should be allowed to be their new sole guardian. Afterwards, she remembered the debates that she and Neko had overheard between her mom and Rocky, her new stepdad, about permanently adopting them and what impact it would have on their gypsy lifestyle. Eventually little Rosa and Neko began to learn the ways of a grifter as Rocky began to incorporate them both into some of his scams. He even taught them how to pick pockets. But mainly Rocky learned that their presence gave him credibility with some potential "clients," and he taught them how make pertinent points that helped move his lies along.

Her thoughts reverted to better memories when she thought about how big brother Neko would take up for her, violently when necessary, in the succession of new schools they were enrolled in as Rocky and big Rosa moved from town to town, often adopting aliases, to stay one step ahead of the law or a disgruntled card buyer. ... Or a disgruntled bookie since Rocky's interest in sports was not confined to memorabilia. Rocky was a compulsive gambler on sporting events. Unfortunately his talent

Conclusive, All-Inclusive Confusion

for picking contest winners was not even close to his expertise in memorabilia.

Then the occasional scenes came to mind when Rocky and big Rosa would unwind by throwing a sometimes extended drunk. Some of the drinking bouts occurred when they were flush from a recent lucrative score, but sometimes they were brought on by depression when they had had an extended period of bad luck. At these times little Rosa would just hunker down and try to stay invisible as she and Neko babysat each other.

These sometimes-volatile benders gave little Rosa the opportunity to rake off cash from her wiped-out parents and begin to amass a secret stash that only she and Neko knew about. She had no specific plans for the money, but it was comforting to know that it was there if she needed it. This changed one day, however, when eighteen-year-old Neko got the hots for a cocktail waitress in Reno and took off with her, taking little Rosa's stash with him. That was the last Rosa had seen of Neko until now. While she had missed her brother, she did not miss his violent temper that had gotten him arrested more than once in incidents that involved not only his fists but guns and knives as well. She suspected that Neko had possibly occasionally gotten away with murdering some of the people who had crossed him.

Since then, her occasional forays into Google had never given her an update into Neko's adult life. He might have been dead for all she knew. With his violent history, anything might have happened.

✍

Foxy-Roxy went out to the front desk early the following morning and pulled up the registration data.

Clayton Potter, according to Nick, nickname Potsy. So that's the name Neko goes by these days. Showing an address in Hialeah, Florida. Figures. That's where the racetrack and casino are.

And Neil says he's already on Monte Connors like shit on stink.

Well, I guess the dung don't fall far from the bung, or should I say, the poop from Potsy's pooper.

Rocky — if you're looking down from heaven — excuse me, ... looking up from hell instead ... you trained your son well.

Maybe it's time for me and bro to have a reunion. Let's see now — room 502.

Foxy-Roxy took the elevator to the fifth floor, located the room, and knocked on the door.

"Mr. Potter?"

"Who's there?"

"Rosa."

"Rosa who? I don't know any Rosa."

"I think you do. ... Rosa Caputo."

The door immediately opened. Potsy stood there in his skivvies and a t-shirt.

"You look a little older, but you're the same Neko I remember. You seem to have aged well. Scamming must still be profitable."

"You don't look so bad yourself, sis. What the hell're you doing here?"

"That's why I'm standing here ... to ask you the same thing. ... I happen to work here."

"Doing what? I didn't know hotels hired pickpockets."

"I see you're still funny — or think you are. You must have inherited Rocky's sense of humor — or would his sense of bullshit be more appropriate. I'm a singer, by the way, not a pickpocket."

"Well, I'll be a horse's ..."

"Ass? Aren't you going to invite me in? Or do we have to have our family reunion in the hall?"

"Come on in. Let me put on some shorts. I wasn't expecting company."

Foxy-Roxy sat on the suite sofa while Potsy tried to locate some shorts in the pile of clothes on the floor.

"Good to see you, sis. Sorry if I was a bit abrupt, but I'm still half asleep, and you're about the last person I thought I'd ever see in Jamaica."

"Good to see you too, but I'm here partially on business. You were seen talking to one of our guests. If you're thinking of ripping him off — don't."

"What guest?"

"Monte Connors."

"Why? You want him for yourself?"

"Actually, I do have some plans that involve the Connors family."

"Then we ought to team up."

"I already have an associate. ... Someone who knows you."

"Who's that?"

Conclusive, All-Inclusive Confusion

"Neil Hackinrider."

"You've got to be shittin' me! Neil-the-Heel — that dreamer! Sis, let me give you some brotherly advice. Watch yourself, and don't let him drag you into his dreams. Cause that's all they are, and all they'll ever be. He can be awfully persuasive. But, I'm telling you right now, they never work out.

"Now that I know that we've definitely got to hook up and work together so I can look out for you. Besides, I have some unfinished business with that boy. He owes me some money."

"Way I heard it was he outsmarted you."

"Eat me."

"No thank you. Brother or no brother, ... I'm warning you. Stay away from my fish. Or else."

"Or else what?"

"I'll let you wonder about that. By the way, you still owe me some money. Probably other people as well. Wouldn't doubt that you're a compulsive gambler like Rocky was."

"Hah! I figured you'd forgot about that money. I do like to pick up a little easy cash occasionally on a sporting event. By the way, who's a good bookie down here?"

"Don't know, and don't care. Christ! Didn't you learn anything from watching Rocky? But I guess stupid is as stupid does.

"Anyway, enough of this sibling happy horseshit. Good to see you, brother. I hope you enjoy staying at Seascape. And I hope you'll take my good sisterly advice to heart.

"Now, if we, the staff, can do anything to make your stay more comfortable, just let us know."

She rose to leave.

"Sis, a tournament's not won until you land the fish and he's safely in the net. Until then, it's an open game. ... Great seeing you again too."

45

REST ROOM OUT OF ODOR

CHAPTER 10

Unknown to them, Foxy-Roxy and Neil's Rum Runner's Cove meeting was being observed by Bessie Prince Blount, another hotel guest, who silently listened unobserved from an adjacent table. Bessie Prince's ears perked up at the mention of Monte's recent windfall. Monetary matters recently ranked very high on Bessie Prince's list of concerns.

She silently evaluated the situation.

He's really not a bad looking fellow. Has kind of a sweet, kind look. And we're probably about the same age. And he appears to be a single. That must be his family with him.

Her ears perked up again when Foxy-Roxy suggested that Monte and his family take a hotel-sponsored field trip to Dunn's River Falls and Shaw Park Gardens in Ocho Rios the following day. She decided to make sure before the evening was concluded that she had reserved a seat on the bus for herself as well. Queisha made the reservation. Bessie Prince silently wondered about Roxy.

I've seen that woman from the hotel somewhere. She looks so familiar. But where? …. It'll come to me.

A long time Montego Bay resident originally from Ireland, Bessie Prince was very familiar with the falls since she and her husband had picnicked there many times over the years. She was now at a crossroads in her life, and with a recent insurance settlement, she had taken advantage of a locals' special package to book a mini vacation for herself at Seascape so she could map out a game plan for herself going forward.

Conclusive, All-Inclusive Confusion

Her former life had all but disintegrated in a puff of smoke over the previous year.

Until that prior year, Bessie Prince had never dreamed that her once settled, comfortable life could disappear like it had done. She had owned her own business, owned her own home, and had been married to a successful husband. Now she had none of the above. All that remained from her former life were her pharmaceutical and cosmetician licenses. And currently, due to adverse circumstances and a disappointing husband, she wasn't using either one of them.

What piqued her interest and stimulated her to decide to have her evening cocktails in Rum Runner's Cove was her almost recognition of Foxy-Roxy in the hotel lobby. She had overheard her using the house phone with Neil to coordinate a meeting. When he stepped off the elevator, Roxy even called him by name. Bessie Prince silently watched them greet each other when he came into the building. After a brief exchange, the man slipped her some rolled up greenbacks. Foxy-Roxy had then smiled and bussed the man on the cheek.

Interesting! Why does she look familiar?

Foxy-Roxy lit a cigarette. The distinctive way she used her hands to dramatize her every move reminded Bessie Prince of someone, but she couldn't remember who. The woman seemed like an amateurish actress giving a bad performance.

Neil took a seat in the lobby and pretended to people-watch while Foxy-Roxy stubbed her cigarette and went into the lounge. The lounge area where nightly performances took place was a piazza style space with a stage at the end. The chairs were all standard plastic furniture. It did have waiter service. The performances were generally average and designed, as was the case in most all-inclusives, for wide appeal using widely recognized musical standards from varying eras.

A few minutes later Monte and his family arrived, and Roxy greeted them. Neil then arose and went into the bar. Bessie Prince followed. But then when she saw Neil sitting at the bar alone instead of immediately joining Foxy-Roxy's guests, she knew she had been right. Something must be afoot.

Why is he pretending he doesn't know her? I just saw *them in the lobby together.*

The scene intrigued Bessie Prince. She seated herself at a table as close as possible and ordered a drink.

Until the previous year Bessie Prince had owned a neighborhood pharmacy that also contained a combination rum bar and unisex hair and nail salon. She called the drug store "Bessie Prince's Fix-You-Up Apothecary." She called the rum bar/hair salon, "Bessie Prince's Sip 'n Snip." She was primarily a pharmacist but was also licensed to work in the hair salon when it was necessary. Yes, Bessie Prince's home life and business life had both been stable, or so she thought, until both had collapsed one after the other in short order.

The first thing to go bad was Bessie Prince's business. Fontana Pharmacy was Jamaica's leading retail pharmacy with six stores located in Jamaica's major cities. Until recently, this had not been a concern for Bessie Prince. But then Fontana opened their first 20,000 square foot superstore in Waterloo Square in Kingston. It was almost like a Wal-Mart with a pharmacy. The store quickly caught on and became wildly successful. It even had a grocery store, a fast-food restaurant, and a rum bar on the premises. There were rumors that it intended to add a gas station and auto repair shop at some point down the road.

Since Montego Bay was Jamaica's second largest city, it was only natural for Fontana bring this winning formula to Mo Bay. When they did, Bessie Prince's business all but collapsed as black ink turned into red ink.

But then to make matters worse, Bessie Prince's stable domestic life collapsed as well. Her now deceased husband, Oliver, had been a local attorney who was on retainer as the house counsel for the Jamaica National Bank. He was also an intangible property specialist who represented reggae artists in their contract negotiations with recording companies. If their careers blossomed, he was also instrumental in assembling a team of competent and honest investment professionals and accountants to evaluate investment proposals, manage and diversify the artist's assets and protect and shield them from the multitude of swindlers that seem to magically appear out of nowhere with pie-in-the-sky, get-rich-quick schemes.

Many of the recording companies were controlled by underworld figures like Dudus Coke of Jamaica's notorious Shower Posse. After Oliver facilitated a major reggae artist's effort to switch from one posse-controlled recording company to an equally savage competitor, the losing posse decided to put him out of business once and for all. They hatched a scheme to make it appear that Oliver was aiding his clients in filing false

Conclusive, All-Inclusive Confusion

loan applications and defrauding the bank he was supposed to be representing. They then coerced posse-friendly board members in the Jamaican Bar Association to recommend the revocation of Oliver's Certificate of Legal Education from the Norman Manley Law School, thereby shutting his practice once and for all.

With no income coming in from either side, the Blounts began to rely more and more on the lines of credit that they had on their home and her store. The debt ballooned, and their payments got further and further behind. They considered selling, but the only offers they got wouldn't even cover the debt. The bank finally foreclosed, and everything was lost. Now their only source of income was the meager amount Bessie Prince brought by using her cosmetician skills with local funeral homes. Oliver began to suffer from depression and turned to rum as a solution.

The last asset of any meaningful value that the Blounts owned was Oliver's paid-up life insurance policy. This is the money that Bessie Prince was living off of now. Oliver had died when he tried to cut across a busy road on his bike as he drunkenly weaved home from a rum bar. The insurance company ruled his death as being an accident and paid Bessie Prince the proceeds. Even though she would never say so to anyone else, Bessie Prince would always wonder if Oliver's accident had been a drunken, depression-driven suicide mission.

Now Bessie Prince watched Foxy-Roxy and her mysterious partner with interest. After everyone's drinks had been served, the man at the bar nonchalantly walked past the Connors party's table. Foxy-Roxy appeared to recognize him and rose to hug him as if she hadn't seen him in a long time. She said how great it was to see him again and how glad she was that he was back in Jamaica. She asked if his trip was business or pleasure. He replied some of both. Then Foxy-Roxy seemed to remember that she hadn't introduced him to her other guests. They talked until Monte invited the man to join them. He immediately accepted and pulled up a chair next to Monte.

As she continued to sip on her drink, Bessie Prince kept looking at Foxy-Roxy.

I know that I know this person. Was she a customer at the apothecary? Or maybe the hair salon? Hair! ... Of course! That's where I've seen her. She's just older now. And she has her clothes on.

Bessie Prince's thoughts reverted to a temporary job she had stumbled into a few years back. A low-budget, soft porn film company had decided to do some films in Mo Bay and had contracted with her "Sip 'n Snip" to be the hairdresser for their players. To fully utilize the rented costumes and movie sets, they had shot three movies back-to-back using the same players. The first film was entitled "Pirates of the Caribbean - A XXX Parody," and followed by "Orgy Pirates of the Caribbean XXX." The last movie in the trilogy was simply called "Pirates XXX." A fourth movie with a working title of "Harlots of the Caribbean XXX" had never gotten made. Bessie Prince had been hired to do both hair and makeup for the actors. Foxy-Roxy had been one of the actresses. These movies had been the thing that had originally introduced Foxy-Roxy to Jamaica. After several months of shooting, she had decided she liked the country and stayed.

Well! Well! Well! Still the actress. I wonder if she remembers me. Probably not. I was just local temporary help, not an actor. And she was just a bit player. The star was Long Dong Silver.

Bessie Prince smiled as she remembered how the actor got his name.

... She went by Remy LaCroix in those days best I remember. ... But just to be on the safe side, I'd better wear sunglasses and a floppy hat when she's around.

But then Foxy-Roxy looked straight at her and didn't give her a second look. Bessie Prince breathed a sigh of relief. It was obvious that she had been right. There was no recognition.

When Queisha came in the lounge and told them and gave them six tickets to Dunn's River Falls for the following day, Bessie Prince suddenly knew exactly where she'd be spending her day. She followed Queisha back out to the front desk and booked an excursion for herself to the Falls.

"Oh, you'll enjoy the falls," Queisha said. "And by the way, I'll be on the bus as your guide."

CHICKEN DRUMSTICKS
(BACK LEGS ONLY)

CHAPTER 11

The following morning, they all gathered in a designated section of the hotel lobby to wait to depart with Queisha, their guide. Once everyone was aboard the hotel minibus, she read out the names of each guest to ensure that no one a being left behind. Each seat sat two people comfortably leaving Monte momentarily in a seat to himself. Bessie Prince made a beeline to that row before someone else could take the seat.

"Do you mind if I sit next to you?" Bessie Prince asked.

"Of course not," Monte replied. "Welcome aboard. My name is Monte."

"And I'm Bessie Prince."

Monte had a favorable first impression of his new seatmate. She was an unpretentious, neatly dressed, mature woman who seemed to be about his age. She was shapely, slightly busty, and looked good in her clothes. Her hair was neatly and conservatively styled, and her smile put him at ease. She seemed to be a person that, while she was naturally attractive, didn't fully realize how beautiful she possibly was and hadn't tried too hard to artificially enhance her appearance. She had a soft accent that made her seem well educated and well bred. Her tan made him think that she was not a stranger to the outdoors. He noted that she did not wear a wedding ring.

Bessie Prince was silently appraising him in return. Now that she had gotten close to Monte for the first time, her first impression was favorable as well. He seemed to her to be a genuinely nice person.

After one last passenger got aboard, the bus departed.

"Welcome aboard," Queisha said. "I'll be your guide today to and from the falls. And yes, I'm the desk clerk most of you have seen in the hotel. Our driver, Nakomis, should be familiar to you as well. He brought many of you to the hotel from the Montego Bay airport when you arrived. Going to the falls is not work for me. I've been playing in these falls since I was a small child. It looks like an irie day to go visit them. Not only is the weather perfect, but there are no cruise ships in port so it shouldn't be overcrowded. If you are going to climb the falls, I hope you've got your bathing suit on. ... And I hope you have some water shoes. Don't worry if you don't, you can either buy or rent some water shoes at the falls. And don't let the falls intimidate you. They're about six hundred feet but aren't as challenging as they seem. And you will have an experienced guide taking you up. The guides will be the ones in the blue shirts. By the way, it is customary to tip your guide at the end. The amount is up to you.

"Now, sit back and enjoy the ride. It's not far. We should be there in about twenty minutes. I hope you will all opt to climb the falls, but don't feel like you have to. If you don't, there's a paved path with handrails that will take you all the way up and give you a full view as you go."

"Do you plan to climb the falls?" Bessie Prince asked Monte.

"Of course. I've never done anything like that before. How about you?"

"Absolutely. I've climbed them many a time, but I never get tired of the trek. And the cool water is so ... sooo refreshing."

"Oh, ... so you've visited Jamaica before."

"I live here."

"But you're staying at the hotel."

"Just for a little staycation. They have a locals' package that's very attractive."

"So that's why you have such a great tan. ... And I might add, you have a delightful accent."

"Well, thank you. I'm originally from Ireland."

"Married?"

"Widowed. How about you?"

"Single. Maybe we can get together for a drink or dinner at the hotel. Maybe tonight."

"I'd like that. My room number is 423."

Conclusive, All-Inclusive Confusion

Jax and Eve were sitting across the aisle from them. He was munching a gummy bear. Jax's ears and radar perked up when he heard that Monte and Bessie Prince might see each other again.

What you wanna bet the broad's up to something? And if she's not, I bet she will be when she finds out Monte's loaded. But he's too big a putz to see that. I better keep an eye on things.

Queisha stood and began to speak again about that time.

"While we are all still together, let me give you a brief history of Dunn's River Falls. As I'm sure you know, Jamaica is where Christopher Columbus originally landed in the New World in 1494. He was greeted by about 60,000 Arawak Indians. Their name for the island was Xaymaca, which stood for the land of springs. That's how Jamaica got its name. When you see the falls, you'll understand why they called it that. The Spanish were the first European settlers, but then the British came along and challenged them. In 1657, not far from the falls, the British, in what is called the battle of Las Chorreras, ... Chorreras is the Spanish word for waterfalls ... defeated the Spanish expeditionary force from Cuba and took over the island once and for all. Jamaica then remained part of the British empire until 1962, at which time it became an autonomous nation.

"Dunn's River Falls was once privately owned but now is owned by the Jamaican government. It's considered a national treasure. Its image is even on our one-hundred-dollar bill."

"Since neither of us has a partner, would you climb the falls with me?" Bessie Prince asked Monte.

"It would be an honor."

"Believe me when I say the honor is all mine."

This is beginning to work like a charm.

"We've arrived," Queisha announced.

The falls started from the top of a hill and ran under the main road directly into the sea. The driver had to go off the main road and up a hill to the parking lot. Once they got to the entrance, they then went back down the hill in order to reach the bottom of the falls and the pristine beach that was the beginning of the sea.

"Take as little as possible up the falls with you. You are going to get wet," Queisha advised. "Leave the rest on the bus. Nakomis will watch out for your things. And I would not take my cell phone to take pictures. You may ruin it. You can buy a waterproof camera at the gift shop."

Everyone got out of the bus and after Queisha paid their entrance fee, she led them single file down the path to the bottom of the falls.

When they all arrived at the bottom, she said, "Attention, everyone. Hold up your hand if you plan on climbing the falls."

She took a headcount, and then introduced them to their dreadlocked guide.

"This is Delroy. He will take you safely up the falls. But be careful. Many of these rocks are covered with algae and can sometimes be quite slippery. And there's a lot of force to the water in some places. You will hold hands and form a daisy chain on the way up. I know climbing while holding a stranger's hand is a lesson in trust. But injuries are few and far between. Don't abuse that trust and have your carelessness cause someone else to fall. You'll encounter some pools that can sometimes be quite deep, and sometimes the current will get a little strong. You'll find footholds in the rocks that'll help you climb. Delroy knows where they are.

"Now, line up, follow him, and enjoy your climb. Relax and have an irie day."

Monte lined up behind Bessie Prince and grasped her hand. Bessie Prince suggested that he go in front of her so he could help her if necessary. Jax noticed the handholding and frowned. A tall goateed black man with a shaved head and a petite Asian woman in a two-piece bathing suit with dyed red hair lined up behind them. From their speech patterns, it was obvious that they were Americans. Klutzy Jax tried to push ahead of them causing the woman to stumble slightly. The man frowned and stepped in front of him again. Jax looked at the muscled arms that protruded from the man's sleeveless t-shirt and backed away, tripping over the woman's foot. Her partner now glared at him and said, "You got a problem, buster?"

Banks tried to lighten the scene and said, "Don't mind him. He's just my spastic, clumsy brother-in-law. In fact, clumsy is why he's my brother-in-law. He fell in love."

"Oh, yeah?"

"And we cut him some slack because he sees flying saucers."

"You trying to say he's crazy?"

"Nah! He's just an extremely clumsy wader. ... We cool now?"

"I guess."

Conclusive, All-Inclusive Confusion

"Yeah," Jax said. "I'm cool."

Eve rolled her eyes at her sister Viv. Viv smiled and rolled hers back as if to say, *Don't look at me. You married him and his gummy bears.*

The climbers started at the bottom like a sea of humanity flowing upriver. They were reminiscent of a school of salmon at spawning time. But, unlike spawning salmon, these waterfall climbers would live to tell the tale. Jax was a possible exception. Each relatively large group made their way upstream from one pool to the next. There, their guide entertained them as he bought time while he waited for the group ahead of them to clear the way so they could continue their upward ascent. Once moving again, their line seemed to travel fairly quickly as they traversed the next section of the falls. Then they would bunch up again when they reached the next pool.

As they waited in one pool, Bessie Prince told Monte, "It's too bad that we won't be in Ochi tonight. If we were, I'd take you to one of my favorite little restaurants not too far from here. Do you like Italian food?"

"Love it."

"Well, there's a good Italian one here. It's in a lushly landscaped, eighteen-hundreds built, gingerbread house on top of one of Ocho Rios's steepest hills. In fact, cars have to downshift into first gear to get up the last part of it to the parking lot. But once you get there, you have one of the best panoramic views of Ochi and the bay you'll ever see. It used to be an inn, but after Evita moved here from Venice, she turned it into an exquisite Northern Italian restaurant and piano bar."

"Sounds wonderful."

"And you'd adore the owner, Evita. I'm not sure how many languages she speaks, but she loves to charm her patrons with her old-world ways to make sure they have an unforgettable experience and come back. Two of her devoted fans are Mick Jagger and Keith Richards."

"Do they perform there?"

"Not officially, but they have been known to join the piano player for a few tunes when the mood or the rum strikes them."

"Bessie Prince, I'm really glad we met. There's nothing like having a local tell you what's what."

He squeezed her hand; she squeezed his in return. Jax noted both gestures and frowned. He tried to move closer in order to overhear their conversation just as the guide told them it was time to move on. Jax was so preoccupied with snooping and eating a gummy bear that he didn't watch his step.

Instead of wearing water shoes as had been recommended, Jax had worn a ratty pair of high-top sneakers. The tread had partially been worn down from use, making them somewhat slick. He stepped in an underwater hole and pitched forward. He tried to regain his traction but failed. His flailing arms pushed Monte and Bessie Prince out of the way. He continued to plunge forward, burying his head in the red-haired Asian woman's butt-crack, pitching her into her husband. Making matters worse, the thumbs on his flailing hands lodged under her bra strap dragging it down. She immediately tried to cover herself. Her athletic, black companion was in no mood to be gracious again. He came back around with a roundhouse punch. Since Jax was tumbling, the man missed him on the first punch and grazed Banks. He partially connected with Jax on the way back. Jax reached out again to try to stabilize himself, but this time he pulled down the man's bathing suit with one hand while he grabbed his private parts with the other. When Jax realized what he had done, he released his handhold, just as the man's knee caught him in the belly. He twisted around in the other direction to avoid a second blow from a kick, but it caught him in the groin.

Jax screamed in agony and his gut released in a projectile the mound of the undigested pancakes and sausage he had eaten for breakfast plus the gummy bears he'd been munching on since then, covering Viv, Banks, and the large breasted, chubby woman behind them. About this time, the black guy connected with Jax's backside with a second kick. Jax clawed the stout woman's boobs as he pitched forward. She bared her teeth like a rabid dog and responded by clawing down his bathing suit and lacerating his already throbbing midsection and thighs with her long nails. He screamed again as the water hit the exposed bleeding gashes. Two local men pulled knives that mysteriously seemed to appear from nowhere in their hands.

In the meantime, Delroy, their guide, rushed back to try to defuse the deteriorating situation. The still moaning Jax slipped again and caught hold of Delroy's dreads, pulling him backwards into the rest of the line of falls climbers. They began to go down like dominos, many taking pieces of other climber's clothes with them. Skinned knees and elbows abounded, but fortunately no one was seriously hurt.

Conclusive, All-Inclusive Confusion

When Jax saw the drawn knives, he took off streaking in the nude down the falls, stumbling into the group below them. An assemblage from both groups began to chase him, screaming epithets as they did so. He dashed across the beach area at the foot of the falls and out into the ocean, knocking Queisha down along the way. An angry mob lined up along the shore and began to throw things at him. Delroy ran back and forth as he tried to calm the seething throng down.

Queisha wasn't sure what had happened, but she knew she couldn't put Jax back on the bus. She called to get a hotel hospitality car to take him back to the hotel. There was no way she could allow him back on the bus and guarantee his safety.

Eventually with Nakomis' help Queisha was able to get the angry horde to go to the locker room and change into dry clothes for the trip back to the hotel.

When everyone had left except Eve, she signaled Jax that it was safe to come out of the water. She turned to Eve and said, "Are you his wife?"

Eve sighed and nodded.

"I've called the hotel hospitality car to take him back. I think that's best. I assume you'll be riding back with him."

"Thank you. I don't think I could face those people on the bus."

"I understand. Accidents do happen."

"With Jax, all too often."

"Well, get out of those wet clothes and wait by the locker room. The car's on its way. I need to get everyone else loaded on the bus. Are you going to be OK?"

Eve nodded, and Queisha left them there.

As everyone reboarded the bus, Bessie Prince whispered to Monte, "Why don't I plan to bring you back here another day — just the two of us?"

"I'd like that. We still on for dinner?"

"Wouldn't miss it for the world. What time?"

> # TRESSPASSERS WILL BE ~~PROSEC~~ ~~PROSEC~~ ~~PROUDSIC~~ HEAD BUTTED

CHAPTER 12

As they rode back to the hotel, Bessie Prince commented. "I see Calamity Cal's seat is vacant."

"Actually, his name is Jax Magnus," Monte replied.

"You know him?"

"He's my son-in-law."

"Oh, I didn't know. I'm sorry I made fun of him."

"No problem. Jax made his own bed today."

They sat in silence, each wondering what to say next.

Monte finally spoke first and said, "Bessie Prince, I don't know about you, but I'm hungry now. Instead of waiting until dinner since we're in dry clothes, why don't we have a late lunch together. You like pizza?"

"Love it."

"Would you join me in one, then? My treat."

"It'll be a treat. Love to."

When they arrived back at the hotel, Monte and Bessie Prince walked over to Dolce Vita, the hotel Italian restaurant. Potsy had been prowling the lobby hoping to run into Monte alone. Neil had found out from Foxy-Roxy that morning what the bus's afternoon estimated time of arrival was, so he was waiting on a love seat as well on the opposite side of the lobby pretending to read. Maybe he could catch Monte. Neither man noticed the presence of the other.

The automated door to the lobby opened and the returning falls tour group streamed into the hotel. They were still boisterously discussing and

Conclusive, All-Inclusive Confusion

debating the incident that had happened at the falls. Some limped slightly, some had skinned limbs and bruises. Both Neil and Potsy wondered if the bus had possibly been in an accident. Most got on the elevator to go to their rooms, but Monte and Bessie Prince came in and detoured towards Dolce Vita.

"Pizza and sangria sound awfully good," he heard Bessie Prince say. "Do you like sangria?"

"I'm not sure I ever had any."

As Potsy listened, he decided that he was suddenly in the mood for Italian as well. And when Neil saw that, he certainly didn't want to get left out. Potsy had to be up to no good.

This is a perfect time to make Potsy aware of my presence.

Potsy waited for Monte to order before "accidentally" approaching his table.

"Mr. Connors! What a surprise to run into you again. Are you enjoying your vacation? And who is this lovely lady?"

"Bessie Prince, this is Mr. Potter. He's the kind gentleman who found my lost bag at the airport and brought it back to me."

The waiter brought out the pitcher of sangria.

"That looks delicious," Potsy commented.

"Why don't you join us?" Monte suggested. "Uh, miss, would you bring out another glass for my friend?"

"If I wouldn't be imposing …"

"Not at all."

"Shit! Shit! Shit!" Neil mumbled to himself. "I can't let Potsy Potter make brownie points."

He too approached the table.

"Mr. Connors, nice to see you again. I really enjoyed meeting you last night. I was hoping to get to know you and your family better while you're here."

"We were hoping the same thing. We'd love to have you join us now if you like," Monte offered. "We're just having an informal late lunch."

Now it was both Bessie Prince and Potsy who thought, *Shit! And double shit!*

Potsy had a second thought, *What the hell's Neil-the-Heel doing here? Jesus Christ! This Monte summbitch must really be a big fish. Well, just call me Simon*

Peter, the fisherman. Even if I'm not from Galilee, I can put out a net with the best of them. … And then reel 'em in.

Potsy zoned back in when Monte asked if the two of them had ever met and offered to introduce them.

"Oh, no," they both blurted out simultaneously.

"Waitress, can you add another pizza to our order, and I think we'll need another pitcher of this delicious — what'd you call it, Bessie Prince? — sangria? … Yeh! … And we'll need one more glass. This is turning out to be quite a party."

You can damned well say that again, Bessie Prince, Potsy, and Neil all thought as they eyed each other.

Bessie Prince had an additional thought, *Now's not the time to be unpleasant or demanding. You almost messed up once on the bus criticizing Monte's dumb son-in-law. Better cool it, girl.*

She then smiled and agreed with Monte.

"Many hands make light work of having fun. Gentlemen, vade ad victor spolia (to the victor belong the spoils)."

The three men looked at other two and momentarily wondered, *I wonder what she means by that. Surely she doesn't wonder if the pizza'll be spoiled.*

Bessie Prince flashed what she considered to be her best smile knowing that no one understood.

Before lunch had concluded, between the two of them, Potsy and Neil had expertly systematically picked out of both Monte and Bessie Prince pretty much everything they thought they needed to know about both of them. Or they thought they did.

Bessie Prince's bio was partially fabricated. When Monte talked about his long career working for the church, Bessie Prince saw opportunity. On the spur of the moment, she composed a story about once being a church secretary herself and how her deceased husband had been a choir director. She even threw in a story that she had a deceased brother who'd been a minister. And when Monte mentioned being a caregiver for his mother, Bessie Prince told a similar tale about taking care of her cancer-ridden husband.

Go for it, girl. If you're going to lie, lie big.

Monte's response was silence, but Bessie Prince could tell by the way his eyes lit up and his head nodded that she'd hit paydirt.

Conclusive, All-Inclusive Confusion

Wow! This lady and I have so much in common. And I think she likes me. It's going to be so fantastic to have someone other than my family to pal around with. It's got to be providence. Thank you, Lord. You must have sent me to Seascape for a reason.

Of course, Neil and Potsy's own bios were totally fabricated or embellished. Neither of them refuted the other man's personal history even though they both knew better. Both felt good about the luncheon even though they wished their competition hadn't been there. Neither suspected Bessie Prince of having a nefarious motive, but both were sure that if this proved to be wrong, they would be up to the challenge. After all, they were professionals.

Both were careful not to make up a story around the other one that could later be used by their adversary to undermine them or to tip their hand prematurely with Monte. After all, this was only a fact gathering session — a strategy session if you will. They would each now do their real work on Monte in private.

Bessie Prince felt that the luncheon had been a success for her as well. She learned more about Monte and was glad she hadn't been the one probing him for information.

Sometimes it's best just to listen and let these nice boys do the heavy lifting. … Though, I've got to wonder what their angle really is. Maybe, girl, you're just getting cynical in your old age. … Hope so.

I don't want him to think of me even remotely as a gold digger. And I find it interesting that Monte's three daughters are all adopted since he's never been married.

Both Neil and Potsy were each now totally convinced that "Operation Monte" was a go, but that it would be necessary for each of them to somehow eliminate or discredit their competition. Bessie Prince was convinced as well that she had made the right choice to go after Monte. Her woman's intuition told her that both men were a potential threat, even though she wasn't sure how.

But I've got one advantage over anyone else at this table. I'm a female. … And not such a bad looking one, if I say so myself.

Monte was having thoughts of his own.

I've met some of the nicest people at this hotel. I can't wait to tell the girls about them. And also, about this sangria. It's delicious.

> SCHOOL
> DRUG
> FREE
> ZONE
> ENFORCED

CHAPTER 13

After their luncheon with Neil and Potsy had concluded and they were alone again, Bessie Prince asked Monte, "Does this lunch date mean that dinner tonight is cancelled?"

"Not unless you want it to be," Monte responded.

"I was hoping you'd say that. Do you like to dance?"

"I ... uh ... guess so. I've never had much of an opportunity to get good at it though."

The truth of the matter was Monte was a wallflower's wallflower. He had never attended a formal dance as a participant, only chaperoned a few parish functions. His mother had shown him some basic steps when he was young, but he had never actually put them to use.

"My guess is that you're better than you think. I think you'd make an excellent partner."

She squeezed Monte's hand. Her warm hand really felt good.

By the time Monte got back up to his room, he was in dreamland.

Oh my gosh! This beautiful lady actually referred to me as her partner. I've never been anyone's partner before.

Monte had never had a girlfriend. He had been an awkward teenager who had always been afraid to talk to girls. And none had ever sought him out for social reasons. He had never dated anyone as an adult. He had never moved away from home — not even to go to college. His whole grownup life had been consumed by taking care of his divorced mother as her health had deteriorated and she came to depend on him

Conclusive, All-Inclusive Confusion

more and more. He had helped chaperone church sponsored teen dances at St. Benedict's, the Catholic Church that employed him, but he had never actually participated in any of them.

When Monte got back up to his room, Nan asked him what he wanted to do about dinner that night. He hesitated at first but couldn't wait to tell her that he had a date that evening and asked her if she and her sisters minded if he didn't join them for dinner.

"Of course not," Nan said.

Nan later reported to Eve and Viv that she had never seen her dad this infatuated with anyone before. Both Jax and Banks grimaced they listened to what Nan was telling them.

This old Blount broad's got an agenda, and it can't be good for any of us.

But Monte felt differently. He felt like his life up to this point had been just like any other. There was nothing special, and he hadn't even wanted to feel special since every day had been methodical. He would wake up, get ready for his day, do his mundane job, eat, take care of his mother, or maybe watch TV with his daughters, and then go to bed. Everything had been on repeat. His mom had cautioned him for his whole life about doing something stupid, and after all, mama knew best. *Her* marriage hadn't worked out. He could hear her now. Don't risk the status quo. And she had been right until now. There had been no reason to upset the applecart because this routine had been easy. He didn't have to try hard. And nothing kept him up at night. He didn't have to worry about making mistakes because he never searched for anything that might make him look like a fool. On the few occasions where he gave his life any thought, he couldn't understand why people were willing to risk their inner piece for a momentary or short-lived rush of happiness. Why cloud your future by putting any obstacles in the way?

But now the thought of Bessie Prince lit up his eyes. Her smile lit up the whole room. Her eyes were a perfect blue. He thought about her touch when her hand touched his on the bus and again at the falls. He thought about the prospect of holding those hands again that evening as they danced. He thought about watching her walk across the hotel lobby and how it made his heart stir. He didn't know why, but she made him feel feelings that he had never felt before. He wanted to spend the rest of his time at Seascape with her even though after this week was over and he returned to Detroit and she returned to Mo Bay, he might never see her again. Now was the time for him to share as many special moments with Bessie Prince as the days allowed. He wanted to immerse himself in her. He wanted them to share jokes and thoughts and to learn as much as he could about this marvelous creature.

Suddenly he was no longer content with just being normal. And his mom telling him not to do anything stupid just made him want to search for something more than the boring life he had lived up until now in Detroit. Since he had met Bessie Prince, a fire had been lit and seemed to grow in intensity. For the first time in his life Monte felt willing to risk something that might make his future blurrier as he now kicked possibilities back and forth that would have been unthought of until now. And for once, the possibility of magnificence outweighed fear of the unknown. He felt suddenly inclined, before it was too late, to leap into that maze of uncertainty and then negotiate his way out of the maze again, even at the risk of getting hurt and possibly destroying his inner peace. And now, thanks to his lottery winnings, he had the resources to do so. Surely his girls would understand. He wouldn't love them less. In fact, if he were truly happy, he would have the ability to love them more.

```
ANAL EGG HUNT
APRIL 10 10 AM
FREE FAMILY EVENT
```

CHAPTER 14

"Guys, Dad won't be joining us for dinner tonight. He has other plans. He tried to play down how much this evening out means to him, but I think he may be smitten by this Bessie Prince person he met going to Dunn's River Falls," Nan reported to her siblings. "They had lunch together when they got back, and now he's taking her to dinner tonight."

"That doesn't sound like our dad," Eve said. "I don't remember him ever having a date."

"Me either," Viv agreed, "but I'm happy for him. Some company will make his vacation experience complete and memorable."

"I just don't want to see him get his feelings hurt," Eve said.

"I'm not sure I've ever seen Dad giddy about a woman before," Nan continued. "I don't know much about her, but I think she's local and that's she a widow."

"I wouldn't worry about it then. Let them enjoy themselves. We'll be going back to Detroit soon, and she'll still be down here."

Jax and Banks weren't so sure. In fact, they were pissed. Royally P — O — ed. They had both hoped to spend the week solidifying their relationship with their now loaded father-in-law with no unnecessary distractions.

"I guess we're on our own for this evening," Nan said. "You guys want to do anything special?"

"I saw a flyer in the lobby that there's packaged show doing a limited run here at the hotel called 'The Best of Broadway — A Musical Revue'. It'll only be playing for the rest of the week."

"Sounds like fun to me," Banks said. "I'll go down to the lobby and get us tickets to the eight o'clocker. We'll have an early dinner and then go to the show."

"Since it's just us young folks, why don't we try Don Pablo Gourmet Restaurant," Jax said. "I understand that they do kind of an experimental, modernistic cuisine. That's probably something Monte wouldn't want to go to anyway. The foods he eats are pretty cut and dried. You know, a meat and potato man."

"He certainly isn't venturesome. He hesitates to eat a steak if any pink is showing."

"Let's face it. His ruts have ruts. Do you know what a rut is?"

"What's that?"

"A grave with both ends kicked out."

"Well, ruts aren't for me," Jax said. "As you know, I like to be adventuresome when it comes to food."

"As long as the portions are big," his wife said and patted Jax's ample waistline.

The group laughed as Jax blushed.

Later, when they arrived at Don Pablo, they found its cuisine to indeed be the unexpected. The two soups of the day were cream of shrimp soup and a caramelized onion soup. They sampled both. This led to an imaginative array of entrees. Jax had salmon tartare, while Eve and Nan had a surf and turf dish consisting of beef sirloin in rosemary sauce served with prawns in champagne. Banks went with prawns on pineapple carpaccio and port jelly. Viv had breaded crabmeat with black truffle mayonnaise on top of a garden salad.

"I'm getting stuffed," Viv said as they finished.

"Not me," Jax said. "We've still got desert to go."

They ended up ordering after-dinner Blue Mountain coffee and a variety of deserts — a banana flambé, an apple tart on a caramel sauce with homemade vanilla ice cream, a passion fruit crème brûlée, and a Jamaican baba.

"What's a baba?" Jax asked.

Conclusive, All-Inclusive Confusion

"Oh, you will find it to be delicious, sir," their waiter replied. "It's a sweet yeast cake made in a mini bundt mold. It's soaked with spices and Appleton rum and topped with a berry infused cardamon compote and chocolate sauce."

"Wow! I'll take that, and if it's a good as you make it sound, I may go for seconds."

The group smiled. After all, Jax's appetite *was* well known.

As they waited for their deserts to be served, Monte and Bessie Prince came into the restaurant holding hands. They were so involved with each other that they didn't notice Monte's family until Jax called out to them.

Monte then brought Bessie Prince over to their table and said, "Bessie Prince, this is my family. Guys, have you met my new friend, Bessie Prince?"

He then introduced everyone. Jax and Banks both tried to be gracious even though neither of them felt that way.

"My darlings, don't wait up," Monte said and winked. "I may be late. Bessie Prince and I are going dancing. And after that, we're planning kick off our flip flops and walk on the beach for a spell. Bessie Prince's going to show me how to identify some of the constellations. Have you noticed how brilliant the stars are down here in the Caribbean when you get away from civilization's artificial lighting? ... Certainly different from Highland Park."

Monte taking a romantic walk on the beach? Holy shit!

They looked down at his feet. He *did* have on flip flops. They had never seen him go sockless before at home, and he didn't even own any loafers except for his bedroom slippers. He was strictly a black lace-up, cap-toe man. He wouldn't even go barefooted at home unless he was getting in the shower.

They were speechless.

The waiter then led Monte and Bessie Prince to a table. Monte pulled out Bessie Prince's chair before the waiter could do so and then sat down himself.

They heard her say, "Thank you, dear. You're such a gentleman."

Bessie Prince ordered a bottle of wine. After Monte and Bessie Prince were each served a glass of it, they began to examine and discuss the menu and finally ordered. Both started with the amuse bouche. Monte's entrée was duck with a black truffle sauce and roasted parsley potatoes served with a Bordeaux infused apple compote and vegetables à la meuniere; Bessie Prince ordered lemon parsley buttered meuniere with black rice, shrimp, and a medley of vegetables.

"What was that you were saying about Monte being unadventurous and lacking imagination?" Banks commented. "Looks like that woman is already curing that."

To himself, he thought, *I gotta do something about this shit. I gotta fix her little red wagon before I lose control of this situation. There's too much at stake. ... I just don't know how to do it yet. But something'll come to me. ... It always does.*

Jax was barely paying Monte and Bessie Prince any mind since his attention was riveted on the baba the waiter placed in front of him.

Oh, what a smell!

He was already thinking about a second one.

After dinner, the group waved at Monte and Bessie Prince and took a leisurely stroll to the hotel's theater. The show was very professionally done and worthwhile. It featured popular tunes from "Oklahoma." "RENT," "Footloose," "The Wiz," "Chicago," "A Chorus Line," "Dreamgirls," and more famous Broadway shows than they would be able remember later.

"These are some of the best singers I've ever heard," Nan commented. "Every one of these young people could be on Broadway making tons of money, but instead, here they are playing at a tourist hotel for probably next to nothing."

When Banks heard "next to nothing," a light went off in his head.

That's the answer I was waiting for. I'll hire one of the actors to try to scare Bessie Prince off. I can't risk doing it myself because if Monte caught me, it'd be all over with him and me and probably Viv as well. One of these people ought to be able to do it right. After all, they are professional actors who I'm sure can use some extra dough. Wonder what'd it'll cost me? Doesn't make a lot of difference. I'll pay him with Monte's money. ... Ain't that ironic!

Banks spent the rest of the show memorizing the faces of the singers so he could identify them later. The following day this paid off when he saw one of the actors reading by the pool.

"Excuse me, sir. My name is Banks Bridges. And yours? ..."

"Kemp Morrison."

"Kemp, weren't you in the show we saw last night? It was excellent, but you were especially outstanding ... really stood out. How'd you like

Conclusive, All-Inclusive Confusion

to make a little extra money doing something that won't take long? There's a professional con artist staying at the hotel who has targeted my naïve father-in-law. I want to scare her off without him finding out about it. And don't worry about her recognizing you. She hasn't attended one of your shows."

For three hundred dollars, Banks hired Kemp to be an "insurance investigator," showed him a picture of Bessie Prince that he'd taken with his Smartphone, and outlined the script he wanted the actor to use.

"Use the names Ben Casey and Guardian Insurance. I looked Guardian up on the internet, and they really have an employee by that name."

Then they rehearsed it a few times to make sure Kemp covered the points that Banks wanted him to.

Banks told Kemp that Bessie Prince liked to read alone out by the pool in the mornings before it got too hot.

"That's where you ought to find her."

The very next morning he hit paydirt. There was Bessie Prince right on schedule, right where she was supposed to be, and she was alone. He moved in. Neil-The-Heel was also skulking about in case any opportunities of any sort presented themselves.

"Uh, excuse me ma'am. May I have a few moments of your time? My name's Ben Casey. I'm an insurance investigator for Guardian Insurance."

Neil instantly recognized Kemp.

What the hell is he up to? I think I'll hang out here for a while.

"What do you want with me? I've never dealt with them before."

"It's not you I'm investigating. It's someone I have seen you with. A Beauregard Montgomery or BM Connors.

"BM? ... B. Montgomery? ... Oh, you must mean Monte. ... I just met him here at the hotel."

"Yes, ma'am, but he sometimes goes by Bo or somewhat appropriately when it serves his purpose, BM. What do you know about him?"

"You make him sound like an offensive bodily function, but he's not noxious at all. He's really quite agreeable. Actually, he's a church social worker from Detroit who recently came into some money."

"Did he tell you the source of that money?"

"He won the lottery."

"That's what he said?"

"Yes. That's not right?"

"Uh, no, ma'am. The source of that money was a large life insurance policy with my employer, Guardian Insurance, on his now deceased wife."

"But Monte's never been married!"

"That's what he said? Hmmm! ... Actually, he's been married several times, and each of his wives was very well insured ... with double indemnity clauses for accidental death, I might add ... he collected the maximum amount on each of 'em."

"Are you sure we're talking about the same person?"

"Yes, ma'am, I'm sure. That's why the insurance company sent me down here. They think it was a little too coincidental. We have cause for concern because he took out a policy on each of his unmarried daughters as well with him being the beneficiary, but when they got married, he remained as such instead switching it to their husbands."

"Monte would never do anything to hurt those girls. He loves them. That's why he adopted them."

"That's not quite accurate either, ma'am. They're his stepdaughters who were a result of his wife's previous marriage."

"Are you trying to infer that Monte is a black widower — a serial killer?"

"I don't want to go on record as saying that, but off the record, you might be wise to distance yourself from him. ... Just to be on the safe side. He met each of his previous wives at a resort much like this one."

Neil overheard the exchange. He knew Kemp Morrison was a performer not an insurance investigator name Ben Casey.

Who the hell put him up to that? And why?

He followed Kemp through the lobby as he tried to think matters out. He didn't have to wait long before his questions were answered. Banks was sitting a couch in the lobby waiting for Kemp. Kemp joined him there, and an earnest discussion was soon underway as Banks debriefed him. Then Banks paid Kemp the remainder of the money he had promised, Kemp said something about it being a pleasure to do business with him and then he walked away.

Well, well, well! I didn't have to wonder long. So a member of Mr. lottery-winner's loving family has a greedy agenda of his own.

Well, as my old daddy used to say, money doesn't change people. It just unmasks them. ... Which is what keeps people like me in business.

Conclusive, All-Inclusive Confusion

Neil's ego took hold as he thought about swindling Banks using a plan he'd successfully used many times before.

Greed leads to S-W-A-G time. Steal without a gun. Yeah, boy, S-W-A-G. If I had to take a SWAG, a stupid wild-ass guess, I have a SWAG opportunity, i.e. show the world all my greatness, to SWAG, steal without a gun, and SWAG, sell without a guarantee, anything including the London Bridge to this SWAG, square with amateur goals — a five swagger.

Hot diggity damn, Neil, you're good. Gooder than sex and getting gooder all the time. ... Thank you; thank you very much ... and for my next number ... by popular request .... My popular request.

Yes siree, Bob! Wait'll I tell Foxy-Roxy. It's time for another operation SWAG. We'll put the team on notice. This mark'll never know what hit him as we lighten his load.

> Rough
> Road
> Remove
> Dentures
> Tighten
> Bra Straps

CHAPTER 15

After Ben Casey left, Bessie Prince sat stunned. She tried to return to her reading, but the words wouldn't sink in.

Monte? Bo? BM? Multiple marriages? Suspicious deaths? Insurance policies? He's the most polite, meek-mannered man I've ever met. But Mr. Casey's an insurance investigator who doesn't even know Monte. Why would he go out of his way to slander a nice man like Monte? And does this mean I'm in danger of becoming a victim of my own greed?

She pulled her iPad out of her beach bag and tried to find Monte on the internet. She found very little he hadn't told her already. However she did find a Ben Casey who really worked for Guardian Insurance.

He must be real.

When she finished, she was more confused than ever.

Oh, Monte! I'm really starting to kind of like this guy!

Neil positioned himself on a chaise lounge behind Bessie Prince and pretended to read a magazine as he watched and listened to her mumble to herself as she scanned her computer for information about Monte.

I wonder what this broad's game is. I gotta feeling she's not the sweet widder woman she pretends to be. But at least she's an amateur. If push comes to shove, she'll be no match for me.

After Bessie Prince gave up her research project and went back up to her suite, Monte came downstairs hoping to run into her. He found a vacant umbrella-covered table out by the pool and ordered coffee and a bagel while he waited to see if she'd show up. Neil started to move in

Conclusive, All-Inclusive Confusion

until he saw Potsy Potter. Potsy had spotted Monte alone and decided that this would be a good time to move in himself.

Dammit to hell! Old Potsy's faster than shit going through a goose. Well, ... let's see what happens next. ... Maybe this is good. I'll find out what Potsy's game plan is, and he won't know that I know. Nothing like having surprise on your side.

"Mr. Connors ... Monte, isn't it? ... Wonderful day, wouldn't you say? ... At least for some people. ... Mind if I join you?"

"Yes, it is a pleasant day, Clay. Sure. Have a seat, but I don't know how long I'll be down here. Why did you say, 'for some people?'"

"Oh, ... I'm sorry. That just slipped out. Forget I said it."

"Is something bothering you?"

"I ... Uh ... I ... Uh ... Uh ... I don't want to bother you ... But I guess you are kind of a social worker."

"I do work for the Catholic Church."

"It's Po Junior. Remember I told you he was in a bad car wreck that left him permanently impaired?"

"Yes, I remember. Has anything happened to him?"

"I got a call from the nursing home telling me that Little Po had a panic attack because I'm not there, and it led to a seizure. ... And that the insurance company is saying it's not covered. They might send him to a state facility ... which is horrible ... unless I can pay them while I try to work things out with the insurance company. ... I don't have the kind of money it takes for go after a big corporation. ... Of either sort. Maybe I should cut my stay short here and rush back, but I'm not sure what I'd do if I did. I don't know what to do. Junior wouldn't know me anyway since they say he's in a semi-coma."

He began to cry. His alligator tears were contagious. Monte shed some tears as well.

"Maybe praying would help. Would you pray with me, Monte? Maybe God will answer."

Neil-The-Heel was sitting a few tables away unobserved.

What a crock of shit! Good old Potsy's dramatic skills are as sharp as ever. And that sap Monte's falling for it! Whatever I'm going to do, I better get moving on it, or I'm going to get left out in the cold.

Neil wasn't the only witness to Potsy's display. Jax witnessed it as well. He decided he needed to join them and hurriedly took his coffee over to

Monte's table before Monte and Potsy could pray together. Jax had his own thoughts.

No! No! No, sleazebag! Monte's money is my money, not some stranger's. After all, I'm family, crumb-bum. Go pray with someone else, and I'll pray too. My prayer is why don't you drown while you're doing it?

Jax plopped down and began to dominate the conversation with anything that came into his mind. When Potsy saw that Jax wouldn't be leaving, he excused himself.

I'll catch Monte again when his shithead son-in-law's not around. I now see it's pretty easy to get his sympathy. Despite the interruption, I'm moving ahead. I've planted a seed. What I need to do now is water that seed.

Neil had his own thoughts on the situation … or situations.

All these muthas absolutely got to go. And Kemp Morrison? How'd he get in this picture? How many damned competitors do I have? This ain't a resort; it's a Grand Central Station grifter's convention. But … they're all just cheap rip-off artists. Not like me. I'm an artiste and master of the long con.

Neil suddenly thought of the old Natalie Wood song that he occasionally performed from the movie "Inside Daisy Clover." He couldn't help altering the words slightly and singing a few lines.

> *My comet's on fire; I've got to go higher.*
> *Watch the world over.*
> *Start coming up clover.*
> *That's how it's gonna be, you'll see.*
> *Yes, they're gonna hear from me.*

"Damned straight. Any of them mess with Neil the bull, and I'm gonna give them the horn."

> WE ARE COMMITTED TO EXCELLENSE

CHAPTER 16

Monte gave it another thirty minutes to see if Bessie Prince might make an appearance. When she didn't, he returned to his room and called her from there.

"Missed you downstairs."

"I miss you too. I'm just running behind. Got a matter to resolve. May take a while."

"No problem. Take your time. Why don't we do happy hour in Rum Runner's Cove in the lobby later today and dine afterwards?"

"Sounds great. We haven't been to Orquidea, the international restaurant yet."

"Then let's give it a try. Six OK? I'll pick you up at your room."

"Pick me up, and I'll try not to let you down."

"Cute. I think that'd be impossible."

Monte once again begged off of having dinner with the family. Jax quizzed him about his plans, and Monte outlined the upcoming evening with Bessie Prince. After Monte left his room, Jax knocked on Banks' door and said, "Dad's taking that woman out again."

Promptly at six, Monte knocked on Bessie Prince's door and escorted her down to the lobby. When Monte and Bessie Prince walked into Rum Runner's Cove, Foxy-Roxy was already into her set, singing "Rum and Coca Cola." They found a table and ordered the drink of the day, Jamaican rum punch. Monte waved at Foxy-Roxy and she waved back. When the number ended, she texted Neil that Monte was in the bar.

"Let's do our friends routine when you get here. That always impresses people."

Neil made a beeline for Rum Runner's. Potsy noticed him hurrying through the lobby and followed to find out what he was up. Coincidentally, Banks, oblivious to the other two, slipped in as well to also do his take on the situation.

Once Neil arrived, Foxy-Roxy announced, "We have a hotel guest with us tonight who not only happens to be a friend but is talented as well — Neil Hackinrider. I bet if we give him a little encouragement, he'll come up and join me for a number."

Neil didn't hesitate to join her, kissed her on the cheek, and began the shtick that the two had so often used on cruise ships.

"Foxy, you mentioned friends. Do you know what a friend really is?"

"Why don't you tell us your definition, Neil."

"A person who knows you're insane but loves you anyway."

"Well, I guess that is apropos for us."

"The hell of the matter is that we're both crazy since that's the main thing that keeps us sane."

"Since you brought up hell, I might as well tell you that I don't like to commit myself about either heaven or hell."

Why's that, dear girl?"

"Because I have good friends in both places. I can tell the difference because the good ones are the ones who have stabbed me in the front."

"I don't think either of us need a therapist as much as we just need a good friend to be silly with."

"Do you still remember the friendship medley we used to do together?"

"Does the tinman have a sheet metal cock?"

"Being a lady, I'm not going to answer that one. You ready to sing before these people bail out on us?"

"Indubitably ready, my dear friend."

Neil and Foxy-Roxy launched into their seemingly impromptu but actually well-rehearsed medley that began with "You've Got a Friend in Me," went into "Stand by Me," then "That's What Friends Are For," before ending with "I'll Stand by You." When they finished, Foxy-Roxy announced that she would take a fifteen minute break. Neil pretended to

Conclusive, All-Inclusive Confusion

notice Monte and Bessie Prince for the first time and headed over to their table.

"You guys are unbelievable together," Monte gushed.

"Foxy-Roxy's the pro. She just sort of drags me along and makes me look better than I am. And this lovely lady is …?"

Monte introduced Bessie Prince, and they struck up a lively conversation. Monte looked at his watch and told Neil that they needed to leave if they were going to be on time for their dinner reservation at Orquidea.

"Good choice. I would recommend their crème de fuchi soup and their black fettuccine with squid."

Potsy seethed at the thought that his rival, Neil, was making inroads with Monte.

In the meantime, Foxy-Roxy made a beeline for Banks' table.

"Good to see you again."

"You too, Ms. Sparrow. You and that Neil guy make quite a duo. He's gotta be a professional."

"Actually, he isn't. He's an international businessman and real estate developer, here in Jamaica on a business trip."

"If you don't mind my asking, what kind of business is he in?"

"It's kind of hush-hush."

"Illegal?"

"Sort of, but not really. He's mostly very private so as not to stir up controversy since some people might not approve. Neil designs and sells items made of rare, exotic, often regulated materials for wealthy, high society customers."

"You mean things like emeralds?"

"Much more exotic than that. I mean larimar, topaz, snakewood, black and fossil coral, meteorite, tamarind, ivory, mother of pearl — things like that. For instance, he made silverware with meteorite handles for Charles and Di. … And makes sculptures out of black coral."

"Aren't some of those things illegal to harvest? And also to buy and sell?"

Foxy-Roxy just smiled and said, "But very profitable. And easy for him to get out of the country."

"Wow! It'd be cool to own something like that."

"You're right. I have some myself, and the value just keeps going up and up as restrictions continue to tighten."

"So you know some of the people he buys from?"

She nodded. The hook was being set.

"But I only introduce them to discreet people I trust ... and people who aren't afraid to deal with cash."

"I qualify both ways."

"Let me think about it, and I'll get back to you. Anyway, enjoy the rest of your evening." Good to see you. And tell your wife hello."

When she saw Neil later, Foxy-Roxy said, "I think I've set a hook with the sap of a son-in-law. He was easy. If eyes could drool from greed, his would have. I'd love to get him in a poker game. How'd it go with Daddy Warbucks?"

"Fine. I'm taking it slow. I haven't identified his hot button yet. But I will. He's a big fish, the kind I love to reel in."

> *A CASHIER WANTED*
> *MUST BE 18 YEARS OLD*
> *WITH 20 YEARS EXPERIENCE*

CHAPTER 17

Foxy-Roxy and Neil spent the following day reassembling the cast of characters for their upcoming scam and making sure everyone would be at his station at the designated time. This cast was every bit as well rehearsed as the "impromptu" skit Neil and Foxy-Roxy had performed at Rum Runner's Cove. Each cast member had participated in multiple past tourist scams using the same tried and true format and knew exactly the role they were supposed to play. The skit would probably be accomplished in an hour and had never taken more than ninety minutes. Then the cast would meet at a rum bar later to split the proceeds. Not bad for less than two hour's work with very little chance of repercussions.

Act one had begun when Foxy-Roxy had planted the seed with Banks at Rum Runner's. Act two was when she made an off-the-record follow-up phone call to Banks Bridges on the second day.

"We are not having this conversation, but tomorrow Neil Hackinrider has an appointment with a seller to buy jewelry and rare materials from a dealer who specializes in the type of merchandise you and I talked about in Rum Runner's."

"What do you mean? Jewelry? I thought he made his own."

"He does, and I'm sure he will with the some of the material he's about to buy. How do you think he often gets things out of the country without being caught? He wears much of it out, and the rest is mixed in with his legal jewelry in his travel jewelry pouches in his luggage and briefcase."

"Oh, I guess that makes sense."

"The man is a pro — a very wealthy pro, I might add. I can't identify the seller since his suppliers change, but my driver Nakomis knows most of them. If I ask him to, he'll tail Neil into town, and if it's someone he knows, he'll introduce you after Neil leaves. The dealer would never risk dealing with you on the good stuff otherwise since you're a stranger."

"So why don't you get Nakomis to take me to one today?"

"It doesn't work that way. You see, these sellers float around town so that they can avoid the constabulary. They call Neil and let him know where and when they'll be on a particular day. By the way, don't even bother to go unless you have ten or twenty thousand in cash. This is the black market, and they don't deal in penny ante amounts. But don't forget, you'll be buying the rarest items on the planet at wholesale which is twenty to twenty-five cents on the dollar from someone who wouldn't give you the time of day normally. Before I forget, it's also customary to tip the dealer for his services as a matter of respect. And don't forget to give Nakomis something."

"How much?"

"Oh, five hundred or so American to each should do it."

"So, these guys sell finished jewelry, not just rocks. Viv would love showing some off."

"These are not just rocks or just any old jewelry — We're talking rare, priceless jewelry — the stuff celebrities wear. And your wife can wear it home duty free. You'll never get an opportunity like this again. And at home, Viv will be the envy of all her friends. And I don't have to tell you what it'll make you look like in her eyes."

"Well, Monte did say that since he can now afford it, the ladies could splurge and buy some jewelry if they saw anything really special. And this *is* special. So, what do you want me to do?"

"Tomorrow morning, go hang out by the pool. Take a book to read. Have your money with you. You won't have time to go get it, or Nakomis might lose Neil's trail. Nakomis will watch the lobby and when he sees Neil come down, he'll come get you. You'll be back before lunch."

That afternoon, Banks arranged a wire transfer from his Golden Rewards Cash Management account to generate the cash he'd need. The following morning he went down by the pool and waited for Nakomis to come get him. Neil told Nakomis where they'd be going and promised he'd drive slowly enough that he'd be easy to follow. He took a circuitous

Conclusive, All-Inclusive Confusion

route just in case the deal headed south, and Banks did go to the cops. He wanted to make it as difficult as possible for Banks in case Banks ever tried to find his way back. They would end up in an unnamed obscure narrow alley.

Act three was executed flawlessly. Neil parked his car and walked up a set of back stairs where he met their Indian partner, Dakshesh Kapur. Nakomis followed. It was a dingy, rundown, roach-ridden part of town that smelled like urine and garbage. He parked on the main street and told Banks to stay in the car while he found out which unmarked door led to the location of the jeweler they'd be dealing with after Neil departed.

"Be sure and keep the car door locked. There can be some pretty rough people down here. And for God's sake, don't get out of the car until I come and get you."

When he was out of Banks' sight, he conferred with Neil and Dakshesh and checked to make sure that his bucktoothed cousin, Tyree John, was present and ready.

"Do you have your fake eyepatch, Tyree? And make sure he sees your crooked teeth. Hold still and let me sprinkle a little water of your pants to give you that homeless, peed-on-yourself look. Got your knife? ... Good. ... And your knit Rasta hat ... the dirty one ... And fluff out your dreads some. Make 'em look like you slept on them. ... Perfect! ... How much time should we give him until Neil leaves ... fifteen minutes?"

"Hell, if I didn't know you, you'd scare me. You look like a black Blackbeard," Dakshesh said and laughed.

"Let's get on with this. This shit itches," Tyree replied. "What do you reckon he has on him?"

"My guess is a payday of at least ten to fifteen thousand."

Neil waited, finally looked at his watch, and announced, "It's showtime. Break a leg."

"Don't say that ... Or even think it."

Act four got underway. Neil exited the alley in his car and drove away. Once he was gone, Nakomis summoned Banks to get out of his car and led him up the rickety narrow wooden stairs where Dakshesh had supposedly set up temporary shop.

"We lucked out today," Nakomis said. "This is a dealer who I have dealt with previously. That'll make it a lot easier to gain his trust so that he'll deal with you. You wait here while I get the preliminaries out of the way and see if I can get him to trust you enough to deal with you."

Banks did as he was told and through a closed door listened to Nakomis and Dakshesh go through a script that they had performed many times before. Dakshesh at first acted reluctant, but Nakomis was insistent. Dakshesh finally reluctantly relented, and Nakomis cracked the door.

"You can come in now."

Banks entered and saw a bearded middle aged Indian man in a long, collarless, buttoned shirt and loose, pajama-like, kurta pants. Round, full-rimmed metal granny glasses completed the look. Two locked, medium sized aluminum business cases sat on some cinder blocks. Neither had anything of value in them. He spoke briefly to Nakomis in patois that Banks couldn't understand. Then he spoke to Banks. His English was suddenly flawless.

"So do I understand correctly that you are looking for some rare jewelry for your wife?"

Just as Banks started to reply, Tyree John threw open the door and rushed into the room. Dakshesh quickly grabbed the two cases and fled out of a prearranged hall door and hid in a storage closet, leaving Nakomis and Banks to face Tyree alone. Tyree held his knife to Banks' throat and demanded his money.

"Give it to him, or we're both dead," Nakomis yelled. "He's a crackhead, and they'll do anything for drug money."

Banks immediately complied. Tyree pushed both men down before fleeing out the door and down the stairs. By the time Banks and Nakomis had regained their feet, he had disappeared down the alley.

"We were lucky not to be killed. These crackheads are totally irrational."

"But what about my money!"

"I'm afraid you'll just have to write it off as lost. The police will never find a homeless crackhead like that. The city's full of 'em. Besides that, you can't risk them finding out you were down here to deal with a black market dealer. Do you want to end up in a Jamaican prison? ... I don't think so. ... I'm sorry things didn't work out."

"Don't you dare tell anyone. I'd never regain the face that I'd lose with my family."

Conclusive, All-Inclusive Confusion

"No problem, mon. We better get going. It's not safe here."

Don't worry. I'll keep the fact that you're a dumbass to myself, and that your money's gone bye bye. I promise you though, we'll make sure your money gets put to good use, Nakomis thought to himself.

"Don't worry. Your secret is safe with me," Nakomis promised Banks out loud as Banks slipped him the only fifty dollar bill he had left to seal the deal.

Once Banks secured Nakomis' promise of silence, he tuned out any efforts at conversation on the drive back. At first Nakomis mistakenly attributed Banks' silence to being the result of a wounded ego, but Banks had a secret reason other than embarrassment for not letting anyone know about this financial fiasco. He knew exactly how he was going to manage to pass the loss back to Monte without Monte knowing about it when they got back home. He had set up a mechanism for doing so back in Detroit but hadn't had a need to test it until now. Nakomis' silence should insure that Monte would never suspect that Banks was diverting funds from Monte's LLC and not using them for their intended purpose. After all, Monte rarely read his statements, and when he did, he usually didn't understand what they were saying anyway.

Banks' secret weapon was a limited liability corporation he had set up with himself having a power of attorney. One of the things so beautiful about it was that the project had been Monte's original idea. Banks had just shown him how to structure it.

Something that had bothered Monte for years was what the church thrift shop did with unsalable soft goods donations — raggedy shirts and t-shirts, torn up pants; stained sheets; blankets, pillow cases, and mattress covers; worn out curtains and drapes — rags of every sort.

Uncaring people constantly donated items that were unsalable to get them on a tax receipt, but the thrift store had no use for these things since they couldn't sell them. So they just ended up in a dumpster and would later clutter up a landfill. In the meantime, the store had a shortage of something that they could use — patchwork quilts and baby blankets that might keep poor or homeless people from freezing to death during the harsh Michigan winters.

There was a large, unused room at the church that could be converted to a factory of sorts. The primary investment would be in washing machines and dryers to clean the items and sewing machines to sew the quilts — plus some miscellaneous costs.

What Monte saw as an additional benefit to the project was that they could train people to sew and would then be providing much needed jobs for the poor Highland Park community. Monte saw this as something in which everyone won. Banks saw this as an opportunity for him to use Monte's windfall in other more selfish and avaricious ways that would avoid most auditors scrutiny when he used the magic of the "miscellaneous" column. Banks' secret personal slush fund had only reached twenty-five thousand dollars, but Banks expected that meager starting balance to begin to grow into a substantial amount in the near future.

Big oaks grow from little acorns.

And best of all was that Monte didn't have a clue about it. All Banks had to do to keep his private annuity growing was to keep Monte's money under his management. And that shouldn't be hard considering that he was married to Monte's daughter, Viv.

Now for the first time, when got back home, he was going to get a chance to use some of this money to cover his recent loss. His secret kitty certainly softened that morning's misstep since he was confident that it would be easy to replace the funds he'd just lost.

You win some; you lose some; and some get washed out. Oh, well. Shit happens. It's not like it was my money.

Nakomis couldn't help but notice the smile on Banks' face and wonder why. He even thought he saw Banks hum and tap his feet to a song Nakomis didn't recognize.

If someone just nailed me for fifteen grand, I wouldn't be smiling.

He had no way of knowing that Banks was smiling knowing how easy it should be to bury his loss — and future ones as well as he enjoyed the inevitable winners he knew would be coming.

All I have to do is keep my father-in-law happy and keep control of his money. That should be a cinch.

Banks began humming and singing under his breath. It was an American tune that Nakomis had never heard before. It was the Whisnant family's familiar gospel song.

I'm getting ready for a new day dawning
I'm getting read for a brand new day

> LEGGS
> OPEN
> AS
> USUAL

CHAPTER 18

In the meantime, since she didn't have a spouse to share things with, Monte's daughter, Nan, like Monte, had been pretty much going her own way since their arrival at Seascape. Being a librarian, on the second day they were at the hotel, out of curiosity she visited the hotel's guest library to see what types of books it stocked, as well how well equipped it was. She was especially interested in books on local history. This is where she met Hans Robin Roman for the first time. She was immediately smitten by the handsome the twenty-seven year old.

Billy Don Brown, aka Hans R. Roman, was an exotic mix of French, Black, and Latin. His complexion sometimes reminded women of a friendly smaller version of Dwane Johnson with hair. The clean-shaven, six-foot Hans was well built. He was trim but had broad shoulders and a deep chest. His hairless olive skin contrasted with his dyed shoulder-length mop of blond hair and his white teeth. He had kind eyes and an engaging smile. He wore a chest-hugging Balinese silk surf-print shirt and slender-fit unpleated linen pants. The drawstring holding them in place was tied in a bow-knot that dangled down the front as if inviting someone to pull on it to expose what the pants were concealing. There was a slight bulge from the hanky folded up in his red lace mesh boxer briefs. Firm but not overly bulging biceps pulled his pants legs tight as he walked, partially further outlining the inviting bulge that crept down his right pantleg. His strong, sensuous arm muscles peeked out from beneath the almost see-through fabric of the shirt. He walked into the library like he was on oiled ball bearings. When he walked past her, she could smell his subtle cologne.

Nan momentarily imagined what it would be like to pull that knot on those pants loose with her teeth and find out the magnitude of the package he was hiding beneath them. Nan didn't see an underwear line under his pants, ramping up her imagination even more. She blushed as her fanciful thoughts embarrassed her.

Is he daring enough to go commando? Are pesky undies a nuisance that just get in his way?

Someone like that would never be attracted to a plain Jane like me, but a girl can always dream.

Hans was aware of the effect he could have on women as well as men. His image and first impression were important. He worked hard to keep his physical condition top notch. His vigorous health regimen included a vitamin enriched diet, extensive workouts, as well as sometimes painful penis enlargement exercises and orgasm prolonging techniques.

After all, his persona and stamina were how Hans made his living. Hans was a professional gigolo. He would willingly service clients of either sex no matter what their age as long as they paid him his $500 an hour fee. His clients had ranged from high level politicians to actors and actresses who were in long-dead loveless marriages that they couldn't unravel without damaging their public image to wealthy people looking for excitement. They had included the wife of a president, the Speaker of the House of Representatives, Arab emirs, and Asian tycoons.

Hans also cultivated the trappings of refinement. He was a wine and food connoisseur and collected valuable first edition books. The finer things in life were his reward for what often was to him nothing more than a job that he sometimes had to just tolerate to add to his investment accounts. He often checked these investment accounts to remind himself of his ultimate goal of complete independence and financial security. Conscience was never a factor.

"I more than earn my money by servicing these aging cows and gelded bulls," he once admitted cryptically. "Most of these people, while enjoying massive power and recognition from their positions, have long since entered into a loveless marriage or relationship with their partner. It's easy to appeal to their vanity, read a few lines of poetry, blow in their ear, and voila, the next thing you know their panty girdle or shorts are lying on

Conclusive, All-Inclusive Confusion

the penthouse room floor in their five star hotel as they can't seem to get enough of themselves being worshipped."

He never missed an opportunity to try to assess the people who he came in contact with off the job. After all, you never knew who had money. He tried to size Nan up just as she was trying to do the same with him. He put on his reading half-glasses. They gave him an intellectual almost professorial look. Her mind flashed to Russell Crowe's professorial role in "A Beautiful Mind."

He peered at Nan over the top of his glasses. They made eye contact, and he walked over towards her. Nan felt flushed.

Surely this resplendent creature isn't coming over here to talk to me.

"It's always interesting to measure the public's tastes by seeing what a library like this chooses to stock," he said.

"Yes, I know. I'm a librarian visiting here on a getaway. Are you in a literary or academic field?"

He noted that she had an RIFD key card instead of the standard key card. That was only used on the penthouse floor. His mental radar was alerted and began to beep in his head. It was seldom wrong.

Penthouse. ... Librarian, my ass. ... This broad's got money. Hans, time to ramp up the charm until you find out otherwise.

Hans sometimes claimed to be a Swiss diplomat who specialized in black ops for dangerous international missions when he thought it made him sound more adventurous or mysterious, but Nan didn't seem to be that type so he told her, "No, but I envy those who are. I'm an interactive social and psychological coordinator and administrator and collector of first edition books."

"Oh," is all she could think to say. "That sounds like a really responsible position for someone as young as you."

"It's a challenge that I relish and have trained extensively for. It seems we have things in common. Would I be being too bold if I asked you to join me for a cup of coffee or tea in Reggae Roasters? Since I got here, I've been dying since to find someone intelligent to talk to. By the way, have you ever had a Jamaican banana coffee cake? It is exquisite. And if you really want to be adventuresome, add a little Kahlua and a dollop of whipped cream to your coffee."

"I would love to."

I can't believe Mr. Handsome wants to spend time with me — Nan Connors from Highland Park, Michigan.

And that's how it all began. After what Hans learned over that first cup of coffee, he knew he was on the right track.

My gut is seldom wrong. After all, I am a professional.

He made a dinner date with Nan for that evening and spent time with her the following day. Once her guard was down, the two of them made a field trip to a bookstore in Ocho Rios. That night they spent a romantic evening under the stars alone in one of the hotel's least used Jacuzzis by one of the pools, drinking chilled champagne that Hans brought there for the occasion and playing soft music with his iPhone. He was careful not to try to seduce her right off the bat, but instead be a perfect gentleman. The right time for seduction would come. And pleasing women ... and men ... was the best part of his game. He knew from much experience all the right buttons to push.

If his research confirmed what he suspected, his plan was to encourage Nan to spend as little time with her family as she could get away with. Hans knew from experience how to make sure of that.

> **BABY CHICKS**
> **FOR SALE**
> **BREAD IN CAPTIVITY**

CHAPTER 19

"Would you like to join me by the pool?" Monte asked Bessie Prince on the hotel room phone.

"I would be delighted to. Half an hour good? Or are you up for doing something a little more daring?"

"Depends on what daring is. I'm not up for parasailing if that's what you're talking about."

"Nothing dangerous like that. The hotel is involved in a special to be televised function they call Skinny Dippin' Beachy Trippin' at their clothing optional beach. Why don't we go to it instead?"

"I'm not a nudist."

"You don't have to be. I saw some flesh-colored bathing suits in one of the hotel gift shops. From a distance, it'll look like you have nothing on, but in reality you'll be just as modestly covered as you've ever been."

"I ... don't know. I've never done anything like that before. My girls and their hubbys would never approve."

"I'm not asking the girls and their hubbys to go. C'mon, Monte. We're on vacation. I've never done anything like that either. But I bet it'll be a hoot. I always wanted to go to a nude beach, but I've never had the nerve. With these bathing suits on we'll fit right in, and our modesty will remain intact. What size bathing suit do you wear? You can wear your regular bathing suit down the elevator, and we'll change in the bath house or cabana before we get there. The family's never going to know, and then we'll change back to our regular suits before we come back to the hotel.

Like I said, it'll be a hoot and our little secret. We won't be doing anything wrong, just living it up harmlessly for a little bit."

"OK, ... you're on. I've never done anything daring like this before. You bring out the wild side I never knew I had. My whole life was spent taking care of mother. Gee, Bessie Prince, ... you know, you're fun to be around."

"So are you, my dear."

Oh, my gosh! Did I just hear her call me dear?

Monte changed clothes, almost bounced out into the hall humming under his breath, and headed for the elevator where he ran into Jax, who offered him a gummy bear.

"You seem chipper this morning, Pops. Where you headed?"

"Just going to meet Bessie Prince. We're going to get some sun."

This gold digger Bessie Prince shit's getting more and more worrisome. Maybe I'd better keep an eye on things.

"Mind if I join you?"

"Thanks, but don't bother. I'm sure Eve's got other plans for you and wants to spend time with you."

"Whatever. Have fun."

What Monte and Bessie Prince did not know was that Skinny Dippin' Beachy Trippin' was a promotional event sponsored by the LOVE FM radio station which was in an ongoing ratings battle with their rival IRIE FM. Their brother television station LOVE TV would be filming the day's happenings. Seascape was participating by allowing their nude beach to be used for the event. In return, LOVE would be promoting the resort as well as themselves. Playboy TV had sent a camera crew as well since they planned to do a segment of their "Hot Babes Doing Stuff Naked" reality show on the event. Playboy had artificially devised some the day's "spontaneous" events to enhance and liven up their program.

Monte and Bessie Prince changed into the skin-colored bathing suits that Bessie Prince had bought, put on a coverup, grabbed a couple of hotel beach towels, and headed for the nude beach. When they arrived, Bessie Prince stepped out onto the hot sand, but Monte hesitated, still confused and unsure. Bessie Prince held out her hand and ordered, "Let's hit it. Don't chicken out now, Monte. Come on. Let's experience this together."

Conclusive, All-Inclusive Confusion

They searched for an open beach spot, maneuvering around an older nude woman with her pet goat and another younger naked one with her chimp. Many in the crowd were senior citizens, and many of those were tanned to the point that they looked like they had had one too many crème caramels. Monte and Bessie Prince silently sneaked peeks at each fresh novelty as they spotted them. There were tattoos, piercings, rolls, and folds. Bessie Prince seemed inscrutable; Monte was fidgety and tried to take his mind off his surroundings by pretending to concentrate on looking for shells.

The ease with which some people lounged in the raw made him feel sort of jealous but also nauseated him as he visualized being naked, haunch to haunch with them. This nausea increased when he felt something rubbery between his toes and saw that it was a condom. He flicked sand over it and said nothing to Bessie Prince. He had a harder time, however, pretending to be cool when he saw a man who reminded him of Tarzan strutting in their direction with his large endowment at half mast. Bessie Prince, picking up a shell, glanced up just in time as his fluffed genitals passed at eye level only a few feet away. She straightened up and pretended to examine her shell find.

Cameramen seemed be everywhere. People actively competed for the cameramen's attention hoping to get on television. Monte and Bessie Prince found an unoccupied bit of sand and staked out a claim by spreading out their towels and anchoring them with their beach bags. A doughy, balding middle aged man with a hula hoop began gyrating, his appendage swinging flaccidly in sync with each hip gyration. Of course, the bodybuilders and their girlfriends strutted by, pausing and flexing each time someone wanted to take their picture.

While they saw a few people discretely playing with their own private areas, there were surprisingly little X-rated activities in sight. No one seemed to mind that Monte and Bessie Prince were not truly nude.

Suddenly Bessie Prince gasped and pointed.

"Monte, look."

Two leathery looking Caucasian twins who looked to be in their eighties pranced by with a black bodybuilder arm-in-arm between them. He appeared to be in his twenties. Their shriveled boobs hung lifelessly at least six or eight inches below where they had originally been when the women were younger, drawing the eye down to their unshaven, hairy privates. In white paint, on their escort's massive hairless chest they had painted "HOUSE NIGGER" in white lettering. When they had passed by and Monte and Bessie Prince could see his back, it said also in white paint "GRANDMOTHER FUCKER."

A nude beach waiter approached them and asked if he could bring them a beverage. He also made no comment as to their attire. They each ordered a Mai Tai. When the waiter returned with their drinks, Bessie Prince asked, "Is it safe for us to leave our things here so we can walk around?"

"Absolutely."

They began to stroll down the beach. They saw a crowd had gathered at one point and decided to check to see what the excitement was. Monte was horrified and turned away, looking out at the ocean. Bessie Prince couldn't help but laugh. A young, attractive nude woman was squatting over a fallen palm tree with her legs spread and her arms flexing as if she was straining, grimacing a fake painful expression, as if the palm tree was the biggest turd on Earth. Her equally nude boyfriend was flexing his fist and cheering her on as he yelled "Go for it. You've almost got it out." Cameras were snapping the scene right and left, and people were applauding and cheering their approval of her performance.

Monte was equally shocked as he stared out at the surf. Two horses with water up to their necks were being led into the beach by a nude Jamaican attendant while the naked white couple riding them leaned over and kissed each other passionately. As the horses walked out of the water, another woman who was nude except for her nun's habit rode a wave towards the beach on a surfboard. She was followed on a second surfboard by a bare skinned man who only wore a clerical collar.

Unbeknownst to Monte and Bessie Prince, Jax was searching for them in his usual misguided effort to protect what he perceived as being his territory, — Monte. He had first walked around all three pools and didn't see them. He inspected the chaise lounges as well to see if he could see them sunning.

Monte said that they were going to get some sun. I wonder where the hell they are. That Bessie Prince broad's getting entirely too much alone time with Monte. Hmmm, ... there seems to be a lot of people walking out towards the beach. Maybe that's where they went. I better check it out.

Conclusive, All-Inclusive Confusion

When Jax got out to the beach, he noticed that everyone doffed their clothing or robes at that point and packed them away in their beach bags. Now he wasn't sure what to do. The white, flabby Jax had never been an exhibitionist and burned easily, but now it seemed that he was going to have to become a sun worshiper if he wanted to continue to track his quarry. He had never even skinny dipped before, but he felt embarrassed to be the only person with clothes on. He wasn't even sure if this lewd behavior was allowed. His heart pounded, and his cheeks burned as he thought. While no one seemed to be staring, he felt that all eyes were upon him.

Look at some of these people! Some look like models, but others really ought to put their clothes back on and only undress in a closet. And nobody has a boner. What do these studs think when they look at me? What would Eve think if she knew I was here?

Shiiit! Monte's worth fifty mil. That's too much money on the line for me to chicken out now and let this gold digger win. Well, ... here goes nothing.

He then noticed what could be his salvation — a rack with hotel beach towels on it. Jax edged over and grabbed a towel. He then went around behind the adjacent trash receptacle to drop down his bathing suit. When he attempted to stand back up, he butted the towel rack, spilling its contents onto the sand. He looked to see if anyone had seen his accident and set the towel rack back up before attempting to reload it. Some seagrass tickled his testicles, making him think that he'd been bitten by an insect or some other beach creature. Jax jumped, losing his flip flops in the process and stomped down on a seashell with his instep.

When he jumped a second time and came down on a limestone rock with his other foot, he accidentally flung his bathing suit into the trash bin. When he went to retrieve it, Jax found it to be slathered with the remains of a sticky, melted chocolate ice cream cone that someone had not eaten. Despite the fact that the ice cream was in the trash receptacle where it belonged, Jax mumbled, "People are such inconsiderate slobs."

Flip flops forgotten, holding the beach towel in front and the brown-stained bathing suit behind him, Jax began to limp across the beach. This time people really did notice him and smiled when he went by since it looked like he had had a runny bowel explosion.

Jax looked around trying to find Bessie Prince and Monte. He thought he saw them in the distance.

My God, what has this harlot done to my conservative father-in-law? They're both running around here in the buff. What else does she have him doing?

He was so preoccupied that he almost kicked sand into the face of a black woman lying on the beach reading a book entitled "How to be Black." She must have thought he had done so on purpose because she said loud enough for all nearby to hear, "Watch it, white boy."

People stared. Jax was so embarrassed that he dropped his beach towel, invading her space with his exposed private parts.

"Are you coming on to me, pervert?"

"No, ma'am. I swear I'm not."

"Then you better get on out of here."

When he leaned down to retrieve his towel, he dropped the brown-stained bathing suit on her book. She jumped as if it contained some kind of disease and threw it back at Jax.

Jax caught it, and as he turned to go, Jax saw something that caused him to drop the beach towel again. A nude woman lying on her back had buried one leg in the sand up to her knee. Her companion had sprinkled ketchup on and around what looked like the leg's stump. He had placed the lower portion of a plastic mannequin leg also sprinkled with ketchup about two feet away. Suddenly Jax felt his own hot, warm urine running down his leg. People began to point and laugh.

Another man had made a sandcastle that looked like an almost two-foot high cow patty and was squatted over it. Jax zigged and then zagged, almost losing his balance, slinging more piss on the man as he went by.

Jax ran towards where he thought he had seen Monte and Bessie Prince while still trying to protect his own modesty only to run over a muscular, bare-bottomed, mock picketer who was walking the beach with a satirical protest sign that said,

> *PLEASE PICK UP YOUR CIGARETTE BUTTS*
> *THE CRABS CRAWL OUT AT NIGHT AND SMOKE THEM*
> *WE'RE TRYING TO GET THEM TO QUIT*

Jax lost his towel again in this latest collision, and the brown-stained bathing suit somehow wound up on the man's face. He looked both shocked and disgusted. He wadded up the bathing suit and stared at it, not believing what he thought he was holding. He wrapped the towel

Conclusive, All-Inclusive Confusion

around the bath suit and tossed them both as far away as he could into the water. With his hands doubled into a fist, he then he turned towards Jax, who threw all modesty aside and fled towards the water to try to retrieve his lost modesty protectors.

After he clumsily waded into the water's edge where the waves were breaking, Jax managed to recover the beach towel and bathing suit, only to be immediately in for another shock — two of Playboy's broadcast enhancement props appeared in the surf. First to his right, was a rubber inflatable couch, with two nude couch-potatoes riding it yelling "Yippee." To his left were sixty-six nude surfers riding a 1,300 pound surfboard. One of Playboy's ploys to move their program up in the ratings was to break the Guinness world record for the world's biggest surfboard. To Jax, it seemed to be a runaway bus coming right at him.

Jax turned to flee, but once again forgot to look down. He tripped over a four hundred pound white merman with an inflatable pitchfork who was wallowing in the sand. The merman, another Playboy plant, was middle-aged, balding, tattooed, and scraggily bearded. His hairy, flaccid, nude belly hung over his plastic merman tail, hiding the top portion of it. It had an unhealthy pallor that made it look almost dead. The collision forced the merman's face down into the sand. He came up coughing sand, screaming obscenities. Visions of the mythical kraken sea monster flashed through Jax's now addled brain.

As Jax once again grabbed his "security blankets" and prepared to flee from his latest foe, a hang glider swooped down like a diving pelican and grabbed his precious items once and for all. Jax turned and watched as it took both items out towards the sea and dropped them in deeper water.

This was the last straw.

"I'm not at a beach. Instead, I've been transported to hell while I'm still living. But why? It's not fair. After all, I ain't so bad," he screamed almost incoherently.

Once again, people stared.

He looked at them and shouted, "Don't look at me like that. I swear, I ain't so bad."

People just stared back.

"Well, to hell with Monte and Bessie Prince. I'm getting my ass out of here before I get killed and really wind up in hell. His money ain't worth dying over," Jax yelled to no one in particular and kicked at the sand which blew back in his eyes momentarily blinding him and causing him to stumble once more.

Bessie Prince overheard this latest rant.

This dumbass is down here spying on us.

This time Jax's victim was a nude man wearing a red and white Dr. Seuss stovepipe hat who was walking around the beach on six-foot stilts. The collision caused him to lose his handhold on one of his stilts. He momentarily balanced on the other swaying back and forth but then crashed spreadeagle through a woman's beach umbrella. She screamed, attracting even more attention, causing Bessie Prince to once again stare. Jax somehow wound up in the middle of the pileup. He screamed profanities. Jax's rant attracted disapproving people near him wondering what this crazy man was screaming about.

"Monte, Monte! Isn't that your son-in-law?"

"You're right. It is. I wonder what he's doing here. Must be an accident or coincidence."

I know what the jackass's doing. Spying on us. I just heard him say as much. Yep, that's exactly what that asshole's doing here, Bessie Prince said to herself.

The devious bastard's here again to try to screw things up with me and Monte because he thinks I'm making headway at his expense. Well, let him try. Miss Bessie Prince's a pro at getting what she wants, and her sights are set on Mr. Moneybags.

Out loud she said, "Maybe you're right. I'm sure the dear boy probably wandered down here by accident. Must be a coincidence."

Dear boy! … Accident… coincidence, my white ass! Two of the things I don't believe in are coincidences and leprechauns.

Jax ran. The last thing he remembered as he headed for the beach towel stand to retrieve another "modesty protector" for the trip back up to his room was running into another nudist carrying a sign that said,

NO SUNGLASSES AT NIGHT
DON'T ACT COOL

Jax felt anything but cool.

God, please don't let me run into anyone in the family before I get back to my room and change.

> YELLOW
> BANANAS
> BONELESS
> $71 JMD
> PERLB

CHAPTER 20

When Jax got back to towel rack, the only beach towel left was a still wet used one that someone had dumped in the sand next to it. He ignored the sand clinging to it in his relief to cover himself up once again. His skin had begun to sunburn, making the sand in the terry cloth feel more like sandpaper instead of sand. He now remembered his flip flops coming off in one of his collisions, but he wasn't about to go back and look for them. He'd just have to barefoot it back up to the hotel. Within a few hip-hop steps, the overweight Jax realized how hot the walkway was for a type two diabetic like himself. After a few steps, his feet felt numb. This was followed by a sharp, stabbing pain as his legs began to feel heavier. He began to sweat. He jumped off of the pavement whenever he could, but the landscaping along the side of the path kept him from being able to stay there.

A crowd suddenly blocked Jax's way. They had gathered to listen to a roving guitar-playing troubadour that the hotel employed to entertain its guests and create ambiance for their stay. Some guests were snapping the singer's picture; others merely listened and applauded him as he finished each song. Women were playfully ribbing their husbands as the performer sang the old Harry Belafonte number, "Man Smart, Woman Smarter."

For God's sake, let me by. My burning feet are killing me.

He began to try to elbow his way through the troubadour's audience, while holding his towel in place with his sweaty hands. The towel caught on a lady's purse. Before he realized it, as he tried get around her, his sweat-slick hand lost its grip on the towel, and he found himself standing in the buff with cameras flashing at him instead of the singer. The singer stopped in the middle of the song he was singing and broke out in Ray Stevens' "The Streak."

People began to laugh, and Jax turned redder than he already was.

Oh, yes, they call him the streak.
Fastest thing on two feet
He's just as proud as he can be of his anatomy.
He goin' a give us a peek

Now they began to clap, and Jax felt more embarrassed than he had ever felt in his whole life. He snatched at his towel to retrieve it, but since it was caught on the woman's purse clasp, it jerked the purse out of her hand. Jax snapped the towel to free it, and the purse flew through the air and whacked an elderly man who had been watching the impromptu concert from his wheelchair. Jax tried to run, trailing the towel behind him, but it caught again in the wheelchair's spokes and pulled free from his grip. He grabbed at it again, only to have the wheelchair and its occupant spin around, causing the old man to spit out his dentures as he lost his toupee.

"Muh mudda fuggin teefh! Muh mudda fuggin teefh! Mudda fugga got muh mutha fuggin teefh!" the old man tried say through his denture deprived mouth.

Screw this! I'm out of here! Towel or no towel!

Jax took off skipping on his hot, sore feet without the towel, but the singer was not going to let him off the hook easily. He continued the song.

Boogity. Boogity.
He ain't lewd
Boogity. Boogity.
He's just in the mood to run in the nude.

Jax stumbled over the wheelchair in his haste, almost knocking he elderly man over. The last thing he heard as he fled up the path ignoring his aching feet was,

Conclusive, All-Inclusive Confusion

Boogity. Boogity.
He likes to turn the other cheek.
... Mister tourist man, you shameless hellion, git your clothes on

as the crowd roared, and other people gathered to try to find out what they were missing.
I'd like to boogity, boogity all their sorry asses.
When Jax was sure he was out of earshot, he paused to catch his breath. His chest tightened, hungry for air. He was breathless and was having a hard time breathing, making him feel like he was suffocating.
This is what a heart attack must feel like. What else can go wrong today?
Jax had to find another towel before he could go back into the hotel. He certainly couldn't walk into the lobby in the buff. He snuck up near the pool and lurked behind a palm tree until he saw a woman on a chaise lounge near the perimeter dive into the pool, leaving her towel draped over it. When he was sure she couldn't see him, he ducked out from behind the palm tree, grabbed the towel, and began to run, only to trip on a low hedge and fall, spraining his wrist as he tried to catch himself. He got up and made it to safety behind a taller shrub, where he stood gasping again for breath.
Maybe I am having a real heart attack.
As Jax approached the lobby, Angel, the hotel Ambassador, saw him.
"Sir, we do not allow bare feet in the main lobby."
At this point Jax lost all of his composure.
"And then how am I supposed to get to my room, cocksucker?"
"Sir, I'll be glad to go get you some disposable slippers if you'll just wait a moment."
"Eat me!"
Jax fled for the private elevator and took it back up to the penthouse floor. As he got off the elevator, he ran into Banks.
"Where's your clothes?"
"Can't you see? I ain't got none, shitass! Somebody took them," he said, letting his towel drop, exposing his scratched up, sunburned, bruised body. And I ain't got my room key either."
"I'll let you into ours. The girls are roaming the gift shop. This is a story I've got to hear. It must be a doozie."

Jax took a shower in Banks' room and donned the bathrobe that came with it while Banks called downstairs and asked for a key to Jax's room be sent up.

"Now, I want to hear what you've been up to, and don't leave anything out."

"Monte's spending entirely too much time with that Bessie Prince woman. I'm sure she knows he's loaded and is trying to get her grubby fingers on some of his money. And we both know he's such a naïve weenie that he might just let that happen. So I decided I need to keep an eye on things, if you know what I mean."

Banks knew exactly what Jax meant. He conveniently ignored the fact that neither he nor Jax had shown the slightest interest in Monte's daughters until Monte's ship came in. Jax had pursued Eve in order to sell Monte a large life insurance policy, and Banks had met Monte through his investment firm and had had no interest in Viv until he had found out about Monte's windfall.

"The woman's evil incarnate — or at least a bad influence. Do you know that she's got Monte going to nudist functions? He never would never been caught dead at something like that before he met her. And who knows what they've done that we don't know about. She can get him to do anything she wants him to . And I bet if she suggested marriage, he'd be all in, and we'd be screwed. So I tracked them to this X-rated event to keep an eye on things."

He once again omitted the embarrassing things that had happened to him that morning. After all, Banks didn't need to know everything. Banks also didn't need to know that Jax would love to increase his take at Banks' expense — if he had an opportunity to do so.

"I've had the same suspicions," Banks said when Jax had finished. "I've been working an angle on her myself."

He continued on and told Jax how he had hired an actor to try to scare Bessie Prince away. He also conveniently forgot to mention how he had slandered Monte in the process, or how if he got the chance, he wouldn't hesitate to eliminate Jax from the equation.

"So, are we on the same page?" Jax asked.

"You betcha, brother-in-law. We're a team — and family."

NO EXIT FROM BURIAL SITE

CHAPTER 21

While Monte and Bessie Prince were at the nude beach, Hans continued to move forward with in his efforts to court Nan. He had been right about her. His research had confirmed that Monty was indeed nouveau riche and unmarried. His life seemed to revolve around his three daughters, and Nan was still single. That was enough to spur him on.

He roamed around the beachfronts near to the hotel until he found a secluded spot for a romantic seaside dinner. The sand was soft and clean and devoid of rocks like he wanted. He then went and found Mr. Angel, the hotel Ambassador, to see if the hotel would be willing to set up a table for him and Nan. When he walked Angel down to the spot he had in mind, Angel tried to talk him into an alternate location that would be more convenient for the hotel staff, but Hans insisted that he would prefer the area he had chosen since he wanted maximum privacy. Angel relented if Hans was willing to pay him a special premium under the table to get what he wanted. Hans hinted that there might be more money coming if things went especially well. The money would go directly into Angel's pocket, and the hotel would never know. Angel didn't plan on splitting a nickel of it with the staff. The two agreed on a price and a time and set a menu. The menu would have a variety of mini courses with a variety of wines and would be followed by dark chocolate covered strawberries for desert.

"I want a linen tablecloth and napkins and also candlelight and red roses on the table. Oh, and set up some tiki torches around the perimeter if you have some."

When they were done, Hans gave Angel some additional tip money as hush money that Angel didn't plan on declaring with the hotel or sharing with Quiesha as she normally expected him to do with windfalls.

"I repeat. My lady and I want privacy," he told Angel. "And once the waiter finishes serving dinner, I don't want him to disturb us again. I don't want to be bothered by any other guests either. Read me? The table can be bussed later tonight or tomorrow if necessary. And have a large beach blanket plus some beach towels and hotel robes down here for us to use in case we decide to take a moonlight dip in the ocean."

Hans gave Angel a knowing wink. Angel smiled to himself and thought, *This boy is seriously going after some poontang.*

They parted ways. Angel sang the Ted Nugent song to himself on his way back up to the lobby,

Wang dang, sweet poontang
He'll be shakin' his thang as a rang-a-dang-dang

Now that the dinner arrangements had been made, it was time for Hans to confirm his date. He went back to his room and called Nan on the room phone.

"Nan, this is Hans. I had a wonderful time with you last night in the jacuzzi. I can't remember when I've had a more pleasant evening. I hope I don't embarrass you if I tell you that you're all I've been able to think about all morning. We talked about a possible dinner tonight. Would you do me the honor of having a sunset dinner with me this evening? I can't wait to see you again. Please say yes."

Nan was floored. Hans' prior invitation had been on her mind all night and then all morning. She had never had a man chase her before. In fact, she had never been with a man. And this absolute dream of a man wanted to be with her. She didn't hesitate to accept.

"Sundown is at seven fourteen tonight. Why don't I come by your suite and pick you up at … say … six forty-five? … I can hardly wait until then to see you again."

Hans knocked on Nan's door promptly at six-forty five. Jax heard him knocking and peeked out of his own door. He did not like what he saw and continued to spy through his cracked door.

Conclusive, All-Inclusive Confusion

"What restaurant did you choose for us tonight?" Nan asked as they walked to the elevator.

"It will be a surprise. I have something special planned, something romantic. I'm sure you'll love it."

Jax continued to spy.

Romantic? That dirtbag gold-digger's up to no good. Is everyone in this hotel on the prowl?

He decided to follow. When he got to the lobby, Hans and Nan were nowhere to be found. He peeked in each of the restaurants and hotel bars but they were still nowhere to be found. He went to the front desk.

"I'm Jax Magnus. You know what my sister-in-law, Nan, looks like, don't you? Have you seen her tonight? She was with another guest. She doesn't seem to be in any of the restaurants. ... You say they went out the rear lobby door towards the beach? .... Thanks."

Since Queisha knew nothing about the arrangements since Angel planned to keep all Han's bribe, she didn't know to cover for Hans. It was too late now to give her a head's up.

Angel overheard the conversation and thought *Oh, shit. Maybe I should have given Queisha a little something after all.*

He quickly approached Jax.

"Is there a problem with Miss Connors, sir? ... No. ... I'm glad to hear that. ... If not, they left word that they were not to be disturbed. You're concerned for her? ... I can assure you that she's in good hands. They are merely having a sunset dinner on the beach. Now, is there anything else I can help you with?"

Angel stood in Jax's way. Jax got the message. He was pissed, but now he at least knew what was going down.

In the meantime, Hans escorted Nan through the pool area and out onto the beach.

"Where are we going?"

"You'll see soon enough. I can assure that you'll be pleased."

What Nan saw took her breath away — a teak table with two chairs. It was set for two. On its linen tablecloth a large candle burned. Next to it was a vase with some of the reddest red roses she thought she had ever seen. Next to the table was a teak serving cart. Atop it was an ice bucket with a magnum of champagne chilling in it. A mosquito trap was on the serving cart; two more were on the ground on each side of the table. A white-gloved waiter stood silently at a discreet distance behind the table. Nan couldn't help but squeeze Hans' hand. No one had ever gone to this extent for her. It seemed like something out of a romantic Cary Grant movie.

The waiter approached the table and pulled back Nan's chair for her to sit down. She was so awed that she almost fell down instead. Hans steadied her, and when she had caught her breath, she wrapped her arms around him and hugged him tightly.

"I don't know what to say. It's the most beautiful sight I've ever seen."

"Then say nothing; just enjoy the evening."

He led her back to the chair, and the waiter seated her. He then seated Hans as well before poring each of them a glass of champagne. The table and chairs had been placed so both of them could take full advantage of the view of the falling sun.

Hans toasted her. They clinked glasses.

They didn't have long to wait before the slanting rays to the setting sun gave a warm orange glow to the sky and sea. This orange was now her new favorite color. The sky was ablaze with the fire of the setting sun. The twilight sky seemed to be aglow, and it was putting on a spectacular show just for them. Sunsets sure weren't like this in Highland Park, Michigan.

To Nan, saying goodbye to the end of the day was like an irony that was telling her that good things sometimes happen in goodbyes. She felt like she was looking through the gates of heaven into its golden streets, and she found herself not wanting for the sun to set. She just wanted it to stay right there on the horizon — not above the horizon and not below it. She wanted it to stay right on it.

As the sun disappeared into the sea, their waiter lit the tiki torches and then brought out their first course. Each course would be small, no more than a four to six bite sampler presented exquisitely. The first course was a Caesar salad. The waiter refilled their champagne flutes when he served them. When they had finished it and he had collected their salad plates, he brought out a cup of Jamaican pumpkin soup and gave them a wine glass that he then filled with pinot noir. From there they went to a portobello mushroom with a truffle sauce. This led to a plate that contained modest servings of linguine with clams and shrimp scampi. He once again replaced their wine glasses and poured them some chianti

Conclusive, All-Inclusive Confusion

to accompany these dishes. This led to morsels of lobster, then thin slices of sirloin basted in butter, and finally to a chicken dish which he served with a Riesling.

"Do you know what this chicken dish is called?" Hans asked.

"No, but it's delicious."

"It's called 'Marry Me Chicken'," Hans said.

Nan's head was beginning to swim from both the ambiance and the variety of wines. She blushed and wasn't sure whether the heat and tingle she felt on her cheeks was the wine or her embarrassment. She didn't know what she was supposed to say and wondered what he was really trying to say. No one had ever talked romantically to her before. It felt strange, but she liked it.

When they had finished their last course, the waiter brought out some dark chocolate covered strawberries and refilled their wine glasses with champagne for the last time.

"Did you enjoy your dinner, sir and madam?" he asked.

"Yes. My compliments to the chef," Hans said, "and my compliments to you as well. You have given us impeccable service tonight."

"My goodness, yes, yes, yes! It's been perfect," Nan gushed. "This evening has got to be one of the highlights of my whole life."

"Then I will leave you now to enjoy the rest of your evening. It has been a pleasure to serve you. You are lovely guests and a handsome couple. My staff will be back later to clean up. Thank you for allowing me to serve you. Good night. Have a pleasant rest of your evening."

After the waiter left, Nan said, "Hans you shouldn't have. This must have cost you a fortune."

"It was worth every penny. Let me rephrase that — you are worth every penny. And you know one of the things I love about you is that you're so modest that you don't know what a treasure you are."

The sincere look in his eyes caused Nan to melt completely. Hans knew from experience that the time had come while she was still aglow for him to begin to make his move. While he had been down this road many times before, this was different from anything she had ever experienced. She had never had a man put her on a pedestal before.

She couldn't explain why, but his desire to seduce her had become the most seductive thing about him. Nan smiled, knowing full well that Hans intended to seduce her. Even before he touched her with a soft caress, her lungs expanded in the salty air, and she got goose bumps. His voice now had a lilt that told her of his intentions. She didn't care. His words were soft. A smile played on his face. With the first kiss came more electric tingles. She felt a desire she had never felt before. Hans knew he was getting to her. No, Hans had gotten to her.

Hans smiled knowingly. After all, seduction was what he did best. He moved into Nan's personal space with just the right look of heat in his eyes. He didn't just look at Nan. He looked into her as if he knew her desires. With the kiss came his smooth touch on her body, producing just the right blend of relaxation and tension.

Hans knew from experience that once he began to kiss her neck, any remaining resistance would crumble and collapse. And he was right. After a few delicate touches of his warm lips, her hands began to do his bidding. They fell down on the beach blanket as her head swam and all previous thoughts stopped in their tracks. Now Nan had only one desire, one wish. Hans knew it was only a short matter of time before she was his.

At first Nan tried briefly but unsuccessfully to summon and erect a protective wall of indifference since her intellect told her that it wouldn't do to let someone with Hans' ego know how much power he was exerting over her. She tried telling herself not to lean in and not to make it easy for him. But when he brushed her hair back to expose her neck and his lean, muscular body pressed against hers, her remaining resolve melted. Before he kissed her for a second time, her mind had already placed their lips together. They kissed again, and then his lips returned slowly and gently once more to caressing her neck before working his way back to her ear lobe and then once again to her lips. She wanted more and could hardly bear to wait. She needed his lips again and the rest of him as well.

The seduction was complete. Afterwards, Nan had no regrets. She had discovered a passionate side of herself that she never knew existed, and she wanted more. There was no going back. The sensuous beast in her had awakened.

A different beast was awakened in Hans. It was called the thrill of victory. If he was reading Nan right, he saw the possibility of early retirement and to not have to eventually face the probability that he would become a middle-aged, over the hill aging Romeo, who would be forced to seduce less and less attractive wealthy men and women to maintain his lifestyle and that he would be subject to being displaced by younger,

Conclusive, All-Inclusive Confusion

hungrier up-and-comers. ... An end to future uncertainty could be within his grasp. He could become a king in lieu of remaining a pawn.

If I play my cards right, this could be my final performance, my swan song. And Nan's really not all that unattractive — certainly better than some cynical, bitter old crones that make me hold my nose, close my eyes, and diddle out of desperation. And I'm really not a bad person. I would never marry for money; I want to just go where rich people are and marry for love.

After all, love may not be what makes the world go round, but it definitely makes the ride worthwhile. And since I'm going to ride, I would love to use a wise affiliation to ride with the 'country club' set.. Money might not buy happiness, but one thing's for sure. Poverty certainly won't.

Hans decided now was a good time to maybe start baiting the hook, and if he got lucky, he could even possibly begin to set it. He looked Nan straight in the eye as he held both of her hands.

"Darling sweet Nan, I don't think I've ever been so drawn to a person in such a short period of time. God meant this to happen. It's only been a few days, but I already feel like I've known you forever. You've become my best friend. But do you know what I'd change about you?"

"No, what, Hans."

"Absolutely nothing. I enjoy you just as you are. And one of the things that is most endearing is that I don't think you realize how much there is to love about you. And to top it all off, I trust you implicitly, and I hope one day in the future you'll allow me to prove to you that I can be worthy of being a part of your life. You, my dear, have no way of knowing just how much you're appreciated. Just being with you makes me happy."

"Hans, I don't know what to say. I've never met anyone like you either, but we'll be going our separate ways in a few days. I don't think I can stand it."

"I don't think I can either."

"Then we don't have to hope about one day in the future. We can make that day today. Marry me. Make me a happy woman. Make me Nan Roman — Mrs. Hans R. Roman."

"I don't know what to say."

"Say yes."

He began to kiss her again. He started with her lips, but then worked his way down her body. Just his kisses caused Nan to climax again. She had never felt like this before. Tremors ran through her whole body.

If this is love, I never want it to end.

They made love again. This time Hans was slow and methodical, enhancing every phase, and making it last.

"Please Hans, make me a happy woman. Marry me while we're both here at the resort."

"Yes, my darling Nan. Maybe I will."

"Maybe?"

"This is so sudden. You're so sudden, and I'm so inexperienced."

"Hans, darling. Life is short. You can't wait for the perfect time so you can strike when the iron's hot. Sometimes you have to strike to make the iron hot."

He wrapped his arms around her, pulled her in close, and said "OK, if you're sure you want me, I will marry you."

"You promise?"

"Yes, I'm certain.... If you'll have me."

Hans wanted to scream *Mission accomplished. And I didn't even have to ask. She asked me.*

"Hans, You're truly a blessing from God. And God will bless this union. Thank you for agreeing to be my partner, friend, and lover for the rest of our lives. I can't imagine spending it with anyone else. Now I have every reason to look forward to each new day and moment with elation because I'll have you to celebrate them with me. I'll be forever thankful that out of all the women in the world you chose me."

"We'll need to start to make the arrangements immediately."

"Yes, we will."

"I can't believe this is happening to me. I never dreamed a girl like you would fall for me. I've always been so unsure of myself around women."

"But it is happening, my dear. It is. And *I'm* the lucky one."

"I don't feel like I deserve you. I could turn backflips"

I can think of about fifty million different reasons I deserve to do backflips, and they all have dollar signs in front of them.

Check and checkmate! Billy Don, a strategist like you should have been an Army general or a politician. Hell, my instincts have instincts. And my end don't stink either. I've proven more than once that those instincts are usually right, and my bedside manner ain't too shabby either.

> ALL-DAY
> BREAKFAST
> SERVED UNTIL
> 11.30 AM

CHAPTER 22

"Dad, you look a little pink. I know I got some sun yesterday as well. I was thinking about going in the sauna, but I talked to the massage therapist, and she told me that was the worst thing I could do. She said that since sunburn is a common problem with hotel guests, the hotel offers an aloe vera rub. I've never done anything like that before. Want to join me?" Jax asked.

"Maybe later," Monte replied. "Bessie Prince and I have made other plans."

That damned Bessie Prince woman again. I wonder what disgusting new path she's leading Monte down today. That lewd, nude beach was bad enough. And if it weren't for her, I wouldn't have gotten this much sun.

He put on an innocent face and asked, "Oh yeah. What've you two love birds got planned?"

Dummy! You shouldn't have said 'love birds.' I don't want to be the one planting any ideas with these two. Hmmp! As if the conniving bitch didn't already have plans of her own.

"First, we're having breakfast together," Monte continued. "Then there's a James Bond trivia competition out by the south pool at ten. After all, we are in Jamaica, and this's where James Bond was created. Bessie Prince thought it'd be fun to take part in it."

"Well, you guys have fun."

Jax made a beeline back up to his room. Neil had overheard their exchange and thought he'd attend the competition as well. He sure would like to "bond" with this rich pigeon.

"Eve, we have any plans for this morning?" Jax said when he got back up to the room. "If we don't, why don't we go to the trivia contest out by the pool. Your dad wants to go. It's at ten."

"Is he going with us?"

"Nah, he's taking Bessie Prince. He'll meet us there."

Monte and Bessie Prince had a pleasant breakfast at the hotel's Palmyra Restaurant where they ran into Neil Hackinrider. When they saw Neil was alone, Monte invited him to have breakfast with them.

"So what are your plans for the day?" Neil innocently asked, as if he didn't know.

"They're having a James Bond contest by the pool," Monte answered.

"I saw that," Neil replied, acting as though that was the first he had heard about it. "I was thinking about going myself. Maybe I'll see you there."

By the time Jax and Eve got down to the pool, Monte and Bessie Prince were already there. Each table seated four people. Most of the tables had already been claimed. A waitress circulated, taking drink orders. As he munched a gummy bear, Jax walked over to where Monte and Bessie Prince were seated.

"The tables look like they've pretty much been taken," Jax commented. "Dad, mind if Eve and I join you?"

"Not at all."

Bessie Prince felt mildly irritated, but she said nothing.

This guy sticks to Monte like glue.

About that time, Neil walked in and saw that Jax and Eve had taken the spot at Monte's table that he had hoped to get. He ground his teeth.

That's fat slob has a way of always turning up like a bad penny. He constantly shows up and exasperates me as bad as if he were an unwashed hog in church on Easter Sunday or a bastard at a family reunion.

Foxy-Roxy had been assigned by the hotel to emcee the competition. Since Monte's table was taken, Neil sat down beside her and volunteered to be her assistant.

"Good morning, guests. We've begun another fya irie day here in beautiful Jamaica. If you're wondering what fya means ... that's spelled f-y-a, by the way. ... In Jamaica it means extremely good, amazing, or on point. Now, is everyone enjoying their week at Seascape thus far?"

Conclusive, All-Inclusive Confusion

People hooted and clapped. Foxy-Roxy went on with her canned pitch on how James Bond was created at Goldeneye just a few miles away towards Port Antonio in 1953 and how it subsequently took both the literary and the film worlds by storm.

"I'm not sure there's ever been anything in either medium quite like it," Foxy-Roxy continued. "Or a ladies man quite like Mr. Bond."

"Before we begin the competition, Why don't I set the mood with a tongue-in-cheek skit about Bond's legendary love life ... with apologies to a 'Saturday Night Live' skit from several years back. The credit is rightfully theirs. ... Now, let me introduce our players. Miss Amanda Hugginkiss will play nurse Connie Lingus. Mr. Kemp Morrison will play Dr. Hardy Boner. His friends just call him Dick. And the star of our show, Mr. James Bond, will be portrayed by Mr. Buster Cherry. Now, give our cast a welcoming round of applause."

Kemp Morrison! The bastard told me his name was Ben Casey from the Guardian Insurance Company. Bessie Prince thought. *What the hell is going on here? Mr. Morrison has some explaining to do.*

"Our skit entitled 'Today Is Never Yesterday' begins with Mr. Bond's annual physical at MI6's private clinic in Helsinki. "

"The doctor will see you momentarily, Mr. Bond. While you're waiting, is there anything that you need?"

"I'll let you know if something comes up."

Nurse Connie Lingus gave a coquettish laugh and said, "Hold that thought. He'll see you now."

"James, how are you feeling?"

"Never better, Dick. Hale, stout, and erect."

"Yes, erect all right. Please take a seat. I have some ... uh ... secret information for you," Dr. Boner says as he opens a folder.

"You mean for my eyes only."

"James, I don't know how you've managed to do it, but you have 107 venereal diseases. Fifty-three of them have been identified. We've sent thirty-six others to our disease control center in London for analysis, but now we can't get them to return our calls."

"And the other eighteen?"

"The other eighteen are viruses no one has ever seen before, and they have somehow found ways to mutate spontaneously with other bits and pieces of some of the other varieties in your body. ... Uh, they're so rare we don't even have a name for them.... We've decided for the time being to just call them Bond-1, Bond-2, Bond-3, and so forth. Then there are three more ..."

"But you said there were only 107."

"We didn't count three kinds of herpes because they're varieties only found in sharks. James, surely you've suspected something was wrong. Haven't you noticed the lesions on your body ... or the discoloration and tissue erosion? Or the massive testicular swelling? Or the odor? ... How many women have you slept with?"

"Not many. Just a few."

"I don't believe that."

"OK, eight or ten thousand or so."

"You do know that you have an ethical obligation to let these women know about your condition, don't you? I suggest the sooner you get started the better."

Connie Lingus bends down and whispers in the doctor's ear. He shakes his head.

"James, I just got a report that Bond-4 has now eaten through the lab beaker."

By this time, the hotel guests were laughing out loud. After a few more jokes, the skit ended with Mr. Bond propositioning the nurse. The cast got a standing ovation at the skit's conclusion. While Bessie Prince stood up and somberly clapped, she was mainly preoccupied. Morrison didn't seem to recognize her.

Me and Mr. Morrison are going to have a serious discussion, and I'm going to find out why he did what he did. I don't even know this asshole. Somebody put him up to it, and I'm going to find out who.

Jax didn't put two and two together either. While Banks had told Jax about Bessie Prince's prior meeting with Morrison, he had never actually seen him and had no point of reference.

Foxy-Roxy continued.

"Enjoy that? Thank you, cast. Ready to get started? This morning we're going to test your knowledge of Mr. Bond, the world's greatest spy. Looking at the number of people here, I'm going to vary the format from what you might expect. If everyone tried to compete against everyone else, we'd be here all day. Instead, we're going to break it down into smaller, more manageable contests. Each table is seating four. You'll

Conclusive, All-Inclusive Confusion

divide your table into two teams, and you'll compete against your tablemates. If your table only has three, that's fine too. I guess in your case it'll just have to be two and against one. Now, how's that sound?"

"OK, Bessie Prince and I'll take on you two," Monte whispered. "Should be fun."

Roxy continued and said, "Each table will be on an honor system to declare its own winner after each round. We will play four rounds, and each team will alternate answering the questions. You'll get one point for each right answer. A wrong answer will subtract a point. You can keep score with the pen and paper that I have provided for you. You'll be on an honor system. I'm sure your tablemates will keep everyone honest to avoid a booby prize. Or should I call it a booby trap? But since nowadays we're all expected to use polite, socially correct terminology, why don't we just call it a consolation prize?

"Oh yes. You heard me right. There'll be a negative prize for the loser at the end of each round that I will announce when the time comes. The questions will get increasingly more difficult as each round progresses. Now. Any questions? If not, relax and have fun. Good luck."

The first few questions were purposely ones that most people knew. Who wrote James Bond? What was his code name? what nationality was he? What was the first movie? Almost every team was tied at that point. Then the questions became more difficult. What kind of car did James Bond drive most often? What agency did he work for? Who was the original James Bond? Who sang "A View to a Kill's" theme song? Since the Magnus' were more attuned to popular music than the older Monte and Bessie Prince, they won the round by one point.

"As I said before we started, there is a booby prize for the loser of the round. They will start out mild, but the challenge will escalate as the rounds become more difficult. The consolation prize for this round is that the loser will either eat a teaspoon of anchovies or a spoonful of cinnamon or a raw egg. Your choice."

The waitresses circulated with the three items and spoons. Bessie Prince had no problem since anchovies are used sometimes to make the Jamaican hors d'oeuvre Solomon Gundy. Monte went for cinnamon since that seemed harmless. He soon found out that he was wrong. He upended the spoon. At first it tasted strong, rich, and slightly bitter. Then he began to gag and cough. He felt like he was choking, and his mouth began to burn.

"Are you OK?" Bessie Prince asked.

"My chest feels tight like I'm about to die," he gasped.

She quickly gave him some water to put out the fire.

Other people were not as sympathetic. They laughed at the losing guests who were having trouble eating their chosen allotment.

"Are you ready for the next round?" Foxy-Roxy began the questions.

What was Pierce Brosnan's first James Bond movie? What weapon did Goldfinger use in his attempt to kill James Bond? How did Ian Fleming arrive at a name for James Bond? What was George Lazenby's only movie as James Bond?

When the round ended, both Monte's and Jax's team had it's share of wrong answers, but due to Bessie Prince's knowing how James Bond got his name, their team was ahead by one. The booby prize was for the losers to recite a tongue twister in front of the group.

When their team's turn came, Eve went first. She read slowly and mostly made it through her challenge.

"Betty bought butter but the butter was bitter so Betty bought better butter to make the bitter butter better."

The group applauded, and now it was Jax's turn. His recitation did not go as well.

"To begin to toboggan, first buy a toboggan. But don't buy too big a toboggan, for too big a toboggan is not a toboggan to buy to begin to toboggan."

Every time Jax tried to say toboggan, he became tongue-tied, and the group laughed and made fun of him. Neil, still pissed that Jax had interrupted his bonding time, urged them on.

Jax and Eve won the next round. Where was James Bond sent in "You Only Live Twice?" Who sang "Nobody Does It Better?" What was the first James Bond movie to feature Blofeld? What body part is Dr. No missing?

The booby prize was to sing a karaoke version of "Nobody Does It Better." Bessie Prince volunteered for the duty, but Monte insisted that he share the embarrassment and ridicule if it were about to come. They began to sing a duet to the words on the monitor.

Conclusive, All-Inclusive Confusion

Nobody does it better
Makes me feel sad for the rest
Nobody does it half as good as you
Baby, you're the best.

By the time Monte and Bessie Prince got to the end of the song, they were starting to grate on Jax's nerves. They sounded entirely too sincere to him. He nervously bit his tongue as he popped one gummy bear after the next into his mouth.

Baby, you're the best
Bay, you're the best
Sweet baby, you're the best
Darlin', you're the best
Darlin', you're the best
Sweet baby, you're the best
Baby, you're the best
Sweet baby

Then as if to rub salt in the wound, Monte and Bessie Prince got a standing ovation.

"Time for the last round. Are you ready, folks?"

Who played James Bond in the spoof of "Casino Royale?" What was the first James Bond movie not based on a book? Who is Felix Leiter? Which director directed most of the James Bond movies? Which actress is the only woman to play "M"?

Monte and Bessie Prince won that round. Now they were tied, two rounds each. The booby prize was for a member of the loser's group to put on some extremely dark novelty sunglasses and don oversized pajama bottoms over their clothes and walk around the pool backwards. Eve balked and drew the line.

"Eve, honey, you know I'll need you to guide me. You know I don't do well backing up."

The group began to jeer and yell things like "Be a sport." Jax relented and after he saw some other people successfully win the challenge, he finally pulled the PJ's bottoms over his shorts. Part of his journey took him right past Foxy-Roxy and Neil's table.

Now's my chance to get this sloppy, fat turd who keeps getting in my way.

Neil stuck out his foot from under the table just enough to brush Jax's leg. As he had hoped, Jax reacted, lost his balance and went tumbling into the pool. Neil looked around to see if anyone had noticed and smiled when he realized he hadn't been caught. Jax was soaking wet and utterly bedraggled as if he was coming in out of the rain. He reminded Neil of a drowned rat.

This morning's victory is mine. And to top it all off when I got this turd-tapper, the jerk doesn't even know it.

Foxy-Roxy gave Neil a dirty look but said nothing. Maybe the crowd missed it, but she saw what he'd done. She had the waitresses take Jax a towel. Eve began to towel him off.

"Do you want to go back up to our room, darling?" Eve asked.

"No," Jax said through gritted teeth. "I'm not leaving these two here alone."

Monte didn't hear Jax's utterance, but Bessie Prince did.

She gave Jax a hateful look as she took Monte's hand and pecked him on the cheek. She smiled at Jax, trying to make her expression look innocent. He glared back.

When things seemed once again under control, Foxy-Roxy resumed.

"So, how many ties to we have?"

Several teams held up their hands.

"It just so happens that I have a tie-breaker."

Jax looked at his wife like "No way. I've been embarrassed enough for one morning."

"Don't worry. This is not a booby prize. As you all know, James Bond was a martini gourmand, but he drank a very specific type of martini. I've had my waitresses set up makeshift bars with a number of ingredients that are often used to make martinis. Some are ingredients that Bond would have specified. Others are merely to muddy the waters. ... Muddy is not the best adjective I could have used considering that martinis are clear. ... Let's just say muck things up.

"My waitresses will bring a cart with these ingredients to each table. Whichever team makes a pitcher of the most authentic James Bond martini will be the winner for that table. But even the losers will be winners since they will get to share in drinking the winning concoction. ... And maybe the losing concoction as well. Let me caution you, however. Don't make a bigger pitcher than you want to drink. ... As if that'll be a problem. ... We should all have these problems.

Conclusive, All-Inclusive Confusion

"My assistant and I will be the judges. ... Hey guys! I know it's tough work, but I'm getting paid to do it. Dirty work, but someone's got to do it. Neil, my friend, are you up to the challenge?"

"Are you trying to hint that they should make a dirty martini?"

"Absolutely not, Neil. I'm no dirty birdie."

"That's debatable, Foxy-Roxy. And I know you wouldn't push Absolut vodka."

"Of course not. But speaking of Absolut, do you know what they call a martini with a sausage garnish? — the Absolut wurst combo."

There was a collective groan from the group.

"Now, now, Foxy-Roxy. Remember, you're a judge. You have to remain neutral."

"That should be easy. After all, vodka is a neutral spirit."

"The way you keep rattling on, you remind me of the two Finnish friends who were sitting in a bar drinking vodka. After a few hours one said to the other, 'Well, that was fun,' to which his friend replied, 'Are we here to drink, or are we here to talk?'"

Some people hissed. Others laughed.

"And you remind me of the person who went on a vodka diet. He lost three days in one week. But enough talk. Our guests are here to drink, so let's let them get to it.

"Oh, and by the way, there will be one grand prize for the team that makes the best James Bond martini. And let me say this, It will not be a booby prize. It's going to be something nice."

"Since there are two people on each team, does that mean they get boobies prizes," quipped Neil.

"Now, now, Neil. Get your mind out of the gutter. This is a g-rated competition."

"Well, you're the one who brought the subject of gutters up. I bet you don't know why gutter men work for free. It's because their work is on the house."

"Enough already. If these people have to listen to one more of your bad jokes, there won't be any martinis to judge. They'll gulp them down in self-defense just block you out."

"This competition should be easy," Jax whispered to his wife. "All we have to do is pick the priciest vodka on the tray and make it as dry as possible."

Bessie Prince overheard and smiled. She had a different opinion.

"We've got this in the bag," she whispered to Monte. "I know exactly how James Bond's martinis are correctly made. They call it a Vesper martini."

"What's that?"

"Watch me, and you'll find out," she said as she measured a healthy portion of Gordon's gin into the pitcher.

"I thought he drank vodka martinis."

"Most people make that mistake."

She then measured a lesser amount of Smirnoff vodka into the pitcher.

"Did you grab the wrong bottle?"

"Shhh! Don't give away my secret. Now's here's the really secret ingredient that most people don't know about. And I see they have some. Good."

She held up a bottle of Lillet Blanc.

"What's that?"

"A French wine used instead of dry vermouth.

"Don't forget the olives."

"No, no, no! Another classic mistake. Lemon zest is what you use. Trust me. This is going to be the winner."

Bessie Prince was right. Jax was once again frustrated and pissed. Bessie Prince had shown him up again in front of his father-in-law.

Monte was completely thrilled. He was not accustomed to winning trivia competitions. In truth, he was not used to winning any kind of competition. While Bessie Prince made a show of congratulating him, inside she seethed and brooded.

I'm going to find out what this Kemp Morrison creep's game is, and who put him up to his elaborate pack of lies.

Jax was not the only person left frustrated at the end of the 007 competition. Neil felt like he a finally come up with an "investment opportunity" that would open the door for him to get to some of Monte's newfound wealth, but thanks to Bessie Prince and Jax, Monte never seemed to be alone along enough for him to begin to set the hook, and each delay was making setting it harder and harder.

Unknown to Neil, Potsy was feeling the same pressure and sense of urgency, but he had devised a dissimilar strategy designed to trigger a different Monte's hot button.

```
┌─────────────────────┐
│ LIVE      EAT       │
│ L̶O̶V̶E̶      SHIT      │
│ L̶A̶U̶G̶H̶    DIE       │
└─────────────────────┘
```

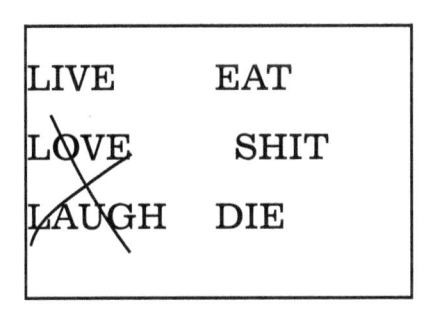

CHAPTER 23

Thanks to Bessie Prince's knowledge of Vesper martinis, Monte and Bessie Prince were the grand prize winners of the James Bond 007 competition. Bessie Prince won a champagne pedicure and manicure at the hotel's beauty salon. Monte's prize was a massage by the hotel masseuse to be followed by some time in the hotel sauna. While Bessie Prince had had plenty of experience with various beauty shop procedures, this was going to be a first-time event for Monte and as such was somewhat unsettling to him. It brought on an unexplainable feeling of guilt.

For a low-paid church worker like him in Detroit, massages were a luxury that until now had been totally out of Monte's budget range. In his subconscious, he imagined that his mother would never have approved. After all, in Highland Park, massage parlors were often used as fronts for possibly dirty (and certainly in his mind diseased) prostitutes and other degradants to perform illegal and immoral acts. Besides that, he wasn't totally comfortable having a complete stranger touch, rub, and knead his body, even though his rational mind tried to tell him that a massage in the controlled environment of a posh hotel was not the same as one in a sleazy, back-alley type sex joint. This close contact somehow seemed like an violation of his personal space, making his palpitating heart almost hyperventilate in dread as he anticipated and imagined what was to come. Instead of making him feel pleasurable, all his mild haphephobic panic was doing was mainly making him feel almost nauseous.

I'm going to be getting naked with a stranger. I'm not sure what I fear the most — having a man or having a woman touch me. I wonder if massages hurt. What if I pass gas or make some other bodily noise? What if my feet get sweaty and slimy feeling and start to stink? What if I get an erection? — I'd die of embarrassment.

While he would be too embarrassed to voice these fears out loud to Bessie Prince, she could tell he was uneasy and tried to reassure him that massages were an enjoyable experience. To take his mind off of the matter, she asked him if he thought she should ask Monte's daughters to join her for her appointment.

"It'll give me a chance to get to know them," she explained.

He agreed.

Viv and Eve readily accepted Bessie Prince's invitation. Nan declined since she wanted to spend her free time with Hans in his room. She didn't want the family to know, but now that she had discovered sex, she couldn't seem to get enough.

I have never felt this kind of high. I tingle all over. And Hans makes me feel so desired. No one has ever made me feel that way before.

When Eve told Jax that she and Viv were going to join Bessie Prince for a girls' afternoon out, he was elated. He immediately began to formulate a list of the things he wanted his wife to learn about Bessie Prince. This was an opportunity he had been hoping for. He was finally going to find out what this gold-digging hussy was up to once and for all. And then analyze and compare Eve's report with what he would spend the afternoon trying to dig out of his father-in-law. And maybe he'd have an answer to his sixty-four thousand dollar question — Was Monte was being taken in by Bessie Prince's pitch?

"I don't think it's fair that Bessie Prince has company while Monte has to spend the afternoon alone. I think I'll join him and get a massage as well. We'll have a boys' afternoon out while you girls are having your nails done."

Monte readily agreed to have Jax join him. He was secretly relieved not to have to face the unknown alone.

I'll let Jax go first. That'll give me time to size up the situation and see how I'm supposed to act so that I don't embarrass myself.

When Monte proposed that Jax be first, Jax acquiesced but insisted that they each keep the other one company throughout both massages.

Conclusive, All-Inclusive Confusion

How else was he going to probe Monte and find out the depth of his feeling for Bessie Prince?

When they arrived, Monte and Jax met the muscular Jamaican masseuse, who introduced himself as Winston. Winston stepped out of the open-air, Bahama-shuttered room so Jax could disrobe. A ceiling fan moved the air, and drew air in from the outside, keeping the room from feeling stuffy. They could hear the soothing sounds of the Caribbean in the background.

Before leaving the room, Winston explained to Jax that he should disrobe to whatever point made him feel most comfortable. He then waited an appropriate amount of time before politely knocking before reentering the room. Monte was impressed with his professionalism.

Maybe this isn't a den of iniquity or Sodom and Gomorrah after all.

Jax had stripped until he was completely nude and had wrapped a towel around himself. His white, flabby stomach and dimpled buttocks didn't seem to faze Winston, who instructed him lie on his stomach and put his face into the face cradle. Once he did so, the masseuse adjusted the towel around Jax's waist.

"Do you have any lower back issues that I should know about? Do you go to a chiropractor? No? Then let's get started. Would you prefer that I use almond oil or coconut oil? Do you want me to close the window?"

"Nah, leave it open. The breeze feels good. Do almond oil. You got any beer?"

"Of course, sir. Will a Red Stripe do?"

"Hell, yes. I had a couple of those with lunch. Monte, you want one? No? Then I'll drink yours for you. ... Beer, beer, good for my heart. The more I drink, the more I ..."

Instead of finishing the rhyme, he took a big chug-a-lug and then ripped as loud a fart as he could manage. Both Monte and Winston looked disgusted rather than impressed.

"I hope you don't exhibit that kind of behavior around my daughter," Monte said.

After the air cleared, the masseuse began to give Jax a complete body massage. Neither Jax nor Winston attempted to make further small talk. Monte just watched and took in the picture. Jax began to doze. As the masseuse began doing Jax's slack shoulders and flabby neck, the silence caused him to become bored and begin to simply massage Jax by rote. Instead, he began to focus on a horsefly that had come in through the open window He began to follow it with his eyes. His head gently bobbed as it zigged and zagged through the room trying to elude a dragonfly that seemed to be chasing it. He glanced back down at Jax, who by now was completely asleep from the fan that was cooling the combination of sweat and almond oil on his body.

The masseuse had become so fixated that he started noticing the pattern the two insects were creating. They would erratically go left and then suddenly go right, then up, suddenly turn left, and then dive down. He wondered if Jah was trying to send him so sort of subtle message and tell him what to massage next. He wasn't the only one fixated on the insects' air battle. A hungry toad was also following their every move.

Winston began muttering silently to himself as he tried to refocus on the job at hand.

You need to do his suprahyoid neck muscles next. OK, now massage left, and then massage right. Now up, down, up, down. Good.

The two insects continued to get closer and closer to the table as if they were trying to tell Winston what to do next. They were now only a foot away. The toad moved closer as well.

And then it happened. In the matter of what seemed to be a second, the horsefly, attracted by Jax's perspiration and a hair growing from a mole on his back, dived towards Jax's sweaty back in a maneuver to elude its adversary, but the dragonfly anticipated the move and followed. The masseuse attempted to swat both away, only succeeding instead in knocking aside the towel that covered Jax's hips. Jax snorted in his sleep but still never woke up.

The masseuse whacked at the horsefly. It bounced off the table and flew straight into the masseuse's nose, biting the inside of it. His reaction was the worst possible one. Without thinking, he sneezed, pushing the horsefly back out covered with a wad of snot. The snot-covered horsefly bounced off the Red Stripe bottle and ricocheted off the ceiling fan straight down into Jax's sweaty butt crack with the dragonfly chasing close behind. Jax suddenly felt the horsefly's sting and his butt crack felt like it was on fire. It was as if someone had taken a pair of nail clippers, turned them sideways, and then used them to punch a hole in Jax's skin. The

Conclusive, All-Inclusive Confusion

horsefly latched on and began to suck Jax's blood. First there was a sharp burning, followed by itching and swelling as the bite inflamed his skin.

He let loose with a wet emission, temporarily immobilizing both insects. As the insects struggled, the hungry toad saw that this was just the opportunity it had been waiting for. He immediately sprang up onto Jax to claim his dinner. Jax felt the clammy, slimy toad hit and peed on himself before his bowels completely let loose.

A three-way battle began in earnest in the brown goo in Jax's crack. The horsefly bit again. This time Jax felt like someone was digging through his skin with tweezers. The sting brought Jax fully awake. With a start, he flipped over and kicked Winton in his burning nose as he fell off of the table The hapless masseuse careened backwards, crashing into Monte. But the horsefly wasn't finished yet. It somehow ended up in Jax's pubic hairs, where the frenzied insect stung him again. Now Jax was on fire both in the front and in the back. The frog finally caught the horsefly there and gobbled it down. As it sat in the bed of Jax's curly hairs, Jax swore that it seemed to be smiling at him.

The dragonfly few back out the open window, and the massage was officially concluded at that point.

Later, after the girls raved on and on about what a perfect outing they had had and how now as a result they were becoming the best of friends, neither Monte or Jax could adequately explain their adventure in the massage room or why Monte had failed to get the massage he had won.

"Cluck! Cluck! Cluck!" the girls chided as they made fun on how they thought Monte had just chickened out.

> **FISHING FOR CHILDRED ONLY LIMIT 3**

CHAPTER 24

Bessie Prince sorely wanted to know why someone would go to all that trouble to slander Monte and try to scare her away from him, but in order to come to any concrete conclusions, she would need to have a serious discussion with Kemp Morrison. First, she had to locate him. She decided to find out if the hotel provided worker housing for some of it staff. A casual conversation with Christian Angel, the Seascape Ambassador, confirmed that to be the case. She didn't risk pursuing the conversation with Angel any farther. She wanted to make her upcoming meeting with Morrison to be as big a surprise for him as their first meeting had been for her.

When she got back up to her room, she dialed the front desk on her cell phone. She knew that she'd probably wouldn't be able to wheedle his room number out of the desk clerk,, so she didn't even try. She'd meet Kemp some place that was public. She wasn't comfortable with a meeting at his room in case he might become irrational or violent. She didn't bother to disguise her voice, reasoning that he probably wouldn't remember hers anyway since the self-centered egotist had done most of the talking during their previous encounter. Once again, she was right.

"Do I have the pleasure of speaking to Mr. Morrison, Mr. Kemp Morrison?"

"Yes, you do."

"My name is Maude Blackwell from the Island Talent Agency."

There was a pause.

Conclusive, All-Inclusive Confusion

Blackwell.... Island ... They must be a part of Island Records. My God! That's big time.

Bessie Prince waited for him to speak.

"Mr. Morrison? Mr. Morrison? Are you still there? I've seen your performance in your Broadway revue show and think you might possibly be a fit for what one of my clients is looking for. Would you be willing to meet with me and discuss it?"

Would I ever!

"Sure. I think I can make time. Where do you want to meet?"

Bessie Prince quickly thought of a public place where she was unlikely to be seen by either Monte or his family.

"The Orchid on the hotel's family side. Would an hour from now be too soon? I'll be the lady in the floppy brim straw hat."

Bessie Prince arrived early and sat with her back to the door. She didn't want Kemp to recognize her the moment he walked in the door and balk. She further disguised herself with an oversized hat with a scarf attached and large sunglasses.

Her disguise worked long enough. Kemp was in the process of pulling out a chair before he recognized her. He turned to leave.

"Sit, Mr. Ben Casey, if you know what's good for you. Otherwise I'm going to track you down in a much more embarrassing location, and when I do, I'm going to make life very difficult for you with both the hotel and the authorities."

She pointed at the chair. He immediately complied.

"How'd you find me?"

"That's irrelevant."

"I didn't mean you any harm. I'm just an actor who was hired to play a role."

"And before you leave you're going to tell me who that was who hired you."

"I'm not sure what his name was."

'Describe him, or tell me what room he's staying in."

Kemp gave her Banks' description and told her that he thought the person was on the penthouse floor.

Banks Bridges! Monte's second son-in-law! So Jax Magnus, the gummy bear freak, isn't my only adversary. This is good information. I'm not sure right now what I'm going to do about it, but at least I know what I'm up against.

"Do you know what this man's motives were?"

"I honestly don't. He just told me what he wanted me to say, and then paid me when it was done"

"And what was I worth?"

"Three hundred dollars."

Figures. Banks is a cheap bastard. Millions on the line, and he only spends three hundred.

"Thank you, Mr. Morrison. I'm going to let you off the hook for now. … But if he hires you to play any future roles, I want to know about them. And don't worry. You will be rewarded. And I'm not a cheap SOB like Banks Bridges. I'll pay you for the information, and I'll never divulge that you were the source of my information. One last thing. If I find out that you have divulged this meeting to anyone … I mean anyone … or failed to relay future information back to me, I'm going to make your life a living hell. Do we understand each other?"

Kemp nodded.

"A nod's not good enough, Mr. Morrison. I want to hear you say it out loud so that we both know I've made myself perfectly clear."

GOT FAR WOOD

CHAPTER 25

Neil was once again frustrated that he had not been able to get Monte alone at the James Bond competition.

Shit! Shit! Shit! That's the whole reason I went. Otherwise, I wouldn't have given a rats ass about 007, 008, or 009.

He had also briefly dropped in the day Monte was scheduled to get his massage, but when he saw Jax was there, he had seen no reason to stay.

There's got to be some way to get this guy alone so I can work on him.

A solution finally hit Neil.

I don't know why I keep hoping a chance meeting's going to take place. That's like trying to see my doctor without an appointment. It ain't gonna happen. What do I do when I want to see my doctor? I make an appointment. That's what I'll do here. And I'll just tell Mr. Moneybags flat out that I have something I want to talk to him ALONE about in a location of my choosing where I won't get interrupted — like in the privacy of my room. Since I've been introduced to him as a successful businessman, his guard should be down and his curiosity should be up. Plus, I'll be able to again use a time-tested prop that's come in handy over and over again. The solution's so simple. Neil, you dumb dodo bird! Why didn't you think of it before now?

The prop Neil had in mind was a set of commercial blueprints of an RV village that he had stolen from a Florida construction site several years back. It showed a pool and a lake as well as a clubhouse, rental cottages and RV sites, a boat launch, a convenience store, a pavilion, and picnic grounds. Truly impressive! They had come in handy on several occasions and were about to again. This time they were what had given him the nugget of the idea he was going to spring on Monte. He had familiarized himself with the plans enough times and made enough similar pitches that he was confident that he could ad-lib a convincing presentation one more time with just the religious spin put on the project that he would trigger Monte's hot button and start the sale process.

His mind reverted back to how he had obtained the plans to begin with. He had staked out a job site off and on for a week, looking for an opportunity to snatch some plans, but the opportunity just didn't seem to want to come. One morning a worker had left his hardhat in the bed of his truck, and Neil was able to steal it. But he was afraid to be caught if he wore it that same day so it went into his car trunk until he could Magic-marker his name into it. Two days later he thought he'd finally gotten lucky. He saw a rolled up set of plans sticking up out of an empty five-gallon bucket, and no one seemed to be around. He donned the stolen hardhat and confidently walked in. He had grabbed the plans and was headed back out when he heard a gruff voice behind him.

"Hey mister. What're you doing with my blueprints?"

Neil knew he had to think in a hurry, or he was in trouble.

"I'm from the architect's office. These plans have some errors in them he wants to correct. I'll bring you a corrected set."

"We need plans today."

"You'll have them. I'll be right back. Lickety split."

Of course, lickety split never came.

He smiled at the memory. Then he scribbled a happy hour invitation on piece of hotel stationary and sent it up to Monte's room via a bellboy. Monte was thrilled that an important businessman like Mr. Hackinrider thought enough of him to invite him out socially and called back to accept the invitation.

"Mr. Connors, thanks for getting back to me. If my name seems unfamiliar, I'm Neil Hackinrider. Do you remember me from the other night?"

"Of course, Mr. Hackinrider. What could I possibly do for someone as important as you?"

"I'm told that you're a religious professional who has sound judgement. I was wondering if I might get your opinion on a project that I have in the works to benefit people in your line of work."

Conclusive, All-Inclusive Confusion

"I'm flattered. You say I'm a professional, but I'm not a priest or a minister. I'm simply a piano player and social worker working for a church."

"I'm not looking for spiritual guidance. This is more of a practical matter. If you'll do me the honor of coming up to my room, I'll be more specific. I'd really appreciate it."

"Uh … Sure. I guess so. … If you think I can be of help."

"I know you can. And please come alone. It might be detrimental to my project if too many people know about it. I'm in 472. Would in thirty minutes rush you too much?"

"No, that'll be fine. I don't have anything else scheduled for this morning."

"I'll be looking for you. … And thank you."

That was SOOO simple. Why didn't I think of the direct approach before now? Because, Neil, sometimes you're a dumbass who makes simple things complex, that's why.

Neil spread the blueprint out on the table in his room and waited for Monte to arrive.

When he heard a tentative knock on the door, he opened it and said, "Mr. Connors, thank you so much for agreeing to share your insight with me. Please take a chair.

"As I think you know, I'm in the jewelry as well as the real estate development business. And they are not as far away from each other as you might think. We live in a changing world, and times ahead will be very different from anything we've experienced in our lifetimes up until now. Ethical transparency is now critical even in the jewelry industry."

Monte had no idea what Neil was talking about, but he nodded as if he understood.

"Consumers, especially millennials, favor products and businesses that have a conscience. A recent study concluded that over eighty percent of customers want conflict-free, environmentally friendly, safe jewelry. The four C's — cut, color, clarity and carat weight — will no longer cut it. Millennials especially want to be assured that what they're buying hasn't had a negative impact on either humans or the environment. Let's face it, illegal mining and recent pandemics have threatened both workers and the environment. This can only get worse since the demand for high-end jewelry continues to increase. Thus far, very few companies in the jewelry industry have taken concrete steps to change the way they traditionally do business. I want to be one of the few who has. Therein, lies opportunity. Do you follow me thus far?"

Once again, a puzzled Monte nodded.

Neil went on to talk about how many environmentally conscious consumers now not only preferred but were actively seeking out lab-made and recycled diamonds that had been produced with renewable energy in lieu of buying mined stones. This trend was causing contemporary jewelers to use recycled gold as well. This e-mined jewelry used precious metals salvaged from technology and dental waste, and unwanted scrap.

Monte wondered how this was relevant to him.

"Now, let me talk about male jewelry. It's always existed, but now it's coming to the forefront and has morphed into gender-fluid, unisex designs that people don't just buy for others on special occasions but jewelry all genders buy more frequently for themselves. Generation Z is especially resistant to classifications or labels.

"Finally, what has emerged is semi-fine jewelry. It nestles neatly between costume jewelry and fine jewelry by using semi-precious stones coupled with fine metals. It has intrinsic value without the high price tag. Semi-precious jewelry is where I'm taking my business, and I plan on making a lot of money. The tentative name for my new company is Filigree & Facet International."

Monte couldn't remain silent and wonder any longer so he said, "So, what does this have to do with me?"

"I'm coming to that. I'm not here to pitch you on the jewelry trade, though if it was an area of investment that interested you, I'd consider maybe taking you in. See that blueprint on the table. That's the master plan for my Tower of Hope Retirement Village. My parents were missionaries who never built a net worth, and even though they did a lot of good for the world, they were destitute when they got too old to work. I don't want to see that happen to other good people. They should be rewarded for their goodness, not penalized. I want to build an assisted living for old folks village for religious workers who can't afford to go elsewhere. I plan to subsidize it with the profits from my semi-precious jewelry business. Do you think that I've got a viable concept?"

"Sure. I guess so. I know there's bound to be a need."

Neil smiled. This was beginning to work.

Conclusive, All-Inclusive Confusion

"Where do you plan to build your retirement mecca?"

"Pinellas County Florida. I've already got an option on the property. And I've already started filing the site plans with the county. So far, the response has been very positive."

"Sounds like you've done your homework."

"Then will you look at these plans?"

He showed Monte the blueprints.

"Can you think of anything I've left out?"

"One thing I don't see is a chapel."

"Excellent suggestion. You wonder why I asked you up here? You're too modest. You're sharp. I knew you'd have some outstanding suggestions. ... And that a good person like you would appreciate what I'm trying to do. ... And, you know, I was right."

"Oh, heck ... You're embarrassing me."

"Would you be willing to put some seed money in the project and then serve on my board of directors? I researched your background, and I was impressed. I need a man like you since my time will be consumed running the jewelry side of the business. Think about it. Maybe we'll name the chapel after you. The Connors Chapel — that has a nice ring to it. Please, give it some thought."

"Thank you for thinking of me, sir. I will. Serious thought. But I will need to run it by my sons-in-law, Banks Bridges and Jax Magnus. You may not know it, but they're my investment advisors. After all, Banks *is* a financial planner, and Jax is a member of his company's million dollar roundtable."

Riiight! And Banks is a jumbo dumbo. And one who I've already "financial-planned" fifteen gees out of on another bogus jewelry deal as easy as pie. I bet if Monte asked him to buy AOL, he'd have to look up the ticker symbol. Old Neil'll get with him and then to him. What you wanna bet?

And as far as Magnus goes, he seems to be even dumber than his brother-in-law. What you wanna bet I can outsmart him as well? He'll be my next target.

But aloud Neil said, "Excellent. They're good men. I understand. Bless you."

Oh, Neil, you're sooo good. No, I'm not good. I'm gooder than good. You're the best. Frank Abagnale and Bernie Cornfeld could have taken lessons from you. Why? Because I'm bad, bad to the bone. I'm living proof that how I sell is more important than what I sell.

David Beckwith

When I walk the streets kings and queens step aside
Because I'm bad to the bone
B-B-B-B-bad to the bone
B-B-B-B-bad to the bone
Wooo, bad to the bone

CAUTION TRANSPORTING LIVE CHILDREN

CHAPTER 26

Neil didn't know just how on target he was with Jax Magnus. Since Jax had conned his father-in-law into overpaying on the life insurance policy, even after Jax had set aside money to pay for the portion of his windfall that he'd have to declare for taxes, he'd still be sitting on a bank balance of over a million and half dollars that his wife didn't know about. This money was already burning a hole in his pocket. He just wished he had a good idea on how to invest it.

Jax came down the elevator and went into the hotel snack shop to make his daily purchase of gummy bears. He strolled out on the patio to find an unoccupied umbrella-covered table to enjoy the fresh air and munch on a few. All along the way, he was thinking that having money provided a lifestyle he could easily get used to. Neil silently followed him out.

After he found an empty table and sat down, Neil casually strolled by.

"Beautiful day, isn't it?"

"That's for sure. As Dorothy would say, I'm not in Kansas anymore — and definitely not in Detroit."

"Mind if I join you?"

"Not at all. Want a gummy bear?"

"Don't mind it I do. You really like these things, don't you?"

"I guess I'm kind of hooked on them."

Neil pulled out a chair to sit in and put his leather messenger bag on another chair. It was a prop that had nothing in it but meaningless papers, but Jax didn't know that. Neil began to bait the trap.

"Did you bring your work with you?" Jax asked, eyeing the bag.

"I was going to go over some documents, but since I ran into you, I think I'll just relax and deal with them later. They concern a new company that I'm starting. Nothing that won't wait."

"If I'm not being too bold and if you don't mind, what kind of business are you starting?"

"I don't mind. I'll tell you a wee bit but only if you promise me that you won't tell as soul. Do I have your word?"

"The CIA couldn't drag it out of me."

"Then, you're holding it in your hand."

Jax looked confused.

"Gummy bears — that's my new business and where I plan to make lots and lots of money. I've done a lot of research on the topic. Do you realize that chewy candy sales will soon reach $5 billion annually and are growing at an annual rate of 15%. And one of the most popular types of chewy candies is gummy bears. They started in Germany over a hundred years ago and were originally called dancing bears. They really caught on in the U.S. in the 1980's — probably in conjunction with Ronald Reagan popularizing jelly beans."

"Wow! I didn't know that."

"I see from the bag that the brand you're eating is made by Haribo. Do you know they make over a hundred million gummy bears every day and sell them in over a hundred countries? And they're just one manufacturer — and not the biggest."

"I had no idea."

"Well, I'm not planning on going head to head with them. That'd be foolish. I'm going to make specialty gummies. I'll have gummies for weight loss, gummies with Viagra in them, gummies for blood pressure control. The potential is mind boggling. Wherever it's legal, I'll even have gummies with marijuana in them. ... And that's just the start."

"You can do all that?"

"I'm not talking pie-in-the-sky. My labs have developed the products. And we've applied for patents on them."

"Gummy bears plus!"

"Oh, no. We'll sell them to look like other things. Maybe gummy giraffes, or gummy butterflies — you get the idea. Maybe we could even

Conclusive, All-Inclusive Confusion

have gummy smurfs. … gummy doctors and gummy nurses. We'll make them look like whatever purpose they're supposed to accomplish."

"I guess the ones with Viagra could be made to look like a penis."

"See. You're getting the idea. You're pretty smart."

"Are you looking for investors?"

"Not right now, but maybe down the road."

"I have money to invest. … Over a million dollars."

"I don't know. …. Better let me think about it. Anyway, … great running into you. Don't eat too many gummy bears."

"Do you have a business card?"

"Sure. I'll give you one of mine if you give me one of yours. And don't you forget? This conversation stays just between the two of us. If I ever find out that you're not a man of your word …"

"You won't. I swear on my mother's grave."

Neil was smiling as he walked away from the table.

So Dumbo Jaxbo has over a million bucks in investable money. Neil, old man, I think you baited that hook pretty damned well. We'll let him stew over what he's missing out on. Then we'll go back and hook this fish and reel him in. By the time he figures out he's been screwed, glued, and tattooed, old Neil's gonna be way down the road using a different name.

"I hate to brag, but damn-it-to-hell, Neil, you're so good that you're bad."

Because I'm bad to the bone
B-B-B-B-bad to the bone

"One more time. … I can't hear you."

B-B-B-B-bad to the bone

"That's better. One last time and bring it on home this time."

B-B-B-B-bad to the bone.

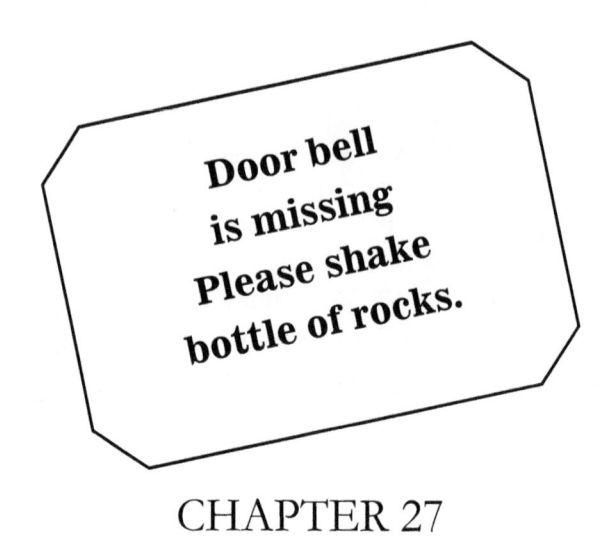

> Door bell is missing Please shake bottle of rocks.

CHAPTER 27

Neil's spiel had hit home with Monte more than Monte let on.

I wouldn't spend all my newfound money if I lived to be a hundred and fifty. I'm just not that kind of frivolous person. I'm an ordinary Christian man, and that's all I'll ever be.

Shoot! I can set aside enough to make sure my girls have a secure future and still have lots and lots of money left over for other things. This windfall was a gift from God, and God gave it to me for a reason, to do good for my fellow man. And what would be more worthwhile than making sure that people who have devoted their lives to helping others can live out their days with dignity. I might even want to end up there myself around virtuous people that I've got a lot in common with.

Monte never would have admitted it to anyone because it would seem too vain, but a picture of a chapel with the name Connors Chapel on it kept popping into his mind. He could see meeting rooms attached to it as well where people would congregate for Bible studies. He could see the nondenominational mini-complex being used for funeral services as residents passed on. And if he lived here himself, he would be a celebrity of sorts. People would point at him and tell their friends that he was the one who had donated the chapel and meeting rooms that they used on a regular basis. He had never felt important before. That would be a fun feeling.

The chapel would become a focal point for the whole community, and this would happen because God provided the financing using him as his delivery mechanism. It would be his legacy, something that would be there

Conclusive, All-Inclusive Confusion

long after he was gone. Maybe it would assure him of his own place in heaven. That gave him a warm feeling.

I need to think this out further — alone.

Monte took the elevator down to the Palmyra buffet restaurant where he went through the line and got a cup of coffee and a slice of coconut meringue pie.

I definitely need to think this through by myself. The girls would probably understand, but ... I'm not so sure about their husbands. Maybe Bessie Prince might give me her unbiased advice since she has no vested interest in either me or my money. After all, she is an educated woman who seems to have a good head on her shoulders. But do I know her as well as I think I do? ... Maybe it's best that I keep this to myself for a while.

Potsy passed by the restaurant and saw Monte in there. He grinned as he looked around and his predator instinct woke up. The restaurant was almost empty.

Yes! For once Monte's alone. Maybe my chance has finally come to test an agenda.

He got a glass of tea, some napkins, and a couple of lemon slices and slipped into a table behind Monte. As he expected, Monte was too preoccupied to notice him.

Potsy went into his act. He rubbed the lemon on his eyelids, causing them to tear up. He began to sniffle and cry into a napkin, occasionally peeking to see if Monte was taking notice. When that didn't happen, he pounded his fist on the table for emphasis. Finally, Monte looked over his shoulder and noticed him.

"Clay ... Uh ... Mr. Potter, is something wrong?"

Potsy turned away from him and said nothing. Monte picked up his pie and coffee and moved over to Potsy's table.

"Don't pay any attention to me. I'm just depressed."

"About what? Maybe I can help."

"I'm not sure anyone can help."

"Give me a try."

"I don't want to burden you."

"I'll decide if you're a burden or not."

"Remember I told you my son was in a car wreck that left him a paraplegic? ... And he had a seizure that left him in a semi-coma? ... That the insurance company was balking at paying? ... Some coverage issue."

"Yes, I remember."

"Well, what I didn't tell you was that as a result I've backed myself into a corner. I had to do it so Po Junior wouldn't die. It started out small, and I intended that it be short term. I gave them the title to my car for my first loan. They told me that there was no monthly minimum payment — that I could pay what I could afford. I didn't realize it at the time, but since the interest was more than what I was paying, and the amount I owed just kept on going up. And the hospital bills just kept on coming in. I needed more money. They suggested that I pledge my house next. ... And I'm ashamed now to say that I did. ... I didn't feel like I had a choice at the time. Now the balance on that loan sho nuff soared ... And they wanted more collateral or for me to pay it down. I liquidated my IRA to buy me time. It was the last thing I had of value. Now I've got two problems. I haven't been able to pay them, and now they want their money — now or else. Plus, the IRS is after me because of the taxes I incurred liquidating the IRA. I don't know what to do. I couldn't let my son just die."

"I'm so sorry."

"It's not your problem. I'll figure something out. There's got to be some kind of government program for people like me. But I don't have any money to hire a lawyer to tell me what it is. ... I'm sorry if I upset you. Excuse me. I've got to go now."

Potsy shoved his chair back and headed for the door still sniffling. His sniffling changed to a smile after he got out of Monte's eyesight.

Potsy, old man, that was a pretty good performance. Act one! Yep, a good show, old man. And you resisted asking him for anything. We'll let him stew for a while before we go in for the kill.

And I've got a good act two coming up to follow. Before I'm done, I won't have to ask him for anything. He'll just be forking it over.

Potsy might not have been so confident if he had known that his performance was coming on the heels of Neil's equally convincing show.

"One more thing to think about," Monte sighed to himself after Potsy left. "I better pray for God's guidance.

"Life didn't seem so complicated before I won the lottery. I just went to work, attended mass, came home and spent some time with my girls, watched some TV, and tried to live a good life. All in all, life was uncomplicated. Now, I don't have just the girls; I have a possible lady friend as well. Boy, I'm sure glad there aren't any other issues with Viv, Eve, or Nan."

SELF CEMETARY

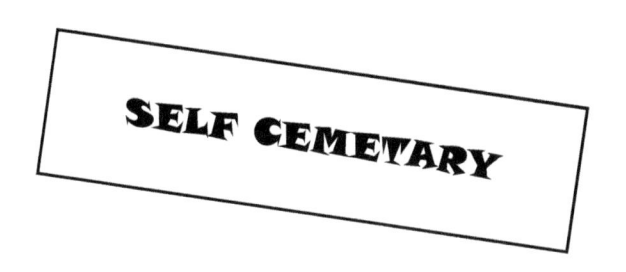

CHAPTER 28

Hans Roman had promised Nan that he would make the preparations for their upcoming wedding, but he still had one obstacle to overcome in trying to do so. He needed some revised identification. Whereas Nan knew him as Hans Robin Roman, his passport was in his real name, Billy Don Brown. Questions about his identity were a can of worms he would rather not open since Hans R. Roman was the most recent of many names he had gone by over the years. If his many aliases were to start coming out, it might well be a deal killer, and even if it weren't, it would be at least make Nan and the rest of her family begin to doubt him in other areas. Credibility was crucial. If his shady background were to be exposed, things would never be the same. Definitely not the way to start a marriage. The pedestal that Nan had him on would crumble and melt away like a sand castle during high tide. And he was sure that the rest of the family was bound to resent his abruptly shoehorning his way into it. He sure as hell didn't need to give them unnecessary ammo.

Thank God for one thing! At least the Jamaican official isn't demanding a certified birth certificate. A copy will do as long as it has the right name on it. I can always say that I misplaced my passport, find it later, and replace it once and for all when I'm back in the States with one that says Hans Roman. I guess it's time to call my buddy Squirrely.

Squandro Levi Possman aka Squirrely Possum was a man of many talents who operated mainly out of Vegas and Reno but sometimes on occasion did business out of his winter residence in Hialeah Florida. On the surface, he was a completely legal entrepreneur with his pawn shop, repo, debt collection, photography, and bail bond operations. But for a very select clientele he had a document creation service as well.

No drugs. No girls. No Porn. Squirrely was adamant on those points. After all, he was a man of principle.

Hans gave Squirrely a call.

"Mr. Portnoy. This is Billy Don Brown."

"Billy Don. This is an unexpected pleasure. How are things with you?"

"Couldn't be better. I'm calling from Jamaica. Something has come up that requires me to have a birth certificate in the name of Hans Robin Roman."

"Now that's an interesting name. I don't remember you using that one before with me."

"No, sir. I don't think I have. I don't need a certified birth certificate. A faxed copy will do for my purposes. Do you think you can handle that for me if I give you the fax number at the hotel I'm staying at? Use the same personal details we've used in the past. I just need the name to say that I'm Hans Roman. That's H-A-N-S R-O-B-I-N R-O-M-A-N. You can charge it to the credit card you have on file for me."

He gave Squirrely the hotel fax number and his room number.

"That sounds easy enough."

"When can you have it?"

"Later today?"

"That's good enough. Perfect. Thank you, sir."

Squirrely was good to his word. The fax arrived after lunch. Queisha pulled it off the hotel fax machine and printed it out.

She wondered about what it meant and what was really happening.

Foxy-Roxy and Neil have been monitoring this Connors family ever since they checked in. And Chris Angel seems to have taken an interest in them as well. ... And this is the room for the guy I keep seeing with the single Connors girl. But I don't think that's the name he used when he checked into his room. Why would he want a birth certificate in this name? Let me check to be sure.

She pulled Hans' file and compared it to the copy of his passport that the hotel had made when he first checked in and found out that the names didn't match. When she saw that, she made an extra copy to show Foxy-Roxy.

> WE
> BYE
> USED
> CARS

CHAPTER 29

"Ms. Sparrow, got a second for me to show you something unusual relating to a guest you seem to have taken an interest in? Maybe you can explain it," Queisha asked.

"Sure, Queisha. What you got for me?"

"It's about Mr. Brown, the gentleman in room 315. I just got a fax in for him in the name of Hans Robin Roman. It was a birth certificate. Why would someone be sending him a birth certificate in that name? Do you think he's some kind of law enforcement officer or private detective or something who's working undercover? Isn't he the one we keep seeing with one of the Connors women? Do you think he might be up to something that could get the hotel caught in the middle of something embarrassing? Or maybe up to something illegal? Maybe he's not who he says he is. I just don't know what to think, but I don't like someone sneaking around causing trouble."

"Where'd the fax come in from?"

"Vegas, and it wasn't from no government office. It was from a bail bond office. Doesn't that strike you as weird? It did me."

"All your questions are worth getting an answer to. Thanks for being on top of things," Foxy-Roxy said and slipped Queisha two twenty dollar bills.

"Let me keep this and make me a copy of the coversheet that came in with it. I'll see what I can find out. Thanks again, Queisha, for being on the ball. And do me a favor? Let's just keep this between us two for the time being."

Roxie didn't let Queisha know what she was really thinking. Her years of experience in dealing with crooks of every sort was kicking in. She had been watching Hans anyway, wondering what a narcissistic, self-absorbed Adonis like him saw in down-to-earth, plain-Jane Nan Connors. Now she was really suspicious. Was he still another conman or shark on the prowl for Monte's money?

And Neil and I thought we were going to be the only players in this game except for those two dumb-ass, amateur sons-in-law.

She smiled as she thought about how easy it had been for Neil to nail Banks on the jewelry swindle and for them all to pick up a little spending money.

They say money's the root of all evil. Baloney! The lack of money is where evil begins. Money must have a certain odor that shysters can smell. Otherwise why would my brother, Neco, aka Potsy, show up muddying the water. And that sweet widow certainly seems to have set her sights on Monte. Sweet widow, my ass — bullshit! But now this Billy Don Brown or Hans Roman or whoever the hell his name is, is throwing his hat in the ring. Soon I'm going to need a flow chart to keep up with all the competitors.

Sigh! I better call some of my old buddies in Vegas who always seemed to be wired in and know about the players worth knowing. I bet Mitchell Freeman'll know this bail bondsman. I'll give old Bitchin' Mitch a call.

Foxy-Roxy dialed Freeman on his unlisted Las Vegas phone number. He answered immediately and burped into the phone.

"Is this Mr. Freeman?"

"Maybe. Who's this, and how'd you get my number?" he burped out.

"Foxy-Roxy Sparrow."

"I don't know any Foxy-Roxy Sparrow."

"I apologize for the confusion, Mr. Freeman. I'm little Rosa Caputo — Tad Green's … Uh … Uh … You know … Rocky and Rosa Caputo's daughter."

"Oh, yeah? How's old Rocky?"

"He died several years ago. Mom's gone too."

"Oh yeah! Sorry. I remember that now. My belated condolences anyway. They always made a good couple," he said, burping again. "I still remember him teaching you three card monte. So, how's things with you?"

"Fine, and you?"

Conclusive, All-Inclusive Confusion

"Not so good right now. That damned pastrami and sauerkraut I had for lunch is backing up on me. What can I do for you, little Rosa?"

"Well, sir. I know you know everyone in Vegas worth knowing. I'm hoping you can identify someone for me. Does the name Squandro Possman ... I think he's a bail bondsman ... mean anything to you?"

"Squirrely Possum. Sure, I know that low-life. He's not just a bail bondsman. He's into all kind of stuff."

"Like possibly falsifying ID's?"

Freeman laughed and said, "That's one of his sidelines. Why? You need an ID?"

"Not me. I think he may have made one for someone else that I'm interested in ... Billy Don Brown."

"That scumbag? Lord, I haven't heard that name in a coon's age. What's he up to now?"

"So you do know Mr. Brown?"

"Oh, hell yeah! Summbitch still owes me money. What's that fruity bum calling himself this time?"

"Hans R. Roman."

"Sounds like a name he'd come up with."

"What can you tell me about him?"

"Hang on. I'm pretty sure I've a file on him. Hang on."

Freeman burped again.

"Yep! Here it is. The only reason I'm telling you this is because of my respect for your mom and dad and that I can trust you to keep what I tell you in confidence."

Freeman then proceeded to tell Foxy-Roxy more than she would have ever been able to learn through conventional channels. He filled Foxy-Roxy in on Hans' past as both a grifter, a bisexual gigolo, a blackmailer, a card shark, and a female impersonator. Some of the stage names he had worked under included Ben Dela Crème, Detox, Baga Chipz, Pandora Boxx, Hedda Lettuce, Spikey Van Dykey, and Mo B. Dick. And those were just the aliases Freeman remembered to put in his file. Billy Don Brown did whatever was necessary to make a buck with the exception of resorting to violence.

As Freeman explained, "Billy Don's always been a lover not a fighter. But I'll say this, he's damned sure a competitor."

Foxy-Roxy's line of work had accustomed her to dealing with some pretty unethical and unconventional people, but even she found herself being shocked and amused by what she was learning. All she had to do now was to figure out how to work what she had just learned from Mitchell Freeman about Billy Don, aka Hans, to her advantage.

"Thank you, Mr. Freeman. Great to talk to both you and your pastrami."

no unortherized parking

CHAPTER 30

"I made both my semi-fine jewelry and my retirement village presentation to Monte Connors, and he seemed interested but at the same time reticent," Neil told Foxy-Roxy.

"I'm not surprised. After all, he's an unsophisticated, novice investor who's never had any money to invest until recently. Until he won the lottery, he was only a social worker without a pot to piss in or a window to throw it out of."

"Very true. However, I did get exposed to one additional thing that I'm up against."

"And that is?"

"His son-in-law, the one they call Banks Bridges. He relies on Bridges to be his investment advisor. Says Banks is a financial planner."

Foxy-Roxy began to laugh. The jewelry robbery scam that Banks had thought to be his secret flub, only known to him and Nakomis, was anything but that since, unknown to him, Neil and Foxy-Roxy had been the brains behind Nakomis' team.

"What's so funny?"

"The irony of the situation. We already screwed Bridges on a jewelry scam once. Do you think he'd be dumb enough to fall for a second one?"

"Well, this one will have a different twist. And looking at it from his perspective, he didn't have a jewelry problem. He just got robbed by being at the wrong place at the wrong time. But who knows. Maybe using the medium that cost him money the first time around to get back to even may introduce into his mind a rationalization of some sense of balance or sense of justice."

"You never know. Speaking of balance, what you want to bet Banks probably isn't as good at his job as his father-in-law thinks. While I wouldn't exactly accuse him of being bad at his job, I did hear that when Monte asked him to check his balance, and Banks hemmy-hawed around. He was as nervous as a long-tailed cat in a room full of rocking chairs. Yuk, yuk!"

"It's all going to hinge on our approach and finesse. Don't forget that in an alien's eyes all humans look the same, but we know how different we are from each other because of our perspective. We should stay committed to our game plan; we just need to be flexible with our approach. That being said, I have an idea. Let's employ a little psychology and then test his greed level."

"We better do it in a hurry before Monte talks to the useless USIL, that's my acronym for useless son-in-law, and he shoots us down just to make himself look good, since this investment wasn't his idea," Foxy-Roxy advised. "For some people saying no is just a way for them to avoid making what could be a bad decision."

"Just leave it up to me. Speaking of the devil, I see him coming now — alone. Excuse me, my dear. It's time for me to go to work."

Banks walked into the Palmyra Restaurant and began to go through the buffet line. Neil did so as well.

After Banks got his food and found a table, Neil sprang into action.

"Mind if I join you, Mr. Bridges?"

"Not at all. You're the jewelry designer aren't you?"

"Yes, that's one of my enterprises and one of the things that brought me here. I've been quite pleased with some of the raw materials that I've been able to buy on this trip. Are you interested in precious gems?"

"I've considered it but then decided it might not be for me," Banks said as he recalled his recent robbery loss.

"I understand that you're a financial planner. Your father-in-law was very complimentary of your knowledge and ability. He told me your ongoing guidance was crucial to his decision making processes. He approached me for some ideas and seemed interested in some of the mediums that I specialize in. Has he talked to you about one of the current projects that I have in the pipeline?"

Conclusive, All-Inclusive Confusion

"I think he did mention something."

"After we finish breakfast, if you have a few minutes, I'll show you what Mr. Connors found so intriguing. And I'll have to admit that it's in an area that is sure to be one with enormous growth potential. Otherwise, I wouldn't be bothering with it."

Fortunately for Neil, the materials he had used to pitch Monte on Filigree & Facet International and the Tower of Hope Retirement Village were still just as he had left them out in his room after their meeting's conclusion. Once he got Banks up to his room, he simply repeated the same presentation he had used on Monte.

When he was finished, he said, "Unfortunately something has come up so I may not be able to include Mr. Connors in this project."

"Why not?"

"An investor I have partnered with in the past, has recently shown an interest. Our past associations have made a lot of money for both of us. If he can generate the liquidity he needs in a timely manner, I'm obligated to team up with him again. The bottom line is that I'm loyal to my friends. I couldn't live with myself otherwise.

"His involvement also hinges on his attorneys being able to set up an investment framework acceptable to both of us. I owe Mr. Connors an apology. I didn't know this investor had an interest when he and I talked, or I never would have whetted his appetite by showing him what I've just shared with you."

"Wow! You've married two concepts that both appear to be homeruns. Let me say this, Mr. Hackinrider, if you decide to accept my father-in-law, he has both the liquidity and a corporate entity that could be used as a holding company. Both are already ready to go. He has a limited liability corporation that he and I are involved in that is currently seeking investment opportunities."

"Did I hear you say that you're involved?"

"Yes, sir. I'm an officer in the corporation."

"Then you would become an officer in Filigree & Facet International and the Tower of Hope Retirement Village as well, and you'd have an equity position in both corporations and could be compensated handsomely as an officer and member of the board of directors of each, entitling you to a board honorarium as such in addition to a salary and an expense account from both companies. Too had it couldn't have worked out. Well, we'll see if my other investor can get his affairs in order. If not, I'll keep you in mind."

Equity position! Salary! Expense account! Maybe stock options and a company car! Holy mother of God!

"Let me talk to Mr. Connors, and we'll get back to you," Banks said.

Banks was trying to hide his greed and to appear to be methodically analytical, but since Neil was a longstanding grifter who knew how to read people, he was sure he had gotten through to Banks. He couldn't wait to report back to Foxy-Roxy. He could almost see Banks singing the Janis Joplin anthem to greed, "Mercedes Benz" as he thought not so much about Monte but what could be in the deal for him.

Oh Lord, won't you buy me a Mercedes Benz
My friends all drive Porsches, I must make amends
Worked hard all my lifetime, no help from my friends
So, Lord, won't you buy me a Mercedes Benz?

no one under 21 must have ID

CHAPTER 31

Monte and Bessie Prince relaxed in two upholstered chairs in the hotel lobby.

"You seem preoccupied," Bessie Prince said. "Is there anything wrong?"

"I wouldn't call it wrong. Some people are after me to do something, and I'm not sure what I ought to be doing. I'm not accustomed to having to make decisions of this nature. Would you mind if I bounced some things off of you and get your unbiased opinion?" Monte asked Bessie Prince. "You're a business woman, and I'm just a poor social worker."

"Correction. You *were* a poor social worker. *Now* you're a man of means. And would I mind? Not at all. In fact, I'd be honored."

"You remember that nice Mr. Hackinrider that Ms. Sparrow introduced us to, don't you? ... You know, the man who makes and sells exotic jewelry? The guy's who's been so successful? He's starting two new companies, and he may be willing to take me in as a partner. Banks is really pushing me to consider it. ... And you know, maybe I should listen to him. After all, Banks *is* a financial planner."

"What kind of companies?"

"Both will do God's work. One will make what Mr. Hackinrider calls semi-fine jewelry primarily manufactured from recycled materials that help save the environment, and the other is a retirement village for former church employees and social workers like myself who don't have large retirement programs — people who have put serving the Lord and helping their fellow man in front of avarice and moneymaking."

Before he could continue, Queisha Hamilton approached them.

"Mr. Connors, excuse me for interrupting, but Mr. Potter just called the desk and asked me to page you to come up to his room. He said it was important. Pardon me for saying so, but he didn't sound exactly right."

"What do you mean by not right?"

"To be blunt, he sounded like he was drunk as a skunk. Do you want me to get Mr. Angel to go with you?"

"That won't be necessary. What's his room number again?"

"509."

"Bessie Prince, will you go with me?"

"Of course."

When they got up to Potsy's room, the door was ajar. Monte and Bessie Prince let themselves in. Potsy had carefully orchestrated the scene for maximum effect. The drapes were drawn almost all the way, and the room was semi-dark. The bed was unmade. He had scattered clothing and towels on the floor to give the place the most disheveled look he could. He sat wavering at the room's hotel desk singing a slurred version of "Amazing Grace." An empty Wray and Nephew overproof rum bottle and an empty bathroom glass sat on the desk. Beside them in plain sight was an unloaded Glock pistol. Another empty bottle was on the floor.

Potsy's hair was mussed, and he sat in his underwear and a t-shirt. Even though he was actually sober, Potsy had poured some rum on his clothing to give the impression he had been on a bender.

He almost gave himself away when he saw Bessie Prince since he had expected Monte to come alone. Monte didn't notice. She said nothing but did take notice.

"Clay! My God, what's wrong?" Monte gasped. "You know you're not supposed to be drinking."

Monte moved Potsy's weekender bag off of a chair and pulled it up close to the desk.

He turned to Bessie Prince and said in way of explanation, "He's a recovering alcoholic."

"This is the wors-ss day of my life. The bank's foreclose-s-sing on my hous-s-se. I'll be homeless-sss if I can't get the money to pay them ss-soon – as in imm-immediately," Potsy said, pausing for effect.

Conclusive, All-Inclusive Confusion

Neither Monte nor Bessie Prince said anything. So Potsy threw out a new zinger, "And the insuranc-sse co-company gave me their final determination about … Po's coverage."

"His only son is a paraplegic as a result of a car accident," Monte explained to Bessie Prince.

Potsy began to wail drunkenly and pretended to bang his head on the desk. Bessie Prince looked at it and thought, I've seen an overnight bag just like that before.

At just the moment that his head was supposedly hitting the desk, Potsy would bump the underside of it with his knee to produce the desired sound effect. Both actions gave him a kind of spastic look. Once again, Monte didn't notice this, but Bessie Prince did. She picked up the empty rum bottle off the floor and turning away from him, held it upside down.

Dry as a bone. No one's dumped or drank anything out of this bottle for some time. Let's test his sobriety.

She pretended to stumble towards Potsy's outstretched bare foot. He quickly moved it before she could step on it.

Not bad reflexes … for a half passed out drunk. Pooh! This shitbag's not any drunker than I am.

Then something else hit her.

That overnight bag is identical to the one Monte had on the bus the day we went to Dunn's River Falls.

Potsy sensed he was losing the battle and decided to up the ante. He grabbed the unloaded pistol and stuck it in his mouth.

"I'm just going to end it all. I can't take the pressure any longer. Take me into your kingdom, God, where there's no more pain and suffering."

He waited to see what either Monte or Bessie Prince would do next. As he expected, Monte reached out to try to take the Glock away from him. But then the unexpected happened, Bessie Prince caught Monte's arm and swept it aside. Without saying a word, she was calling Potsy's bluff.

What you want to bet that this joker is a drama king with one nefarious purpose — getting his hands on some of Monte's money.

And what a ham actor! 'Take me into your kingdom, God, where there's no more pain and suffering.' Gimme a break! A seventh grader could write better dialogue than that. If a person seriously wants to kill himself, he doesn't call the front desk and have them page someone to witness it and hear him pontificate like a bad Shakespearian actor. I'm surprised he didn't order a cameraman while he was at it. If you really want to kill yourself, you just do it.

Potsy saw the look in Bessie Prince's eyes and panicked.

Oh, shit! Now what do I do? Pull the trigger on an empty gun and destroy my credibility once and for all? Or pretend I'm going to shoot them? The only thing I'll kill is all the time I've spent working on this mark. And forfeit the win to Neil. Nope! As they say in football, we have to keep the drive alive.

So Potsy did the only thing he could think off to exit the scene. He spastically jerked his body too far backwards in the desk chair and purposedly upended himself, accidentally "throwing" the Glock across the room before pretending to black out from banging his head.

Maybe this isn't the most graceful way for me to end the scene, but it's time to fade to black.

> **WE HAVE FROZEN ICE**

CHAPTER 32

"Viv, I've got a secret, but I'm going to pop if I don't tell someone," Nan gushed. "But it's got to stay with just the two of us. And you can't tell daddy yet. We'll tell him when the time's right."

"Don't tell me Hans has gotten you pregnant," Viv replied.

"No, even though I can't get enough of him. Our sex is great ... no ... better than great. Greater than I ever imagined sex would be. I get chill bumps just thinking about it. And while it's marvelous and fantastic, it's more than that. ... We're in love."

"Whaa the hell ...? Nan!... You just met this guy!"

"What can I say? It just happened. And it's changed my whole world."

"You said 'we.' Are you sure it's not just *your* infatuation with having a steady someone to go out with? After all, you've never even had a boyfriend up until now. And so now you're in love with the first guy you've ever climbed into bed with and the first guy who's ever proposed to you?"

"He didn't propose to me. I proposed to him."

"You proposed to him? Oh, come on now, Nan! For God's sake!"

"He was reluctant at first, but then he finally agreed because he loves me as much as I love him."

"I don't believe I'm hearing what I think I'm hearing. Nan, didn't you get it backwards?"

"Oh, Viv, you just don't understand. Sometimes the rules don't apply when someone is shy and tender like my darling Hans is. This really is a two-way love affair. I'm telling you. ... He's been bitten by the love bug worse that I have. And when he makes love to me, every nerve in my body tingles. At last I understand what it means to be loved by a man — to be a complete woman, not just a daddy's girl. ... I don't think I could ever go back to being the girl I was before Hans and I met. We're going to get married. We've already started the process. And Viv, there is a possibility that I might be pregnant. I'm late. But I've always been irregular."

"Is that why you're doing this? I wish I could slow you down, but it sounds like it's too late for that."

"No, Viv, I'd marry him anyway. Please be happy for me. After all, you didn't go out with Banks long before he proposed. You knew when it was right."

"I'll have to admit that we didn't date for long. I sometimes wish we'd known each other longer. Maybe I shouldn't have let him push me. But at least he was a local boy, not someone I met at a resort."

"We'll work these things out. Please congratulate me, and don't try to make me feel guilty."

"Come here and give me a hug. If you're sure Hans will make you happy, then I'm happy too."

"I'm sure. Thank you Viv. I knew you'd understand. I love you, sis."

"When do you plan to tell daddy?"

"I don't know. I'm still working on that."

"You know he's going to be hurt and might even be crushed."

"Lord, I hope not. I hope he'll understand."

✍

When Viv got back up to her room, Banks noticed how quiet and reflective she seemed to be.

"Something wrong, dear?"

"Nan just confided in me something she doesn't want daddy to know about."

"And that was?"

"I'm not supposed to tell."

"Viv, ... I'm your husband. We're not supposed to keep secrets from each other."

Conclusive, All-Inclusive Confusion

"But this is different. It's a sister secret."

"That's bullshit, and you know it. Viv, this is a demand. Tell me. ... Right now!"

So she did.

✍

Banks didn't like this latest development one little bit. Later that day as he and Jax were having a drink by the pool, he brought the topic up. After all, he hadn't promised to keep Nan's secret.

"Looks like our little family might just be getting a little bigger."

"Viv's pregnant?"

"No, worse. Nan's planning to elope with that Hans creature."

"You gotta be shitting me! That slimeball opportunist? He's a sleazy manipulator if there ever was one. What'd he do, get her drunk?"

"She proposed to him!"

They then sat there silently, each evaluating this recent development. Both men conveniently ignored the fact that they were both of the same ilk. Each was obsessed with how they could dump both Hans and Bessie Prince in the creek with Monte while taking the maximum credit at the expense of the other and at the same time not alienate their own wife meal-tickets.

✍

The Hans dilemma was not confined to Banks and Jax. Foxy-Roxy was still silently debating what to do with her knowledge about Hans' background. This info was too good not to be profitable. And she saw it as profitable to her and her alone. Neil didn't deserve any of this action. He had done nothing ... nada ...to earn it since it was her father's past relationship with Mitchell Freeman that had prompted Mitchell to share information he would have withheld otherwise. Neil alone could never have gotten Mitchell to open his bank vault of knowledge.

Going to Monte will probably gain me nothing. All that'll happen is that I'll crap on Hans' parade and get Monte's goodwill but not one thin dime in profits. And I can't spend goodwill. I wonder what Hans would pay for me to keep his little secret until he gets what he wants. ... And I wonder what that want is — a simple score, or is he going for a homerun? My guess is the homerun. Why else would he need a birth certificate in his latest alias?

Well, I'm never going to find out sitting here on my fat ass until the train pulls out of the station, and by then it'll be too late for me to make a nickel. Foxy-Roxy, old girl, you need to set up a meeting with old Billy Don Brown, aka Hans R. Roman, and see what you can squeeze him for.

✍

Banks and Jax each devised a Hans Roman attack plan. Neither shared his plot with the other conspirator since each planned to execute his plan secretly all by himself, and if there was credit to be claimed, take it all. After all, in this war, it was every man for himself. While Banks' plan was one easily executed and would employ a strategy similar to the one he had used with Bessie Prince, Jax's plan entailed amassing some necessary items and then employing them properly.

There was one conclusion that both men arrived at. In both cases, it would be imperative that each remain "publicly" ignorant of Hans' and Nan's secret wedding plans and even pretend to be supportive so no one would suspect their true motive of trying to sabotage the nuptials and risk crapping in their own mess kits with their father-in-law as well as their wives. The other thing they both had in common was a newfound respect for Hans' ability to manipulate Nan and weasel his way into the family in the matter of only a few days.

✍

Foxy-Roxy decided to deliver the fax with the bogus birth certificate to Hans personally instead of having Queisha call him to pick it up at the desk. She waited until she saw him get into the elevator alone to go up to his room and then followed him.

She knocked on his door and when he answered said, "I'm Ms. Sparrow with the hotel. Do I have the pleasure of speaking with Mr.

Conclusive, All-Inclusive Confusion

Brown or is it Mr. Roman? I have the fax that one of you ordered from Las Vegas. I think we need to talk."

"You're reading a guest's private communications? I could have you fired for that."

"But you won't. And the reason you won't is that if you do, I'll make sure that I sabotage whatever it is that your plans are."

"You wish! You're dreaming. Ms. Sparrow, if that's what your name is. You don't want to mess with me."

"Mr. Spikey Van Dykey or Mr. Mo B. Dick or a few more names I could drop, you're not the only one with Vegas connections. And my guess is that mine probably run a lot deeper than yours do."

Hans was momentarily stunned. How did she know about those past aliases?

"Who gave you those names? They don't mean anything to me."

"My source will remain confidential. But I will tell you this, Billy Don, he told me a lot more things about you. Things that I don't think you want your latest girlfriend or her father to hear. Upgraded your business wardrobe recently? Bought any new evening gowns? I'm thinking you might have put on a pound or two. Maybe it's those Baga Chipz. A stylish girl can't go around in last year's fashions, especially if they're getting a little tight. Am I starting to get my point across?"

"Yeah! Yeah! I hear you. Come on in then and tell me what you want."

That's what I'm still trying to determine, but hopefully we'll know soon enough.

"Thank you for the invitation, Mr. Brown. Don't mind if I do."

So I can begin to put a dollar value on what I know.

✍

Banks decided that the most effective way to get rid of Hans was to let Monte do it for him. He would just have to manipulate Monte into doing so. It was time to hire Kemp Morrison again.

Within twenty-four hours, he did just that, providing Morrison with a fresh script for his latest mission. He generously decided to give Kemp a fifty dollar bonus. Kemp didn't question Banks' motives. He silently sneered but didn't openly quibble. This was fine with Kemp since he knew he'd soon be double-dipping with the more generous Bessie Prince anyway. Kemp studied his lines so that he could give a cohesive, convincing presentation.

Since Monte had been present the night that his troupe did the musical revue in the hotel's theater and might accidentally recognize him, Kemp donned a disguise using wardrobe items belonging to the company.

I'll put on a hound's tooth newsboy flat cap, an eye patch, and a goatee. That ought to do it.

When he felt like he was ready, Kemp put his disguise in a shopping bag and began to look for an opportunity to catch Monte alone. When he saw Monte, he ducked into the men's room to don his disguise before approaching him.

"Excuse me, sir, but are you Mr. Connors?"

"Yes, I am. May I help you with something?"

"Just the opposite. I can help you. If you'll give me a few moments of your time, I think I can be of service to you regarding one of your daughters."

"Is there a problem with one of them?"

"Not now, but one could be developing. Please give me a few minutes of your time, sir, and I'll gladly explain. Let me also say, sir, that if you choose not to listen to what I have to say, your assets could be at risk as well. Why don't we sit over there?" Kemp said, pointing to a conversation area there in the lobby.

After they sat down, Kemp introduced himself.

"My name is Dirk Gently and I work for Mr. Casey Closéd, owner of the Casey Closéd Detective Agency. Does the name Hans R. Roman mean anything to you?"

"Yes, he's a friend of my daughter, Nan's."

"That name is an alias, and he might not be as good a friend as your daughter thinks he is. I'm here investigating him for a felony violation."

"But he seems to be such a nice young man."

"Maybe on the surface, but not in reality. He's registered at the hotel under a different name. If he's so nice, why is he using more than one name?"

"I don't know."

"Then let me explain. There is a good reason he needs to disguise his identity. At one time, he was a branch manager and a trust officer for the

Conclusive, All-Inclusive Confusion

Harbour Isle branch of the Eminence Trust. Eminence was and is the exclusive banker for Harbour Isle.

"The problem arose after Mr. Roman left their employ and was found to have pilfered the accounts of residents who were old and frail and who no longer had the mental capacity to know what he was doing. Over time, literally millions of dollars were wired out and are still unaccounted for.

"By the way, before I go on, what I'm telling you, I'm telling you in confidence. Can I count on you to respect that confidence? It will be to your benefit. Otherwise, maybe I should stop here."

"Of course. What is Harbour Isle?"

"An upscale sunbelt retirement village that also functions as an assisted living home and ultimately a nursing home for those residents who need those services. The residents do not own their units but instead have a life estate to them."

"So, you represent Harbour Isle?"

"No sir, my employer is an individual whom I'm not at liberty to name, whose parents' accounts were raided by Mr. Roman and who also has a vested interest in the entities involved. It's complicated, but let me explain. Harbour Isle and Eminence Trust both decided not to risk the loss of confidence that would result if word of Mr. Roman's embezzlement was made public before they could catch Mr. Roman and recover as much of the money as possible. In the meantime, they made their clients whole out of their own pocket."

"If Hans has millions of dollars, like you said, why would my assets be at risk?"

"I'm coming to that. It seems that Mr. Roman made some bad investments with people who I suspect took advantage of him and lost an indeterminate amount of the money he stole, and now he has money problems himself with an unscrupulous, lethal Jamaican gang who call themselves the Shower Posse."

"Oh, wow."

"The word on the street is that he needs money, and that he will do whatever it takes to stabilize his own situation. ... And, sir, I understand that you are quite well off."

"So, if I understand you right, Mr. Roman is courting my daughter hoping that it will result her making my money available to solve his self-created problems."

"Yes, sir, that's the essence of it. And if Mr. Roman's in danger, your daughter will probably be so as well. These are heartless people who have no conscience."

"I'm speechless."

"Someone needed to explain to you what's going on while we try to resolve this matter."

"My once simple life seems to just be getting more and more complicated. Thank you for giving me a heads up. Quite frankly, I'm not sure *what* I should do next."

"All I can say, sir, is that you can more effectively deal with things you know about instead of things that you don't."

**TABLES ARE FOR
EATING CUSTOMERS ONLY
NO LOITERING**

CHAPTER 33

Monte was stunned after meeting with Dirk Gently. Was there any truth to what Gently had told him? Nan would be crushed if her Sir Lancelot turned out to be a Mordred. He didn't know what to think, and besides that, he didn't know what to do about it anyway. At least, he and his family would hopefully be returning to Detroit before Nan's infatuation became even more serious.

But Monte was about to find out that another shock was just around the corner.

"Daddy, I've got something to tell you," Nan said, "and I hope you'll understand and be happy for me. Hans and I are going to be married."

Monte was speechless. This was his worst nightmare coming true. His thoughts raced over everything that Dirk Gently had told him. Was his future son-in-law really a soon-to-be convicted felon?

"Daddy, please wish us well."

Monte was at first speechless and sweat broke out on his brow. He finally caught his breath and spoke hesitantly.

"Are you sure you've thought this through, darling? You just met Hans. What do you really know about him?"

"I know I love him, and he loves me. ... And I don't think I can live without him. But I also love you and hurting you would break my heart."

"And it would break my heart if something came between us as well. I don't know what to say. I guess I'll go along with and support you if you're completely sure this is what you want. But please, Nan, I beg of you, give this some more thought and make sure. Do your sisters know about this?"

"I told Viv, but I told her that I wanted to be the one who told you."

I can't even depend on my daughters to keep me informed. Is Bessie Prince the only person I can trust? And can I truly trust even her?

Bessie Prince was having a different set of thoughts after debriefing and paying Kemp Morrison for his report.

What in the hell is that Banks Bridges up to now? First, he hires an actor to try to scare me off with Monte by slandering his character, and now he's doing a character assassination with Monte's daughter's boyfriend, Hans.

She got on her computer and began to Google some of the names Morrison had given her. She couldn't find a Harbour Isle retirement community or an Eminence Trust. Then she tried looking for the Casey Closed Detective Agency. That didn't seem to exist either.

Everything Banks told him to tell Monte was apparently a pack of lies. He's just making stuff up as he goes along that fit his agenda. I wonder if Billy Don Brown really exists. Did he make him up too?

The Billy Don Brown search was more successful than her previous searches had been. She first found a Facebook page for "Billy Don Brown-Entertainer." It cross-referenced her into Billy Don Brown's personal Facebook page. She was shocked by what she found.

My God, Hans isn't a banker. He's either a singing crossdresser or a drag queen. Or both.

There was a phone number to call if a person wanted to hire Billy Don to do a show. He was also available to be an escort. His page stated that his pricing schedule was flexible and would depend on time, location, travel costs, and special requests. It said he'd set the terms of his employment on a case-by-case basis. She started to page through some of the pictures of Hans in various past costumes and noted the names of some of the characters of both sexes that he had previously employed.

And now this ... this ... whatever this creep is ... has his sights set on Monte's daughter, Nan. Jesus God! What a mess!

Conclusive, All-Inclusive Confusion

Bessie Prince was glad to see a true picture of the real Hans R. Roman, but she was going to have to think long and hard to decide what to do with what she now knew.

✍

Before Bessie Prince could think the matter out thoroughly, she got a call from Monte.

"Bessie Prince, we got interrupted yesterday by Mr. Potter before I could finish telling you about some things, and some new things have happened since then. Would you mind terribly if I asked your advice? I'm overwhelmed. Sometimes I wish I was just a simple church worker again. I didn't know life could get this complicated. And don't know who I ought to be talking to or getting advice from."

You poor man! In way over your head. Well, one thing I'm sure of is you can't depend on those sons-in-laws of yours who are actually sons-of-bitches instead. Now the question becomes, how frank should I be with him?

"Sure, Monte. You can depend on me. Meet me on the patio by the pool."

When Bessie Prince got to the pool, Monte was already there. When he saw her approaching, he jumped up to greet her.

"Thank God I have you to depend on."

Monte then proceeded in a stumbling, rambling manner to tell Bessie Prince about his meeting with the private investigator, Dirk Gently. ... And how Hans was a criminal and embezzler who could be arrested at most any time. ... And how Hans was courting Nan only to get his hands on some of Monte's money to bail himself out with a Jamaican gang who might kill him and possibly kill Nan as well. ... And now to make things even worse, Nan was about to marry this guy. ... And how he couldn't even trust his other daughter not to keep secrets from him. ... And all these people wanted him to invest money. ... And how he was being pushed to do so by his son- in-law as well. ... And how on top of everything else, the suicidal Potsy was depending on him to bail him out. ... And how he just didn't know what to do any more. ... And how he wishes he had never come on this trip.

"I think I can at least trust Jax's honesty, Monte said, "but I'm not so sure about his judgement. He did come up with the solution to my future tax issues by selling me a life insurance policy at a bargain price. But sometimes he doesn't seem to be all there. You're the only person I know who has never tried to take advantage of me."

Honey, I'd hate to have to be the one to tell you, but you can't trust either Jax's brains or his integrity.

Monte rushed and blundered from one thought to another, not completing any of them, in a series of run-on half-finished statements almost like a desperate person.

At first, Bessie Prince smiled.

I'm in the driver's seat since he trusts me. Good things come to patient people like me. Now, how much do I want to tell him? I can't hit him with everything at once. Why don't I concentrate on undermining Banks and Hans right now.

"You dear man. You've certainly had a lot of confusing things thrown at you. And I'm glad you realize that you can't be too trusting. Now I'm going to throw a few more at you that I hope will clear up some matters. You're not going to like most of what I'm about to tell you, but the things you know will probably harm you less than those that you don't know about. There's been some questionable things happening behind your back. Are you ready to listen?"

"I think so."

"Well, you better know so. I too was approached by Mr. Dirk Gently, only he didn't use that name. And he didn't work for Casey Closéd Detective Agency. He called himself Ben Casey, and said he was an fraud investigator for Guardian Insurance. And that he was investigating you."

"Me? Why me? I never even heard of Guardian Insurance. Why would he say that?"

"I know you haven't. You're going to be floored when I tell you why. He said your money came on a fraudulent claim on a life insurance policy on your former wife."

"But I've never been married."

"Mr. Casey said that you've been married multiple times and over-insured each wife, making yourself the beneficiary every time. He also said that you've taken out large policies on each of your daughters as well, with you being the beneficiary in lieu of their husbands. He also said that if I got involved with you, I would be in danger since you would probably

Conclusive, All-Inclusive Confusion

set me up as well. He advised me to stay away from you. He inferred that you're a serial wife killer."

"Lies! All lies! Why would this man say that? I didn't even know him. You didn't believe him, did you?"

"Of course not. His story was completely implausible, so I got to the bottom of things. You'll never guess what I found out."

"Tell me."

"I won't go into details on how I did it, but I tracked Mr. Casey down, cornered him, forced the truth out of him. He's a professional actor whose real name is Kemp Morrison who was hired to play this role."

"Who would hire him to do this?"

"You're not going to like what I'm about to tell you, but it's the truth. Your son-in-law, Banks Bridges."

"Banks? What possible reason could he have had?"

"Because he's afraid you might get serious about me, and that if you and I married, I would convince you to make me your heir at his expense. This is the son-in-law you trusted. Monte, there's nothing you can do about his marriage to Viv without risking your relationship with her, but you need to know that Banks Bridges is not your ally and deal with him accordingly."

"I don't know what to say."

"Don't say anything. Just keep your eye on him and plan your affairs appropriately. Now, let's move on to Hans. Hans is not what he seems to be either, but he's not what your Mr. Dirk Gently, otherwise known as Kemp Morrison, is representing him to be. I know all about what he told you because I forced Morrison to report back to me after he met with you."

"How'd you do that?"

"Don't ask. Let's just say that he knows if he crosses me, I can make life very unpleasant for him. Do you want to know who hired him to tell you the lies about Hans? You get three guesses and the first two don't count."

"Banks again?"

"You're on a roll! Ring the bell and give the man a teddy bear! The biggest one on the shelf. And would you want to guess why?"

"For the same reason he was hired to talk to you?"

"Brilliant, my dear Mr. Holmes! That would be my guess as well."

"So, what should I do about it?"

"At the moment, nothing, my dear man. Let's keep the element of surprise on our side. Let's the two of us keep Mr. Bridges under surveillance and wait for him to screw the pooch."

"Maybe we can recruit Jax as our ally."

"Don't even think about it. I've had my eye on him as well. Take my word for this. He's not on your side either."

"I feel so alone … and vulnerable. So, back to Hans. You say he's got a troubled background?"

"Hans R. Roman is Mr. Billy Don Brown's latest alias. He goes by many names that I won't mention right now. Like Mr. Morrison, he's also an entertainer, but one of a different sort. He entertains sometimes as a man but other times as a woman."

Bessie Prince then proceeded to fill in the details about Hans' background. Monte listened silently.

"Is he gay?" he asked when Bessie Prince had finished.

"I don't know for certain, but I suspect he's bisexual."

"Jesus, God! What should I do?"

"I've been giving that some thought. Nan thinks she's really in love with this guy, so I don't think you'll be able to talk her into dropping him. And if you do try, you'll probably only succeed in making her want to embrace his advances even more fervently. But if Hans is the money grubber I suspect he is, you may be able to bribe him into dumping Nan. Are you willing to spend some money to stop this marriage?"

"Of course. You know I'll do anything to save my daughter."

"You've got two rotten sons-in-laws. You certainly don't need a third. Let's give this matter some more thought before you do anything."

"I'm so glad I have you on my side. Without you, I'd be all alone."

"Monte, you're such a nice man. You deserve better than what you're getting. Let's see if we can't work things out together."

"What about Neil's investment proposal? Or Mr. Potter's problems? Will you help advise me there as well?"

"Of course, but let's deal with one problem at a time. You need to give things some thought and maybe do some soul searching."

Bessie Prince was beginning to soul search as well and doubt her own motives.

Conclusive, All-Inclusive Confusion

Maybe I'm not cut out to be a ruthless, rapacious predator. I was once a professional person.

Her thoughts turned inward. She thought back to the days she was both a pharmacist and a beautician who owned "Bessie Prince's Fix You Up Apothecary" and "Bessie Prince's Sip 'n Snip" and how the Fontana Pharmacy chain had put her out of business. Her thoughts also reverted to her disgraced and now deceased husband, Oliver, who had been controlled by Dudus Coke and the Shower Posse and how after Oliver had crossed Dudus, his license to practice law had been revoked because of Dudus's influence with the Jamaican Bar Association. She winced as she thought about how the family's debts had then careened out of control, causing her to lose everything except Oliver's paid up life insurance policy. She cringed as she recalled how Oliver had fallen into a deep depression and turned to rum as a solution to his problems, and how this had led to his death, forcing her to become the predatory person she was today.

Yes, I need to do some soul searching as well. I think I'm really beginning to like this guy for something other than his money. He's so gentle and kind. Not predatory. … And trusting. … And straight as an arrow. He's a real gentleman. I'm even starting to like the way he looks.

Watch it, Bessie Prince! Don't get distracted and sidetracked. You thought your last husband was a prince of a guy too and look what he turned out to be.

Do I deserve this nice guy? Or to rephrase the question, does he deserve someone else who doesn't have the baggage I do?

But then maybe he does deserve someone who can keep the sharks of the world from eating him alive and then spitting out his bones.

**DARYL'S RADIATOR
A GREAT PLACE TO
TAKE A LEAK**

CHAPTER 34

"Hans, Nan has told me about your nuptial plans," Monte said in a flat, monotone voice.

"Oh," Hans responded as he tried to mentally evaluate whether this development was good or bad. Nan hadn't told him that she had confided in her father, but Hans wasn't surprised, knowing how close they were. He didn't know that Nan had also told Viv who had told Banks who had told Jax who had told Eve.

So much for secrets and the element of surprise.

"I hope you'll wish us well. Will you?"

"I have concerns. Certain facts about your past have been brought to my attention. While I haven't verified them … which I will … I can only assume that there's a certain amount of truth in what I've been told."

Hans was caught flatfooted and didn't know how to respond. After a delay, he said, "But I'm a different person now."

"So you don't deny your checkered past? Pardon me if I say that I have my doubts since you're not even going by your real name. I'm told that it's Billy Don Brown. My dear daughter doesn't even know who she's really marrying. As a father, I have to try to prevent her from possibly making the biggest mistake of her life."

"Sir, I'll admit that in the past I've occasionally done some things that I'm not now proud of, but I had to in order to survive. But believe me when I say that I love your daughter, and I'll do everything in my power to be a good husband."

Conclusive, All-Inclusive Confusion

"Assuming you get my generosity. But what if I'm not as generous as you think I'll be? Will your character flaws reemerge? I think there's a very good chance that'll happen, and I'm not willing to risk Nan's safety, security or happiness on someone so questionable."

"So, what are you trying to say?"

"I'll give you $100,000 to call this thing off."

"Sir, I can't do that."

"Two hundred?"

Hans was silent.

"Three hundred?"

Silence again.

"Five hundred?"

"Sir, I love Nan."

"Hans ... or Billy Don ... or whatever you want me to call you, think of a number, and we'll talk again. What if I throw in a Cadillac Escalade as a signing bonus?"

After Monte had left, Hans sat there in silence wishing that he and Nan could have gotten married before Monte found out about him. Then he could deal from a position of strength instead of being in the iffy situation he now found himself in.

He was really torn on whether he should take Monte's money and run. After all, Monte was offering a lot of money, and it was apparent he would up his offer. And also, he was worth fifty million bucks. But then Hans' conscience started to bother him. Nan was so naïve and trusting, and she idolized him. He had never had this happen before with anyone including some of his past drag queen lovers. It was a new feeling and one he liked.

And on top of that, I'm really starting to fall for her. She's not like anyone I've ever dated before.

Hans thought back to his own childhood when he was still Billy Don Brown. His strung-out parents had never married and lived mostly apart. Both had done whatever it took to feed their habits. He never knew stability since he was shuffled back and forth. He had hoped that one or the other would see value in him instead of telling him he was an inconvenience they regretted and that he was a loser who was always destined to be a loser. The multiple molestations by both his parents' boyfriends and girlfriends had confirmed and reinforced this self-image in his mind.

When Nan finds out the truth about me, will she run me off before I can land Monte's money and then I'll have nothing to show when all's said and done for this venture? How much more money can I squeeze out of Monte? Would it be enough for me to set up an investment program that would insure my future? How much money would that take?

Hans' thoughts vacillated back and forth from plusses to minuses like a ping pong ball.

And Nan told me she might be pregnant. What would it be like to be a father? One thing for sure is I will never be like my parents were. I'll do whatever it takes to be a good parent.

What should he do?

Even if Monte hates me right now, he'll soften his stance for his grandchild. And he won't live forever. No matter what he offers me, maybe I'll come out ahead in the long run if I'm married to Nan. And I really do like her. She's smart, witty, easy going, morally sound. And she's really a lady. And the sex has been awfully good. Let's face facts. She's a better woman than I deserve.

The more he thought about it the more he thought maybe he should take his chances.

If Nan really is pregnant, surely she'll think twice before becoming a single mother if she has another alternative. Maybe that fact alone will make her willing to take a chance on me and overlook the person I was. And if she will, I'll make a pledge that I won't make her sorry.

Billy Don, let's go for it. Risk it all.

Hans' decision was made.

Thank you for the offer, Monte, but no thank you. I'm going to go with Nan.

Even though his future with Nan and the rest of her family was muddier than ever, Hans felt like a weight had been taken off of his chest.

Announcing Mr. and Mrs. Billy Don Brown.

DO NOT ENTER ENTRANCE ONLY

CHAPTER 35

Jax's plan for Hans differed radically from the undermining strategy Banks had employed.

Yes! Itching powder! That's what I need. When I get through with Hans, he'll feel worse than a dog passing peach pits and be as full of pains as an old window.

Jax had resurrected his idea from his own past by listening to the lyrics in a rousing, upbeat song by C.W. Colt, an American tropical rock performer who was working at the hotel.

Mi amigo mosquito, adios
Makes you want to scratch and itch
And scratch and itch
Little son of an itch

Colt had encouraged the audience to join him and dance doing exaggerated comical imitations of scratching and itching as he sang the song. He had gotten peals of laughter and applause at the song's conclusion. He responded by toasting his well-oiled audience, instructing them to drink up at the count of three, only to upend his own glass after he yelled one.

The gummy bear popping Jax then began to research the ingredients to make an effective itching concoction. After that, it had taken him the better part of a day to amass the items he needed to put his plan to annoy Hans R. Roman into play. But it was time well spent. The materials Jax had assembled should do the job first of all of satisfying his own paranoia when he embarrassed and tormented his assumed adversary. He then hoped this would result in Hans showing his true nature to Nan in the worst possible light and turn her off or at least make her think twice about what her future would be like living with a volatile husband. And he hoped she would ask another question. What kind of father would such an individual make?

When Jax was in school, a rival had used an itching powder on him in the school cafeteria. The whole cafeteria had sniggered at his distress. He vividly remembered the miserable experience and how he had lost the respect of the girl he had hoped to take to the homecoming dance after he ultimately embarrassed himself publicly to the point that he had alienated her permanently with his out of control rants and raves in front of her and her girlfriends. His rival had laughed at him to the point that Jax had started a fist fight right there in the cafeteria and had ended up in detention. The girl had later gone to the dance with his tormentor.

Well, now that miserable experience was at last about to come in handy and hopefully would show Nan a part of Hans' personality that she hadn't seen previously.

He had spotted a blue mahoe wood pestle and mortar set made by one of the local woodcarvers who carved souvenirs to sell to hotel guests. It was the only one the woodcarver had for sale so he bought it without even trying to negotiate the price.

According to Google, dried rosehips and maple seedpods worked the best, but he didn't have either of those items available. It also mentioned that finely cut up hair and toothbrush bristles, finely ground black and white peppercorns, and dried chili peppers also caused itching. Crumbled up dried biscuit crumbs were also sometimes effective. All of these things were things he could probably easily find. Then it suggested that the chosen itch generator should be mixed with a base of either talcum powder or baking soda. Since he didn't have the most highly recommended ingredients of rosehips or maple seedpods, Jax decided he better not take a chance on any one ingredient. Instead, he'd just use them all.

On several occasions he collected the hair out of his electric razor, shook it onto a piece of paper, and carefully stored the hairs in one of his larger empty Walgreens plastic pill bottles. He then went to the hotel

Conclusive, All-Inclusive Confusion

pharmacy and bought several of their stiffest toothbrushes and a package of single-edge razor blades to mince other bristles into even finer pieces. These were then added to the bottle. While he was at the store, he bought some talcum powder. The peppercorns and the baking soda turned out to be easy to acquire. Now it was just a matter of using pestle and mortar, grinding them to a fine consistency, and combining the ingredients. By now the volume of his witches' brew far exceeded what would fit into any prescription pill bottle so Jax poured it all into one of the dry twenty-six ounce plastic tumblers that he had been drinking lemonade from the day before. Now he was ready to go.

"I can't wait! This is going to be so much fun," he muttered. "When I get through with Hans, he'll be a loony coconut running around like a headless chicken. Damn, I feel like singing."

He couldn't resist singing out loud,

I'll get him to
Scratch and itch, scratch and itch, that son of an itch.

This was followed by another song from Colt's repertoire,

I'm a loony coconut
I'm a loony coconut

Since he didn't have access to Hans' room key, he decided to administer the concoction by sprinkling it on items Hans would be using out by the pool.

Oh, this should be good. Nan and the whole family are about to see the unsavory, nasty side Hans Roman's real personality.

Now he just had to make sure that Hans was the one who got a good dose. He knew Hans and Nan often went down and sunned by the pool in the mornings. He'd just go down and wait for them to take a dip in the pool and when the opportunity presented itself — voila.

When he reached the patio, the heavily perspiring Jax carefully held the glass with the itch-powder out in front of him so as not to spill it. It was almost full. Foxy-Roxy saw him and wondered why he was carrying it so gingerly. Twice a well-meaning waiter, thinking Hans was carrying an empty glass that needed refilling offered to take it away from him and get him a fresh drink. Jax nervously shooed the waiter away each time.

Strange, Foxy-Roxy thought.

Jax looked around but Hans and Nan were nowhere to be found. He did, however, see both Neil and Potsy individually taking in the salt air. Neil was on the second level sipping a drink and examining a copy of "Modern Day Pinup" magazine. Potsy stood below as his yoga class began. Neither seemed to be paying the other any attention. Both of them took note of Jax when he walked in, and they each began to monitor him silently and separately.

A woman got out of the pool and shook her head to clear the water out of her ears. Jax put his hand over the top of the glass to keep it dry, and as he turned away, some no-see-ums attracted by Jax's sweat bit him on his nose and eyelids. A banana spider, sensing a good meal, went after them. Jax panicked and as he attempted to shoo them away with his free hand, stubbing his toe on a chaise lounge that was below his eyesight level. The glass flew out of his hand and the itch-powder covered a rack of clean beach towels and the area surrounding it. Adjacent portable patio fans began to disburse the fine powder.

Strange, Foxy-Roxy thought again.

A look of horror came on Jax's face along with a gasp as some of the powder blew back on him. Jax turned about-face and almost ran in the opposite direction as fast as his throbbing toe would allow him to go.

This is getting stranger by the second, Foxy-Roxy thought. *What is going on? Why did he have powder in that glass instead of a beverage? And what is it?*

She didn't have to wait long to find out the answer to her questions. The fine powder was being disbursed in every direction caught in the crosscurrents from the portable patio fans.

Some blew towards a Tambu dancing class the hotel was conducting. Tambu is a Jamaican folk dance in which dancers move frantically in isolation to two native drummers using extreme hip gyrations. It is very sexual even though the dancers never touch each other. As the dancers began to itch, their gyrations became more and more frantic. Within moments, they began clawing their bodies.

Just down from them was Potsy's yoga class. Some people stretched as they waited for class to get fully underway. Their meticulous stretching

Conclusive, All-Inclusive Confusion

exercises gave way to jumping up and franticly scratching, and their moves began to mimic gyrations of the Tambu dancers.

Potsy was soon up clawing his own body. His bathing suit fell down around his ankles. As he bent over to try to pull it back up, a Tambu dancer kneed him from behind and sent him flying. By the time he regained his balance, he was spread eagle over a reclining sunbather and his privates dangled in front of her face as he urinated down her ample cleavage. She shrieked and gave a guttural growl. Potsy thought she was about to bite him, but she headbutted him instead in this sensitive area. Stars exploded in front of Potsy's eyes. Her sunglasses broke, and their ragged edge gouged his already itching midsection. The fresh bleeding cuts began to burn and itch even worse. His wind broke and he ripped a cheeser, spraying itching powder into her eyes and open mouth. This caused her to bolt straight up, whacking his sensitive area one more time. Potsy couldn't remember the last time he'd been in so much pain. Being worked over by Vegas thugs hadn't seem to hurt this bad.

One woman with a bikini bra accidentally clawed her own top away. When she saw people staring at her naked breasts, she cupped them a took off running, only to trip over another guest's flip-flops. She careened head-first into a pudgy, hairy, middle aged man. His head was bald except for his thick black beard. His chest and back were so covered with hair that he appeared to be wearing a winter coat. He had been hungrily ogling his double banana split expectantly before being blinded by some of the itch powder that had blown in his eyes. He let out a scream as pain seared his face and as he realized he was spilling his delicious treat down his front and would never get a bite.

As he angrily tried to shove the woman away, she grabbed his bathing suit to try to regain her balance, tugged it down, only to be staring directly into the thickest patch of black pubic hairs she had ever seen covered with ice cream, whipped cream and chocolate syrup with the remnants of a banana poking out of the bristly but gooey bush towards her like the man was two-schlonged with one anemic banana member being erect while the other had wilted. She felt like the phallic symbol from hell was staring at her and was only inches away. A cherry somehow became lodged in one nostril. The woman panicked and sneezed it onto his pair of dual sticky, flaccid uncircumcised-looking penises. As he danced in confusion and pain, high-stepping on the hot patio, he kneed her in her bare breasts, and she bit the gooey banana in half. She was now consumed in as much pain as he was and in order to get away from him and belly flopped with a flying spreadeagled unladylike breast-first splat into the swimming pool.

Neil-the-Heil was smoking a cigar on the second level when some itching powder caught in an updraft got in his eyes. He unwittingly spit out the cigar. He reached over to try to catch it, but it dropped and landed in a lady's straw beach bag beneath him. It began to burn as the Kleenex in it caught on fire. About that time another blinded guest backed into Neil before he could stand back up, sending him sprawling over the rail. He was saved from serious injury when his fall was broken when he miraculously landed on top of a large open beach umbrella, flattening it onto a stack of folded beach towels on the table below it.

A waiter who was balancing a tray with a bloody Mary and a hamburger was hit in the forehead by an errant frisbee haphazardly thrown by a blinded swimmer. The tray went flying, covering an obese woman and her Chihuahua with her morning cocktail as she madly scratched her fleshy arms. Tomato juice, vodka, and horseradish dripped down her massive cleavage. The drink's celery stick protruded from her bra.

A hot burger patty dripping with ketchup landed on the exposed naval of the scratching woman lying on a nearby beach towel. When the Chihuahua smelled the delicious, freshly cooked hamburger patty, it leaped up on the woman to retrieve it. She screamed and began kicking at the dog as she also clawed herself, but the dog was determined to not let this delicious smelling delicacy get away. She tried to stand but slipped down again when she stepped on the tomato and lettuce. Finally she regained enough balance to sling the dog with the burger still in its mouth.

Potsy saved the dog by catching it in midair, but the frightened dog began to yap and snap at him so he lobbed it again. The dog's nine lives had some left because this time it landed feet first and got entangled in the dreadlocks of one of the Tambu drummers.

About that time Nan and Hans, oblivious to everything that was happening, arrived on the elevator, hoping to have a leisurely breakfast by the pool. They had completely missed the trap Jax had set for them. Chris Angel headed them off in the lobby and told them that the pool patio was temporarily closed for maintenance.

Hans and Nan never thought to ask why.

Conclusive, All-Inclusive Confusion

Carnage was everywhere, and Foxy-Roxy, Neil, and Potsy all knew who was to blame. Foxy-Roxy told Chris Angel about how Jax had inadvertently started it all, but as she explained to him, "It'd be my word against his."

The same thought was going through all of their minds. While each person's words and thoughts were somewhat different and each generously sprinkled those thoughts with four-letter words, their bottom-line sentiment was the same.

I will get even.
That Connors son-in-law creep has got to go.

> WELCOME BACK STUDENTS
> WE ARE GLAD
> YOU ARE HEAR

CHAPTER 36

Neil limped into the hotel lobby leaning on a hand carved walking stick. The stick had a Rasta smoking a ganja pipe carved into the upper portion and had a spiraled carved snake entwining the lower half. He wobbled as he walked. His arms and face were covered with scratches and scabs. Foxy-Roxy and Queisha were going over some things behind the desk.

"Boy, you look like a train wreck," Foxy-Roxy commented.

"Like you've been shot at and missed and then shit at and hit," Queisha agreed.

"Oh, shut up, both of you. This ain't funny. If I hadn't landed on that umbrella I'd be dead right now or a quadriplegic."

About that time Chris Angel walked up.

"What a disaster! I've been working my ass off since that pool fiasco happened trying to make things right with the guests who were out there. I'll be surprised if some lawsuits don't happen. And I shudder to think of the doctor bills the hotel is going to have to pay. And I've already had to comp some guests room refunds to pacify them."

"You all know who's to blame, don't you?"

"You told me you saw the asshole who started it. Connors' fat pig of a son-in-law. I just wish I could prove it. What in the hell was he trying to accomplish?"

"You got me. Funny though. I didn't see any of the Connors party on the patio when it happened. Though his daughter and her gigolo boyfriend came down shortly afterwards."

Conclusive, All-Inclusive Confusion

"I know. I headed them off," Angel said.

Foxy-Roxy still hadn't told any of the others all she knew about gigolo Hans. This blackmail venture was hers and hers alone. But so far it hadn't produced any tangible profits, and she was debating whether to give Hans another ultimatum or whether to try to sell the info Mitchell Freeman had told her to Monte. One thing she was still certain of was that there was no reason to share any profits with Neil. He had brought nothing to the table. It was her score. What she didn't know what that there was no score to be had since Bessie Prince had rendered her revelations worthless.

"There's got to be some way to pay that Magnus stupido back."

"I've got an idea," Queisha volunteered. "And we can use our positions at the hotel to make it happen."

"Oh yeah! What've you got in mind?"

"We'll have to all work together, but if we do …"

Queisha explained her plan.

"We better be ready to cover our tracks in case he starts raising hell with the hotel later, or we might all lose our jobs," Foxy-Roxy said.

"We should be fine if everyone sticks together," Neil added.

"Do I have everyone's word that that'll happen?" Foxy-Roxy said.

The yes votes were unanimous.

Step one involved Chris Angel setting up an exclusive President's Club VIP ladies-only shopping excursion into Montego Bay the following day. Foxy-Roxy would host it and accompany them, and one of the hotel's hospitality cars would drive them there. This would isolate Jax from his wife.

In the meantime, Foxy-Roxy would "accidentally" leak to Jax that Bessie Prince had booked a special champagne romantic rafting trip for her and Monte down the Martha Brae River for that same time period. Queisha would then call Jax's room and tell him that the hotel was still trying to identify what had gone wrong on the pool patio but was deeply embarrassed by it. And then as a matter of apology for the unfortunate incident, she had been authorized to offer him a free pass to go rafting on the Martha Brae River as well as his transportation there and back.

Queisha was counting on the fact that Jax could not resist spying on Monte and the "gold-digging" Bessie Prince. When they got Jax to the river, the fun would begin.

In the meantime, Potsy Potter was in his room swigging rums on the rocks as he soaked his bruised privates in the room's Jacuzzi bathtub as he tried to recover from his pool patio related injuries. He was also thinking of all the things he wanted to do to Jax. As the rum took hold, he began talking out loud to Moxie, his imaginary self, who had appeared and joined him after half of the first the bottle and was now soaking across from him in the tub as he smoked a reefer.

"Damn, my balls hurt. Are yours sore?" he said to his imaginary companion.

"Nah! Pussy! My body's tougher than yours."

"I sure wish I could borrow your body. You don't need it anymore. ... Moxie, I'm going to do the same thing to his body that he did to everyone by the pool. You know what a pencil cactus is, don't you?"

"Sure. It's a common plant. There's lots of it around here," Moxie replied.

"Ever gotten any of the cactus' milky sap on you?"

"Can't say that I have?"

"I'm telling you right now, you don't want to. It's poisonous as hell. It causes itching and blistering, and if you get it in your eyes or in your mouth! ... Ooowee! Let's just say you don't want to do that ... not even a little bit."

"I see where you're going. But I don't know how we'd get a room key to plant the stuff. And if he walks in on you and you get caught in his room, you might get arrested," Moxie warned.

"Worry-wart, you fret too much. I'm an expert at breaking and entering. I won't get caught, and if I do, it won't be that much trouble to talk myself out of the tight spot. I've done it plenty of times before."

"OK, then go get some, but I'm telling you, handle it with kid gloves."

"Yeah! Yeah! I know all about that. Hell, I'm the one who told you about the stuff. You know this asshole has it coming, don't you?"

"I agree. Just be careful. Where are you going to apply it?"

"How about in his bathing suit? I think that's appropriate. I want his nuts to hurt as bad as mine do."

Conclusive, All-Inclusive Confusion

✍

"Our jackoff guest from hell, Jax Magnus, took the bait," Queisha said. "I knew he would when he thought Ms. Blount and Mr. Connors had booked a romantic trip to the Martha Brae, and that the hotel would pay for the cheap SOB's own ticket."

"And Chris invited the Connors girls on the President's Club shopping excursion. When they found out I'd be there to show them which stores to shop in, they didn't hesitate to commit," Foxy-Roxy said.

"And I've got Ruddy Puss lined up to drive Mr. Magnus to the Martha Brae," Chris Angel said. "Ruddy Puss practically jumped at the chance to drive when he found out who the guest was."

"Apparently he doesn't like Mr. Magnus either. I'm surprised he even knows who he is."

"Oh, he knows all right. Ruddy Puss wouldn't comment when I asked. He just smiled. Then he mumbled 'Ebry dawg hab him day, an ebry puss him 4 o'clock' *(Every dog has his day, and every cat his 4 o'clock.)*."

"Let me repeat the plan and make sure we're all on the same page," Neil said. "So when Mr. Magnus gets to the river, Ruddy Puss will tell him that another car already delivered Mr. Connors and Ms. Blount earlier and that their raft has already departed, but that his captain can probably catch up to them."

"Right! But they never will because Mr. Connors and Ms. Blount aren't really there."

"Magnus will be told to call Ruddy Puss when his excursion is over, but the phone number he'll have is my cell phone instead of Nakomis'."

"Correct, and you'll answer when he calls, pretending to be the hotel, and promise to send a car to pick him up. But no one'll come."

"And each time he calls again, I'll promise that the car is on its way, but it won't be."

"And voila! Mr. Magnus can get back to the hotel the best way he can."

"Sounds like a plan."

Nakomis aka Ruddy Puss had a plan of his own.

So to Fatso Magnus I'm a chocolate jungle dumb-bunny. Well, this chocolate jungle dumb- bunny's day has come like I prayed it would.

It was common knowledge around the hotel about Jax's infatuation with gummy bears. The clerk in the hotel's convenience store had commented to Ruddy Puss in the past on how he came in daily to buy more. Ruddy Puss called Coolmarket Wholesale in Ocho Rios and found out they sold gummy bears in a three pound package. His next call was to Miss Joy Products also in Ocho Rios. They handled laxative gummy bears and had some in stock. Perfect. Now all he had to do was buy an equal amount of both and mix them together. He decided to cover his own ass by gift wrapping this shit bomb and saying it was an anonymous gift.

I'll show you what a chocolate jungle dumb-bunny can and will do when you dis and embarrass him, you obese racist asshole.

Potsy successfully got into Jax and Eve's room. The pencil cactus was freshly cut and dripping with its milky sap. He had also squeezed some sap into a plastic pill bottle. He smiled as he looked at the concentrated juice in the bottle and tried to determine what to do with it.

Potsy looked around the room trying to decide what to impregnate with the dangerous substance. He didn't have a beef with Eve. She'd always been very pleasant and polite around him. He almost felt sorry for her, but then he assuaged his guilt by reminding himself that nobody had made her marry her jerk of a husband. So he wouldn't rub it on any towels or anything that both Jax and Eve probably both used or might get picked up by room service. No, it needed to go for something of Jax's that was personal. And preferably something he'd be wearing in public.

If I only humiliated him in private, it'd take half the fun out of it. After all, he humiliated me in front of what seemed like the whole hotel. ... His bathing suit! Yes!

Conclusive, All-Inclusive Confusion

… And the UV sun-blocker shirt he wears by the pool. … And that bottle of Banana Boat sunblock lotion in his beach bag.

I can't wait to see him go ape shit in front of the whole hotel.

Please God, let it happen with half the world watching.

Potsy didn't know that he was slated to be disappointed since his prayer wouldn't be answered. He wanted so badly to have the pleasure of witnessing Jax's upcoming over-the-top, award-winning performance. But it was not to be since Jax would be putting the show on for a Martha Brae audience instead of one at the hotel.

✍

The following morning Jax saw Eve off on her shopping excursion while keeping his own plans for the day under wraps.

"You girls have a fun day, but don't feel like you have to buy out the whole country. Save some of it for others," Jax said in a jocular vein as he saw her off. "I'm just going to chill out here at the hotel and work on my tan. Maybe I'll catch up on my reading."

Eve looked at him kind of funny but said nothing. She couldn't remember Jax reading a book the whole time they'd been married.

After Eve left, Jax went back up to his room, retrieved his beach bag, and as he had been told to do, he went to the hospitality desk to catch his own transportation. Chris Angel gave him a phone number to call when he wished to return. Jax programmed it into his cell phone. Within minutes, Jax and Ruddy Puss were in route to the Martha Brae River.

"Looks like you have a marvelous day for rafting," Ruddy Puss observed as he tried to make small talk.

"Yeah! Yeah! Sure! Do you know if Mr. Connors and Ms. Blount have left for the river yet?"

"Oh, yes sir, if they were supposed to. Another car would have picked them up earlier. Were they going rafting as well?" Ruddy Puss answered, even though he had no idea what Jax was talking about. Chris Angel had said nothing about Monte and Bessie Prince when he'd scheduled Jax's trip.

"Then step on it, boy."

*Boy? Suck yuh mudda **(Go fuck yourself)**, you rude bastard. I hope you eat every gummy bear I bought and then shit your brains out,* Ruddy Puss thought.

Out loud all he said was, "Yes, sir. Relax and enjoy the scenery."

When they got to the Martha Brae, Ruddy Puss showed Jax where to change clothes while he checked him in and selected a raft. As Jax got on his raft, Ruddy Puss said, "Oh, sir. I almost forgot. Someone left a package for you at the hospitality desk with instructions to give it to you."

He gave Jax the giftwrapped package with the tainted gummy bears.

"Huh! What's this?" Jax said brusquely. "Who's it from?"

"I wouldn't know. I'm just doing what I was instructed to do. I'm sure it's something nice."

"Then gimme it," Jax said as he snatched it out of Ruddy Puss' hand and tore the wrapping off of it. When he saw it was gummy bears, his face lit up. Now he'd have something to munch on as he went down this God-forsaken river.

"Let's get going. I want to catch up to the other rafts," Jax said to his captain as he chewed on a green gummy bear. Then he popped a red one in his mouth.

"This isn't a race," his captain reminded him. "Just relax and enjoy your day and the scenery. By the way, my name is Captain Kirk."

"Yeah! Yeah! Let's get this spaceship moving," Jax said through green and red stained teeth.

"I hope you have a wonderful day," Ruddy Puss yelled as Captain Kirk poled the raft out into the gentle current.

"Yeah! You too."

And don't eat too much, ass wipe.

"Let me know anytime you want me to stop so you can go swimming, "Captain Kirk said. "Also there's some ropes hanging over some parts of the river if you want to swing out over the water on them and drop in. They can be fun."

"Yeah! Sure! I'll let you know. Now let's get going. I'm trying to catch up to some friends on another raft."

Jax looked up at the sun and thought he'd better put on some sunblock lotion. He began to rub some on his forehead, nose, and cheeks. He ate some more gummy bears but didn't offer to share any with Captain Kirk.

Jax began to experience several things at once. His stomach began to rumble, and then it felt gaseous and bloated. Then he felt a bubbling

Conclusive, All-Inclusive Confusion

sensation followed by a stabbing pain. He passed wind. It felt wet. At the same time, his face began to sting. The sting became a burning sensation that continued to intensify. He passed gas again, this time loud enough to make Captain Kirk turn and look at him just as Jax's underarms and midsection both seemed to catch on fire simultaneously. Jax didn't know what problem to address first. Now his ears began to burn. He rubbed them and his eyes. Within moments tears poured down his face and his vision blurred from eyes that were beginning to swell shut.

Jax stood and began to dance on the raft, not knowing what problem to address first. About this time his bowels let loose and a brownish ooze began to run down his legs.

Captain Kirk stared at Jax disbelieving what he was seeing.

Jax's bowels let loose a second time, and the stench became overpowering. His eyes bulged, and he suddenly let loose with a torrent of undigested gummy bear vomit.

The man's been either possessed by the devil, or a duppie's gotten hold of him. Either way, I'd better get the hell out of here.

Captain Kirk dived overboard and began swimming towards the bank as fast as he could, rocking the raft. Jax lost his balance, belly-flopped overboard, and began swimming behind him. This panicked the captain to swim even harder, and when he got to the bank, he fled into the undergrowth.

The water seemed to dilute the cactus juice, and when Jax reached the bank he felt a little bit better. He felt in his swimming trunks pocket.

Thank God my cell phone's still here. And also thank God it's got a waterproof case.

He dialed the number he'd been given for hotel pickup. Neil answered the phone.

"OK sir, I'll get a car on the way to pick you up."

Neil laughed when he hung up. "GFL. Ain't no way, Jose."

An hour later, his phone rang again, and this time Neil said, "We've dispatched a car to pick you up, but it had a flat tire."

He laughed when he hung up again, "Payback can be so much fun."

Neil would have been even more pleased if he could have seen Jax having yet another diarrhea attack and then could have seen Jax wading back into the river to try to scrub his mottled skin and cleanse himself all over again. This done, Jax dog-paddled out to the raft that by this time had snagged on the shore. He was able to reclaim his beach bag, his wallet, and his money.

Jax freed the raft and began to pole it downstream. Soon he saw some Rastas on the bank smoking ganja and drinking the Red Stripes and rum they had brought out to sell to tourists. When they found out he had money, they closed up shop for the day and decided to get the party started in earnest after he bought their inventory. They allowed Jax to join them in consuming it all and agreed to take him back to the hotel and drop him off but only after he used his remaining funds to treat them at a local roadside rum bar. He finally arrived back at the hotel after dark, both high and drunk, smelling bad, and still scratching his still stinging skin.

The family was frantic by this time, not knowing where Jax had been all day. They had had the hotel call the constabulary to try to find him and had been imagining the worst. When they saw him stinking drunk, their concern became anger.

Even Foxy-Roxy and Chris Angel were perplexed by what they saw, not knowing about Potsy or Ruddy Puss's contributions to Jax's hellish day. Not completely understanding why, it seemed to them that their plan to undermine Jax Magnus had succeeded beyond their wildest hopes.

The drunken Jax didn't even try to explain or justify what he'd been through until the next morning when he sobered up. He merely collapsed in his bed and within moments was out cold.

As far as Neil, Foxy-Roxy, Potsy, Christian Angel, Queisha, and Ruddy Puss were concerned justice had been served, but Neil still wasn't completely satisfied. Plus, he saw opportunity to kill two birds with one stone as he composed a brief note and sealed it in an envelope.

> PRIVATE PARKING
> ILLEGALLY PARKED
> CARS
> WILL BE FINE

CHAPTER 37

When Jax woke up alone the next morning after a restless night in and out of the land of Nod, he still felt like he'd been run over by a train. He felt like the lyric's to Jimmy Buffett's song "My head hurts, my feet stink, and I don't love Jesus" had been written especially for him.

His stomach was weak; his rectum was raw from the previous day's diarrhea attacks; the cactus juice had left his midsection looking like it belonged in a leprosy colony; and he had a hangover worse than any he had ever experienced. As he tried to climb out of bed, he couldn't seem to get his equilibrium as he at first tried to grope his way towards the bathroom. He finally ended up crawling. Once he got there, he used hanging on to the sink to render himself upright again so he could collapse on the room's bidet.

He looked from his perch there on the toilet, but he decided he couldn't move another inch. All he knew was his bladder was screaming for relief. When he tried to relieve it, his urethral opening felt like it was on fire from the cactus juice that had penetrated it. His joystick felt like someone had threaded an alcohol-soaked fireplace match down it and then lit it on fire. Jax had experienced a burning sensation in the past from soap accidentally entering it but nothing remotely as agonizing as this. It stung so bad he almost began to hallucinate.

When he looked down at his manhood, he gasped at what he imagined he saw.

"Willy, you're pissing fire!"

This caused his bowels, which already felt like they were inside out, to begin to run, and he now felt like he had a hemorrhoid the size of a double-yolked egg.

"And now I'm shitting fire too!"

He turned on the bidet's water, hoping it would soothe him, but when the water hit his raw private areas, it only seemed to make them burn even worse.

After forcing himself to take a soapy shower, Jax noticed the envelope Neil had slid under his door. It contained a short but succinct message.

"Meddlers pay! — HRR."

He wadded it up and threw it across the room and shouted at the walls as he shook his fist, "HRR — Hans R. Roman, mark my words. I'm coming for you!"

He sat down at the desk and began to doodle and make a list of ideas to right the wrong that had been done to him.

Why don't I ruin his love life? I'll get a garlic supplement that'll make his breath smell bad and give him BO. And while I'm at it, I'll put some salt peter in his food and render him into a stinking Romeo who can't get it up. I wonder where I can get some of that? Nah! But it's probably hard for me to find. I sure wish I had some poison ivy.

I'm not sure what he did to make me itch, but one itch deserves another.

He Googled itching stimuli.

…. Niacin … says here it's the same thing as Vitamin B3 … now that ought to be easily available. Says here Niacin causes body odor, flushing, itching, nervousness, headaches, and intestinal gas. … Wow! That pretty much covers the waterfront. … Sounds even better than poison ivy. … That'll make Hans one miserable SOB. He'll be scratching like a hound like I am right now. And if it causes him to show his sorry ass around Nan, maybe it'll turn her off of him to the point that she'll dump the gold-digger, and that'll take him out of the big picture once and for all. He'll end up as pitiful as a three-legged dog.

He began to sing the Coasters old song "Poison Ivy" to himself as he looked at his disfigured face and body in the mirror.

Measles make you bumpy
And mumps'll make you lumpy
And chicken pox'll make you jump and twitch
A common cold'll fool ya

Conclusive, All-Inclusive Confusion

And whooping cough will cool ya
But Niacin, Lord'll make you itch … and fart … and stink

Yessiree, Bob! There's got to be someplace, I can buy Niacin. I'll go down to the lobby and ask a hotel employee … and get a light breakfast while I'm at it. My stomach's empty. I'm so hungry I could eat the north end of a southbound scabby horse.

Jax was so excited about his discovery that he left his doodling sheet on the desk. Eve beat him back to the room and saw the doodle notes he had left there. She knew a little bit about vitamins since she had once clerked in a General Nutrition Center store back home. When she saw Jax had scribbled a circle over and over again over the word Niacin, a light went off.

Oh, crap! My husband's planning on playing a dirty trick on someone … to get even for yesterday … but who? … Banks? … I thought they get along. Hans? … He never did anything to Jax. … Oh, my God! He's going after Bessie Prince, which means he might get daddy by accident! I'd better warn Nan, Eve, and Bessie Prince. … And I'll keep my eyes peeled for some B3 here in the room and dump it if I find some. I'll tell them not to tell any of the other guys. I don't want to start a war.

Eve caught both Viv, Nan, and Bessie Prince and told each of them that she suspected her husband was planning retribution against someone, but she just didn't know who. She told them that she would make sure that Jax did not go on any shopping excursions without her being around. She also told them that if he somehow did manage to get hold of some Niacin, she'd flush it down the toilet the moment she found it. They seemed comfortable with trusting Eve to contain the situation until Jax regained his perspective. She said she'd covertly work on Jax in the meantime and convince him just to let the matter drop. All agreed that a family feud could last for years and would serve no purpose. It would simply tear the family apart.

✍

Bessie Prince's attitude, however, was not the same. While she pretended to be understanding and forgiving, deep down she just knew that she must be the primary target of Jax's aggression. Her thoughts reverted back to the pack of lies Banks had told when Kemp Morrison had been instructed to tell her made-up falsehoods about Monte and the subsequent slander he had told Monte about her. She was convinced that both Jax and Banks would do virtually anything to make sure she was never admitted to being a member of this family.

Eve continued to apologize, but Bessie Prince only heard selective words as random thoughts began to zing back and forth in her mind.

I'm not going to take any more crap from either Banks or Jax. They want war — I'll give them war. After all, I'm a licensed pharmacist, and I've forgotten more than these two idiots have ever learned. I know just what'll do the trick — Dulcolax. It's odorless, tasteless, and it works fast.

Do these two morons want to play? They don't know what rough play is. Dis pretty rose got macca jook. And when rat like fi romp 'roun' puss jaw, one day 'im gwine en up inna puss craw **(Beautiful roses have thorns that will hurt you. And when a rat gets too close to a cat's mouth, one day it'll end up getting eaten.).**

And I know the perfect place to get these two — Monte's birthday celebration. And it needs to be somewhere other than the hotel if I'm going for maximum effect. And besides that, I don't want the hotel to take the blame. That wouldn't be fair. They've had to suffer enough embarrassment so far because of Jax's antics.

Bessie Prince smiled at Eve and said, "Thanks for warning me, Eve. Isn't Monte's birthday coming up? Do you have anything planned for it?"

"I'd like to do something special. He's turning fifty."

"Maybe a restaurant in town instead of the same-old, same-old at the hotel."

"I don't know local restaurants well enough to make an intelligent choice. But you do, don't you?"

"I can give you some options that I'd choose if you like, and I'd love to join you."

I really don't care where they go as long as I'm there to administer the laxative to those two jerks."

"Of course, Bessie Prince. We'd love for you to join us."

I just need to make sure she thinks the restaurant choice is hers and not mine so I won't get the blame when the party doesn't go according to Hoyle.

"Well, let me see. There's the Terrace at the Jamaican Inn …"

"No, too much like staying at the hotel."

"And there's the Almond Tree. They don't have bar stools around the bar but instead have swings that come down from the ceiling …"

Conclusive, All-Inclusive Confusion

"No, probably not. Too bar-ish."

"Oh, then Spring Garden Seafood or Oceans on the Ridge or maybe Evita's. ... It's Italian with a Jamaican twist."

"Evita's sounds interesting. Everyone in the family loves Italian. In fact, Monte's mentioned that name as someplace he'd like to go. Did you tell him about it?"

"As a matter of fact, I believe I did. It's way up a steep hill and is landscaped almost like a tropical forest and has a bird's eye view of the whole city. It also has a room with a piano bar."

"I like the sound of all that. I'll make a reservation. I'll let you know when."

"Perfect."

Good! Her choice, not mine. Get ready for a very shitty evening boys.

Eve made the reservations. She called for a hired car to take them since the hotel wouldn't want to tie up one of the hotel's drivers for a whole evening. The road to Evita's was exactly how Bessie Prince had described it to Eve. The winding road up the hill was so steep that the driver had to put the car in first gear to make the final leg up to get to the lushly landscaped random, rustic parking lot. Evita's gleaming, topless, red and white vintage two-seater Morgan was parked near the door. "The Best Little Pasta House in Jamaica" was painted across the fake spare on its trunk. Its actual spare tire was mounted on the hood.

The restaurant itself was a quaint 1860 gingerbread house with bright red eaves. The walkway into the building was decorated with three-foot, hundred year old olive jars. A broadly smiling, deeply-tanned, Italian-born Evita greeted them at the door with some light banter and jokes. She was a pleasantly plump, platinum blonde, mature woman of average height. She was wearing a floor-length, flowing, batik gown and had on one of her signature, wide-brimmed straw hats that had a hatband that matched the gown. The dark-wood paneled front room was the piano bar Bessie Prince had told Eve about. Framed pictures of Evita with the celebrities she had entertained covered the walls from floor to ceiling. A grinning Mick Jagger and Keith Richards must have been in a dozen of them. The main dining room's wooden walls had been painted the same bright red as the outside eaves and contrasted with a white wood planked ceiling. This led to a large open porch that had baskets of blooming orchids hanging virtually everywhere above it. Diners were sheltered from the hot Jamaican sun by giant blue and white striped umbrellas. The porch's railing oversaw a heart-stirring panoramic view of much of the city of Ocho Rios and the surrounding part of St. Ann Parish. Winding stone steps led down to a rustic stone path to Evita's lush, heavily forested private botanical garden. The whole thing rivaled any commercial botanical garden they had ever seen as it stretched out below the porch.

A table had been reserved for Monte's party on the porch. After they were seated, a beaming waiter immediately arrived to take their drink orders.

"My name is Shaka Onfroy, and I'll be your server tonight. Welcome to Evita's. Would you like to order a drink before dinner?"

"Why don't we begin with a round of Cuba libres," Bessie Prince suggested. "Anyone object?"

There were no objections. Shaka left to fill their orders.

"Have you ever seen such a view?" Bessie Prince said. "Why don't you take the steps down to the garden and watch the sun set from there? It's breathtaking. Since I've been here plenty of times, I'll monitor the table and make sure the waiter gets our drink order right. You may want to take some pictures while you're there."

Once they had all gone, Bessie Prince then took the liberty of ordering a variety of appetizers for the whole table to share. She chose fried, breadcrumbed mozzarella in a marinara sauce, an assortment of garlic crostini slices topped with fresh tomato, onions and smoked marlin, and a dish the restaurant called Jamaican Viagra. This was actually salt fish fritters topped by a jerk sauce. She purposely chose rich, slow-to-digest items.

She then waited for the waiter to bring the drinks and food before calling everyone back to the table. The drinks and the appetizers arrived. Before telling them that their order had arrived, while everyone was still preoccupied with the view, Bessie Prince slipped the Dulcolax into Banks' and Jax's drinks.

Let the fun begin, assholes ... or should I say, let the fun begin for your assholes, boys. Bon appetite!

Conclusive, All-Inclusive Confusion

Everyone returned to the table and sat down. They were stunned by the array of appetizers before them.

About that time the actress, Uma Thurman, walked through the restaurant.

"My God! Do you know who that is? That's Uma Thurman — in person," Jax gasped. "She's even taller and more beautiful in person that she is on the screen. She's taller than I am."

"And thinner too," Banks quipped.

Without looking or thinking, the wowed, mesmerized Jax stood up to ogle Uma some more just as a waiter was passing by as he headed for an adjacent table with a tray of pumpkin soup. Soup flew. Fortunately, most went over the rail or on the floor instead of onto other diners, but much of it drenched the appetizers Bessie Prince had ordered, ruining them.

Uma Thurman looked back and couldn't help but smile at the reaction she had caused.

Shaka Onfroy, with the false grin still plastered on his face, graciously moved in to try to save the day. He quickly moved them to an adjacent table, transferring their drinks and other unsoaked items to the new location before seating them.

Jax tried to stutter his apologies but was met by his dining companions by a stony silence.

After Bessie Prince assured Shaka that they would cover any damage, she tried to reinvigorate the group by offering a humorous toast to Monte and his birthday as they waited for the replacement appetizers to be prepared.

"Age is strictly a case of mind over matter. If you don't mind, it don't matter. To Monte! Happy birthday."

Jax thought he'd counter and try to take some of the onus off of himself by being cute.

"Monte, may your liquor be cold; may your women be hot. And may your troubles slide off you slicker than snot."

This mainly caused his wife to give him a dirty look. The rest of the group glanced at each other but remained embarrassingly silent until Hans tried to rescue the moment by saying, "Well, that rhyme was itself slicker than snot. Cheers to Monte."

Hans looked at Nan, and she nodded.

"Now there's one more thing for us to celebrate tonight," Hans said. "Nan and I have an announcement to make."

Before he thought, Jax blurted out, "Don't tell me you've knocked her up."

Eve glared and clenched her fists.

"No, " Nan blurted out. "That turned out to be a false alarm."

"Something even more wonderful, Jax. Nan and I got married yesterday."

Banks and Jax looked ashen, but their wives almost upset the table a second time as they jumped up to hug their sister. Monte wasn't sure what he thought, but he wasn't surprised. After all, Nan *had* warned him.

Bessie Prince's stomach rumbled for the first time. She thought it was gas. Another round of toasts followed.

Further awkwardness was spared when Shaka Onfroy brought out the replacement appetizers and then took their entrée orders. The dinner orders varied. The orders ranged from homemade gnocchi to jerk spaghetti to lobster carbonara to crab cakes. Bessie Prince ordered "One Love" alfredo, which was penne with chicken in an alfredo sauce.

About that time Bessie Prince's stomach began to rumble again as fecal urgency began to lead to the backdoor trots. She knew she'd shortly be headed for a diarrhea apocalypse.

Oh shit! The waiter must have given me the wrong drink. I wonder who got the other one.

She glanced around, but no one else seemed to be in distress.

Maybe the other spiked drink got spilled when Jax ruined the hors d'oeuvres.

She quickly excused herself and headed for the ladies room. It was down a level from the main dining room. She grimaced as she went down the narrow stairs, hoping she would make it in time.

Please God, let the restroom be unoccupied. If it isn't, I've got double trouble.

God must have heard Bessie Prince's plea. No one was there. She rushed into the restroom and barely got her panties down before she the first torrent began to pour out of her rectum into the toilet. A brown and orange Niagara began to pulsate in sharp bursts. It made her asshole feel like someone was welding it shut before firing a laser-bomb through it.

I'll never make it through dinner now. It'll be less embarrassing to catch a cab back to the hotel. I'll leave them a note. I'll say I got a call saying I had a family emergency. But how am I going to make it all the way back there?

Conclusive, All-Inclusive Confusion

The wall-mounted feminine hygiene dispenser gave her an idea. She checked her purse to make sure she had enough money to purchase what she needed. She sighed in relief when she found that she did.

Bessie Prince purchased four Tampax. She put two in each orifice. She then purchased an equal number of Kotex which lined her panties. A stolen toilet paper roll went into her oversized purse. She then waddled bow-legged back up the stairs and headed for the front door. She saw a display containing picture postcards. It was meant to encourage diners to take them for souvenirs of their Evita's dining experience. She quickly scribbled a message on one of them.

"A situation has arisen that demands my immediate attention, and I've had to return to the hotel. Please go on with dinner without me. I'll explain later."

I'm not sure what that explanation is going to be, but I'll think of something.

She handed the postcard to the bartender along with a tip if he'd take it back to the Connors' table once she had left. She lucked out again. A taxi arrived, bringing new diners. Within minutes, Bessie Prince commandeered it and was on her way back to the hotel.

Every time the cabbie hit a bump, Bessie Prince felt like the Tampaxes were impaling her simultaneously both in the front and from behind. She prayed she'd make it before she blew her plug and flooded her Kotex-bulging panties.

When they arrived at the hotel, Bessie Prince threw an American hundred dollar bill at the cabbie and didn't wait for change before fleeing for the lobby ladies room. She didn't have to pull the Tampax plugs. The moment she ripped aside the Kotexes and sat down, the torrent of pressure behind the rear ones shot both of them into the toilet bowl as she peed in relief over the two front ones. She had never felt such relief.

Monte, people say love is the best feeling, but sometimes they're wrong. Right now, this toilet is the best feeling thing I have felt in a long time.

And well, as to Banks and Jax. Maybe, evening the score just wasn't in the cards today. And maybe that wasn't so bad. After all, this attack of the crab-apple two-step has given me pause to have remorse on what was probably a foolish plan to begin with. It really would have been wrong and selfish to spoil Monte's birthday party just to even the score with those two jerks.

Despite her discomfort, Bessie Prince laughed when another stray thought shot through her head.

I read that four out of five people suffer from diarrhea. Do you think that means the fifth one actually enjoyed it.

COWS PLEASE CLOSE GATE

CHAPTER 38

Monte put on a false front for the rest of his birthday party, but he was primarily concerned about Bessie Prince. What could possibly have happened to make her leave the restaurant so suddenly without even so much as a goodbye? She'd never done anything like that before.

When they got back to the hotel later that evening, he quickly excused himself and went up to his room to call her and try to find out the reason.

"Bessie Prince, did you have some emergency? Are you alright? I've been worrying about you all evening. It's all I've been able to think about. Should I come down to your room and check on you?"

"You dear, dear man. No, don't come to my room tonight. It's late. I'll be OK. I promise. I'll explain it all in the morning. If you don't mind, I'd rather have you come down in the morning. I'll call and let you know when."

"I won't be able to sleep a wink worrying about you."

"I'll be OK. I promise. I'll clarify everything in the morning. Now, good night, you dear, kind man."

"If you're sure you're OK."

"I am. I promise."

After they hung up, her words kept replaying in Monte's head.

She called me dear and kind.

Monte showered and shaved earlier than usual the next morning and waited impatiently for Bessie Prince's call. When the call came, he immediately headed for the elevator. She met him at her door after his first knock and hugged him affectionately.

Conclusive, All-Inclusive Confusion

"Come in, dear Monte. We need to have an overdue talk."

His knees quaked and he wondered if this was about to be the end — her dear John.

"I'm so sorry about last night. I can't apologize enough. Please forgive me. Sit on the sofa over there, and I'll clarify it in a few minutes, but right now I've got some other related things to discuss with you first."

Now the knot in Monte's stomach was really beginning to swell. He sat, and she cupped one of his hands in both of hers.

"There's been a lot going on around here behind your back fostered by people who don't have your best interest at heart. You're such a naïve, kind, trusting lamb. They're some of the attributes I love so much about you. I sometimes think you'd hesitate before you killed an insect, but darling, some of the people around you aren't harmless insects. They're nasty, diseased roaches. And there's so many of them I almost don't know where to start."

"I don't understand."

"I think you will when I'm through. When you won the lottery money, you opened the door to become a target for some very greedy and crooked people. Let me take them one at a time.

"Neil Hackinrider. That jewelry company of his he wants you to invest in. It doesn't exist. And he wants you to invest in his retirement community in Pinellas County Florida. I don't think it exists either or ever will. I checked on-line. He doesn't have applications pending with the county and never has. He's nothing more than a swindler. Both of these ventures are a figment of his imagination designed to swindle you out of some of your money. If he was as successful an international businessman as he portrayed himself to be, would he be going into business with someone he just met at a hotel? I don't think so."

"As for your pal Foxy-Roxy Savage ..."

"Oh, she's really a nice person."

"Depends on what you consider to be nice. Didn't she introduce you to Neil Hackinrider?"

"Sure."

"She's been bothering me since the first day I checked into this hotel. I kept thinking that I'd seen her somewhere before. Well, it finally hit me. You remember I told you I was a licensed beautician and cosmetician and had a section of my apothecary that was a beauty parlor called Sip 'n Snip?"

"Sure. What does this have to do with Ms. Savage?"

"You're about to be stunned when I tell you. A movie company from Vegas came to Mo Bay and wanted me to do the hair and makeup of their actors. She was a bit player in the company. The star was a guy who went by the name Long Dong Silver."

"Long Dong Silver?"

"Yep. The first movie was entitled "Pirates of the Caribbean — XXX." It was followed by "Orgy Pirates of the Caribbean — XXX." Seems like there was a third sequel and then maybe a fourth that never got made."

"Porn?"

"H-a-r-d core porn."

Monte was speechless.

"I can't prove it at this point, but I strongly suspect she's somehow in cahoots with Hackinrider, and that she set you up to meet with him in return for a cut out of whatever he can get out of you. And I wouldn't be surprised if their network didn't also include other hotel employees."

"Oh?"

"It's a mean old world out there. Now let's go to Carl Potter. I've suspected for some time that that name was most likely an alias, and I've confirmed my suspicions. Monte, my deceased husband dealt with some pretty questionable characters, but characters who had long reaching tentacles. I hope you won't hold it against me, but I still have an open line of communications with some of them. Potter's real name is Neko Caputo. He's nothing more than a second-generation, cheap, second-rate grifter who has worked primarily out of Vegas. At one time, he partnered with a sister named Rosa, but apparently they parted ways years ago. I'm not sure what happened to her.

"Anyway, once I had his name, I spent some money to buy reports from both the TruthFinder and the BeenVerified websites. He has a police record and a history of violence."

"But his wife and his son ..."

"I can't verify if either of them exist or ever did exist. I think Potter's playing on your sympathy to beat you out of some of your money. You don't know much about guns, do you?"

"I've never even shot one. Don't want to."

Conclusive, All-Inclusive Confusion

"I figured as much. That gun in his room the other day. Did you know it wasn't loaded? I know it wasn't because the magazine wasn't in it and it wasn't cocked. And those rum bottles he was supposedly using to get drunk, they were dry as a bone. I tested him by pretending to almost step on his foot. He sure moved it out of my way in a hurry to be as drunk as he was pretending to be.

"And that bag you moved off his chair so you could sit down. It was identical to the one you took to the falls. At first I thought, what a coincidence. Then it hit me. Didn't you tell me that's how you originally met him? I'm sure he was playing the old bait and switch game to give him an excuse to meet you and gain your trust. Didn't you think it was strange that he bonded with you, a stranger, immediately and took you into his confidence on so many highly personal matters? No, I don't guess you would, you dear sweet man.

"Finally, do you know why he pretended to pass out that day in his room? Because he saw I was on to him."

"I see."

"By the way, do you happen to have anything with Potter's handwriting on it?"

"I believe I still do. … From my first day."

"Good. Then let me have it."

"Let's move along. I hope I'm not crushing your ego, but I'm just getting started. … And am about to get to the sensitive part. Your sons-in-laws. They're not much better than Potter or Hackinrider. In a way, they may be worse."

"But Banks is a successful financial planner and has an MBA in accounting from Michigan. The priest told me so. He manages my money. And he's creative. He set up a limited liability corporation to shelter me from taxes."

"Oh, he's creative all right. He's creative about calling himself a financial planner. A certified financial planner has to pass qualifying exams to get his license and take continuing education to maintain that license. I researched every legitimate financial planning organization's membership rosters. He doesn't belong to any of them. His license is make-believe. I suspect he's found creative way to get access to your money and not get caught stealing it, and I plan to find out for sure. That swindle isn't new."

"My God!"

"Banks may be a CFP in his mind, but that's all he is. Let me repeat, I checked the membership rosters of six different financial planning organizations, and he isn't and never has been a member of any of them. And his degrees from Michigan. He never even finished his freshman year there. Think about this. If he was that successful, why was he running a one-man shop in one of the poorest sections of Detroit? You wanna know why? Because he was only selling low-minimum mutual funds until you came along. Now, I'm guessing that you're his only client, and he'll do anything to maintain control over your money. And that included marrying your daughter.

"Let me tell you the extremes he'll go to in order to protect his turf. He hired an actor named Kemp Morrison to try to scare me away from you. This guy pretended he was an insurance investigator named Ben Casey and told me you weren't a lottery winner but a possible serial killer who was suspected of killing all of his former wives for insurance money."

"But I've never been married even once."

"That's right. Lies and more lies."

"An investigator calling himself Dirk Gently ..."

'Another bullshit alias name."

"... and told me bad things about Hans too. Said he had embezzled multimillions when he was a banker for Eminence Trust from a retirement community banking with them called Harbour Isle."

"That's right. Another pack of lies. Banks hired this same actor to slander Hans because he was scared Hans would marry Nan and become a competitor for your money. I know. I forced Morrison to admit it to me."

Monte looked ashen.

"Now, let's get to your other son-in-law, Jax Magnus."

"Jax really knows insurance. He analyzed my future tax liability and sold me the policy I'll need to pay it."

"You told me. Three million bought fifteen million. And guess what. He took your ass to the cleaners in the process by overpricing it. Do you know how much I think he made on that policy? I know because I shopped them. Take a guess."

"I don't know. He said he gave me a special deal."

Conclusive, All-Inclusive Confusion

"Oh, it was a special deal alright. A special deal for him. I figure he made somewhere between a million and a half and two million by gouging you on that policy."

"How'd he do that?"

"Through a high commission and then by controlling the billing. You paid the money directly to him, so you told me.

"Monte, you were the biggest sale Jax made in his whole life. Until you came along, he was selling nickel-and-dime debit insurance. Do you know what that is? It's low-end insurance where the agent collects the pissant little premiums on the insured's payday before they can piss their money away because these people can't afford to buy insurance any other way. Five dollars here, ten dollars there.

"And let me remind you, he made about a million dollar commission selling you the policy, but that wasn't enough for him. The greedy bastard squeezed you for roughly another million under the table, all of which is tax free to him as long as he doesn't get caught. I'm not suggesting we turn him in. After all, he is your son-in-law. But I'm telling you, he's not your ally who has your best interest at heart.

"But let me go on. Have you ever wondered why both Jax and Banks pulled out all the stoppers to marry your daughters after you became a wealthy man?"

"I assumed the girls finally met their soulmates, and I was just glad for them."

"Well, the boys were mostly happy for themselves. The girls found their soulmates, but two marginal wage earners found their buck-mates.

"Now let's talk about the newest member of the Connors family."

"Not him too. You just told me the slander on him was made up."

"Maybe the story Banks told Morrison to tell was made up, but the real story is every bit as juicy. Hans Roman's real name is Billy Don Brown, and do you know what he does for a living? Whatever it takes to make a buck. He's been a gigolo and a male prostitute who has former clients of both sexes, ... "

"Whaaa ...?"

"Oh, yes. But let me go on. A female impersonator, and a runway beefcake who also entertains for private parties.

"Guess what he saw in Nan. If you can't guess, I'll tell you. He saw a permanent homerun."

"I'm speechless."

"I'm not surprised. Oh, I could tell you more. There's been a lot going on behind your back. Now let's talk about last night. Doesn't it seem funny to you that so many accidents have seemed to happen since you've been here? That's because they weren't accidents but dirty tricks being played by all of these people with various motives to try to eliminate their competition for your money. And do you wonder why Jax seems to be present so often when things get off the track? Because he's paranoid and stalking you to make sure no one else gets to you. In many cases he's trying to get rid of yours truly — me.

"Think back. He was present at the incidents at the nudist beach, the 007 competition, Dunn's River Falls, the Martha Brae. Starting to see a pattern? Well, last night someone tried to sabotage me again at Evita's. You want to know why I fled out of the restaurant? Someone put a strong laxative in my drink. It had to be either Banks or Jax or maybe the two of them working together. I don't think it was Hans. He's gotten what he wanted, Nan."

Monte was speechless. He just stared at the floor.

"But this has to end. You've got to turn the tables on all of these shysters. And I'm here to help you do it."

"But how?"

"Between the two of us, we'll come up with either one plan or a series of plans. I already have some ideas. Monte, you can depend on me. I think I'm the only person you can depend on who doesn't have a hidden agenda. Mull over my comments overnight, and we'll talk again tomorrow. OK? And keep our meetings confidential — even from your daughters.

"And Monte dear, chin up. We *will* win. Don't forget that it's not the size of the dog in the fight, but the size of the fight in the dog."

KIDS WITH GAS EAT FREE

CHAPTER 39

Monte's night was a turbulent one. His insomnia was as relentless as a blood-crazed feeding shark. It constantly nourished and renourished itself on any kind of thinking, even thinking about not thinking. This money had seemingly brought with it trouble that would inevitably lead to more trouble. Was his ordered life gone forever? Should he just give all the money away and retreat back to the simple but orderly life he had had before? Probably not! He'd be forever publicly branded as being a fool. And could he really trust Bessie Prince? If not, who could he trust?

When Bessie Prince didn't hear from him the next morning, she called Monte's room.

"Good morning."

"Morning to you too," Monte said in a monotone.

"You don't sound well."

"I didn't sleep. I'm groggy ... and confused."

"I'm not surprised. I hit you with a lot yesterday. Why don't you come down to my room, and we can continue our conversation?"

"Let me wake up and shower and shave, and I'll be on down."

"I'll make us some coffee."

After Monte arrived and Bessie Prince poured him a cup of coffee, he said, "I don't know what to say. It's all so overwhelming. It makes me just want to give the whole caboodle away."

"Then why don't you just let me talk and you listen? Your solution is no solution at all, just a knee-jerk reaction that you'd regret. What you need is a strategy that makes real sense."

He nodded but looked confused.

"First of all, let me clear the air. Monte, you and I didn't meet by accident. I was aware of your good fortune and maneuvered our early meetings. I will admit that avariciousness was my original motivator. But that's now changed."

"Not you too."

"Monte, like it or not, you're a wealthy man. And wealthy men have a target on their chest. But things began to change as I got to know you. I found out that rich or poor you're a genuinely nice, attractive person who deserves better. I'll admit my original intent was land you as a husband as quickly as possible, but now I wouldn't become your wife even if you proposed."

"I'm that bad."

"No, you're that good. I'd be proud to be your wife, but only after we pursued the matter the right way. I now realize that I'm not Banks or Jax or Hans. Or Neil Hackinrider or Carl Potter or Foxy-Roxy Savage. All sharks of the worst kind. Parasites! I'd love to be a part of your life, but I'm going to propose that I play a different role. I want to be your business manager. I'm not volunteering to work for free. I'll let you decide what you'd be willing to pay me. But I'll be your buffer against the world and either slay or chase away the dragons who're going continue to pursue you."

"Uh … I … I … I… don't know what to say."

"This role is not totally foreign to me. I don't think I told you this before, but Oliver, my deceased husband, was an attorney who had an expertise in intangible rights and other matters and who represented Reggae singers in their contract negotiations and put into place teams, after the fact, to protect them from just the sort of people who are pursuing you and your family. That is until he was put out of business by Dudus Coke and the Shower Posse. Let me be your Oliver."

"You'd do that for me?"

"Yes, I would, and I'm not going to push you into a rigged marriage. If something like that were to happen down the road, it'll happen because it was meant to happen."

Conclusive, All-Inclusive Confusion

"Then, yes. You can. Where do we start?"

"I've been giving that some thought. Do *not* expect everything to come together overnight. And I'm going to be accompanying you to a lot of locations over the next few months. And because we can't trust any of your sons-in-laws, you are not going to be transparent with your daughters. I'm not telling you to lie to them, but your business needs to be only our business even if they push on you and try to make you feel guilty. ... You know who'll most likely be pushing them ... the very people I'm trying to protect you from. I'll let you know when and how much you can disclose to them going forward. Do you agree to my terms? They're not up for discussion."

"I agree. How much money do you want?"

"That's up to you. Money is not the issue. I know you're a fair man," she said in a laughing manner. "After all, I'll be living pretty much for free since you'll be paying my expenses. And in the long run, we'll see where things go."

"So, where do we start?"

"Well, I'm not as good a Christian as you. I'd like to begin with a little payback on the non-family shysters."

"I guess I can go along with that. I'm not that goody-goody."

"Then I'll go to work on phase one of Project Retribution. Just call me the Avenger. By the way, do you have any handwritten notes from either Neil or Potter?"

"I believe I do ... from both."

"Good. Then let me have them."

Monte called Bessie Prince the following morning, but she told him she didn't have time to talk and that she'd get back to him later in the day. She was true to her word and reported in late that afternoon.

"Boss, the Avenger reporting in. Sorry I didn't have time to talk to you this morning, but I had a lot of things I wanted to accomplish. As I told you yesterday, Project Retribution is going to fix the little red wagon of your friends — Neil and Carl being first. Things are in motion. Unfortunately, the bad news is we won't be able to witness the scene climax since the proverbial shit's not designed to hit the fan until after we leave. I'll give you a bill for what I spent."

"I'll also cover your hotel bill."

"Thanks. That's sweet of you. I didn't expect you to do that, you darling man. But now the good news. The good news is there's almost no danger of repercussions."

"No one's going to get killed, are they? I don't want to be a part of violence."

"Oh, there may be some violence all right, but it'll be between the two of them. I broke into Potter's room while he wasn't there and stole his passport."

"What if he misses it?"

"He won't because if he looks where he had it, he'll find a passport there, but it'll be a lousy forgery I had made. He'll have no reason to examine it, but it'll be apparent that it's bogus to any customs agent when he decides to leave Jamaica. I'm counting on the fact that once you've left Jamaica, he'll feel that it's time to move on the fresh pastures and look for a new mark elsewhere. That's when his troubles will begin, but it won't be when they'll end. I've got another surprise for Mr. Potter. While I was in his room, I also packed in an obscure place in his luggage a bag of coke and spilled a little as well so that a drug dog is sure to pick it up. We won't be there to see it, but I can't see how Mr. Carl Neko Potter won't be up the proverbial shit creek."

"Wow! Remind me never to get on your bad side."

"I save that aspect of my personality for people who truly deserve it, not people I care about. But I'm not finished yet. Remember those examples of Neil's and Carl's handwriting I asked you for? I put a note written in Neil's handwriting in with the cocaine saying, "This should bring you some walking around money. Have a good trip. Tell the old gang hello. N." This won't mean anything to the authorities, but it'll give them one more thing to give Neko hell about as they push him to find out who the author is. Neco might give Neil up, leaving Neil up a creek, but even if he doesn't, it'll definitely mean something to Neko. It'll tell him the source of both the cocaine and the fake passport and who he needs to get even with. With his history of violence, I'd hate to be in Neil's shoes. And the best thing about it is that Neil will never see Potter's

Conclusive, All-Inclusive Confusion

vengeance coming. He'll be totally caught off-guard. Oh, I'd love to see the outcome."

"Holy moly!"

"Am I earning my money so far? And I also have a surprise waiting for Ms. Foxy-Roxy Savage. That hammer's also gonna fall after you check out of the hotel. Seascape corporate will receive a complimentary copy of "Orgy Pirates of the Caribbean-XXX" along with a note explaining its relevance to them at the same time that the Jamaica Gleaner gets a copy of "Pirates of the Caribbean-XXX" with a similar explanation. Oh, I wish I could be a fly on the wall."

"I don't know what to say."

"You don't have to say anything, my dear man. Just let mama do her job. And I've got other plans to protect you. Mama's just beginning to roll. I've been an underdog much of my life, and I can tell you that we underdogs will eventually prevail. Why? Out of sheer, pure-de-will-power. That's why. Don't you forget, top-cats begin as underdogs."

> **TOILET ONLY FOR DISABLED ELDERLY PREGNANT CHILDREN**

CHAPTER 40

"I hope you like to travel," Bessie Prince told Monte.

"Why's that?"

"Because it's time that we take another trip to put your business affairs in order. How much longer did you plan on staying at this hotel?"

"Oh, I don't know. Another week or so? I've got a feeling the kids will stay as long as I'm paying for it. I know that since Nan's a newlywed she definitely would."

"Then why don't you offer to pay for her to go on a honeymoon either here or somewhere else? You can afford it."

"Good idea."

"As far as the other two, I don't really care where they are just as long as you and I are free to come and go as need be. If you want to send them back to Detroit, that's fine, or if you want to let them stay here, that's fine too. ... No, on second thought, let me retract that statement. I'd personally like to see them go home and get them away from Neil and Carl. It would worry me if either of those two targeted your sons-in-laws and tried to swindle them somehow. Don't they all have jobs they need to get back to? Excuse me for saying so, but Jax and Banks don't strike me as the sharpest tools in the shed. You and I need to go our separate ways from the family for a little while without having to worry about them."

"Your point is well taken. What do you suggest for us?"

Conclusive, All-Inclusive Confusion

"How'd you like to be my guest at either a family wedding or a family reunion. Take your choice."

"You have both coming up?"

"I have neither coming up, but they don't know that. That's merely an excuse for you to go somewhere without them and not have them worry. I wouldn't want you to disappear and have them call the cops or something because they were concerned about you. They might not like you travelling with me, but that's too damned bad. After all, you're free, white, and twenty-one and know your own mind."

"I guess I shouldn't care if they approve or not."

"Then let's attend an Irish wedding. They last for a whole week, and then after the wedding, maybe I'll show you some of Ireland."

"Boy, I've never been there before."

"And you're not going there now. You and I've got business to take care of elsewhere. Now, here's what we're going to do to cover our tracks and disguise our real destination. It'll cost you a little money on the front end, but in the long run, it'll save you gobs of it. We're going to drive to Negril. There we'll charter a boat and captain, and it's going to take us to Grand Cayman. That's about a two-hundred mile trip. We should be able to do it in about ten or so hours."

"What's that going to cost?"

"I figure we'll give the captain twenty grand to take us over there and give him another twenty to dead-head his boat back to Negril. I'm not talking about a little fishing boat. We'll charter one that's fifty feet or so. We might as well be comfortable and get some rest because we'll have business to attend to once we get there."

"OK, and then what?"

"We're going to Cayman National Bank. My husband used to use them for his clients. They handle over a trillion dollars in assets and offer a full array of banking services. Believe me, they're solid as a rock. Then we're going to transfer your money from Banks to them."

"That's not going to make him happy."

"Too damned bad. It's your money, and it deserves better than a mutual fund peddler who is also a bald-faced liar. As I told you before, I strongly suspect he's been milking you and taking advantage of you. And we'll find out for sure later. I plan to have a real CFP and CPA audit your past statements. I'm going to see that you're put in the hands of a *real* financial expert going forward."

"I don't know what to say."

"If you're smart, you'll do what I'm suggesting. Monte, you can afford to hire the best. You don't have to settle for less — that is, unless you choose to because of some misguided sense of loyalty. I can assure you, it's not a two-way street."

"So then what?"

"Not then, now. Most clients don't know this, but lawyers rely on boilerplate documents that they then add to or subtract from to make them applicable to a particular client. I still have those electronic files that my husband used. Before we go to Negril, you and I are going to use his computer to find the document that'll set up an insurance trust to be the beneficiary of that huge life insurance policy that Jax sold you. … And don't forget, ripped you off while he was doing it. You'll sign the trust documents, and then we'll get the insurance company to send us a change of beneficiary form to make the trust the new beneficiary. I've got a feeling that Jax is counting on not only making a mint on the front end but on the back end as well. This will be a stopgap measure until we can get a tax attorney to go over the document and probably replace it with one more current and suitable.

"I'm only getting started, but that's enough for me to heap on you for one day."

"You were serious when you said you would become my business manager."

"Yes, I was. I'm sick and tired of people trying to take advantage of you just because you're a good, gullible person."

> **SHOPLIFTERS WILL BE PERSOCUTED NO EXCEPTIONS**

CHAPTER 41

Monte informed the family that Bessie Prince had invited him to attend a family wedding in Ireland and that he had accepted her invitation. At the same time he told them that he was offering to extend the stay for Hans and Nan to have some time alone to enjoy their honeymoon. As for the rest of the family, since they had all by now probably used up their vacation time and needed to get back to work before they jeopardized their jobs, it was time for them to return to Detroit. He said he'd see everyone back there.

The girls were genuinely happy that their dad was beginning to enjoy the new life his windfall afforded him. Jax and Banks appeared happy for him on the surface but were in reality frustrated because Bessie Prince was continuing to make inroads into the family and possibly construct a generational barrier that could delay or jeopardize the inheritance that they thought should be rightfully theirs down the road. But each of them put on a false front so as not to antagonize their rich father-in-law. And if Bessie Prince was destined to marry Monte and become his soul mate and confidant, they certainly didn't want to create a permanent enemy from the get-go. They'd simply have to find another devious way to discredit her down the road. They were sure at some point she'd leave herself wide open.

And who knows? They might get lucky, and she'd predecease Monte. Yes, right now patience and prudence were the two emotions that should rule the day. They might not have been so outwardly tolerant or confident if they had any idea of the changes Bessie Prince was in the process of putting into motion.

On the following day, Bessie Prince hired a car and driver to take Monte and her to Negril. She purposely chose a JUTA driver who had no connection to the hotel to insure that their destination remained their secret. On the way, they detoured by Bessie Prince's home in Montego Bay to print out the boilerplate pages of an insurance trust from the legal files she had kept when she closed her husband's law office.

Once they arrived in Negril, Bessie Prince instructed the driver to take them to the White Sands Hotel where she had booked a two-bedroom suite for them. Later in the day, she took Monte to the ever popular Rick's Café. It proved to be a breezy and lively locale.

There they watched thrill-seekers jump and dive off the sheer cliffs that ranged from eight to forty feet into the glistening twenty foot turquoise and emerald waters below that hypnotically foamed and lapped at the base of the cliffs. People were letting loose of their inhibitions and simply falling into the ocean. Monte was enthralled as he watched this adventurous sport that he couldn't imagine himself summoning up the bravado to try himself. Most would jump from an area designated as a diving platform with their arms out to the side to keep their balance and land feet first. As they neared the water, they would bring their arms back in as tightly as possible to brace for the impact and enter the water like a tin soldier.

As the sun went down, Monte and Bessie Prince were treated to stunning views of the sky as it caught fire, reflecting off the expanse of water below. After that, they had a romantic dinner before returning to the hotel.

The following morning they located a captain with a forty-eight foot diesel-powered cabin cruiser who agreed to take them to Grand Cayman. When he saw what Bessie Prince was offering and after she assured him that everything about this trip was legal, he practically jumped at the chance to take them there. It was then decided that to prevent nighttime traveling, they would leave early the following morning.

Bessie Prince told the captain he'd get half of his money before they left and the rest when they arrived safely in Grand Cayman. Once again, Monte was impressed since if the captain had demanded it, he probably would have paid him the full amount up front.

Conclusive, All-Inclusive Confusion

Once they got out away from land, the pulsing, riparian-blue sea forged its own sea-song as it kindled its own symphony. The humming of its wave-song beguiled Monte. Bessie Prince let him enjoy the scene in silence for an hour or more.

When she was sure he had drunk in as much of his new environment as his mind could absorb, she decided they needed to talk.

"Monte, would you mind if I brought up some business since we have plenty of time on our hands today? You'll have plenty of time to think about my comments."

"Not at all."

"This is a sensitive subject that I purposely waited for an appropriate time to discuss with you. The topic is Banks and Jax. We both know that if the regulatory authorities were told how Jax feathered his nest at your expense, he would probably have his license to sell insurance pulled and he'd be forced to reimburse you for the money he gypped you out of. On a similar note, from what you've told me, I strongly suspect that Banks could be padding his pocket at your expense on an ongoing basis. There are several ways he could be doing that. I plan to have your statements audited by a reputable CPA and CFP. If they prove me right, I could also turn him over to the regulatory authorities, and at a minimum he'd probably also lose his license, and if you chose to bring charges, he might be convicted of embezzlement. You need to decide what if anything you want to do about both of them."

"Is what they have each done that bad?"

"Yes, it is. If you want to talk about it now, we can. If you want to think about it while we travel, you can do that too. The choice is yours."

"Let me think about it."

"I'm not pushing you one way or the other. As your business manager, however, I wouldn't be doing my job if I didn't let you know what I suspect's been going on behind your back."

Monte retreated to the stern of the boat and silently evaluated Bessie Prince's comments as he looked out over the ocean.

About an hour later, he came forward and calmly told Bessie Prince, "I've made a decision. I'm not going to expose either Banks or Jax to either the authorities or to my daughters. I would risk possibly destroying my family forever, and even if it didn't destroy it, things would never be the same. Whatever damage those two might have done to me is minimal in the scheme of things.

"What are we talking about — a few million dollars? I have a lot more than that. Maybe I'd derive a short-term pleasurable feeling like I'd gotten retribution, but if I was the catalyst that broke up Viv's and Eve's marriages, I'd never be able to forgive myself, and even worse, I might risk alienating forever both of the daughters I love so much if they felt like I was forcing them to take sides. And Nan would feel like she had to choose sides as well. It's just not worth it. I'll miss that money but not that much.

"Does that make sense to you?"

"Yes, it does. You're right. It's minor when all's said and done. But knowing what you know about them, it's more important than ever that you distance your business affairs from your family matters and plug the leaks right now. And you have every logical reason for doing so without disclosing all to them. You need a professional team to run this much money, and I plan to put just such a team in place for you. I still want to get your brokerage statements audited. If I'm wrong and Banks isn't guilty, I think he deserves to be exonerated. And yes, I still want to set up the insurance trust to be your beneficiary."

"Neither Jax nor Banks are going to be happy."

"Make me the heavy if it'd make you feel better. I can take the heat. They'll get over it. And if they don't, tough. Don't forget. This is your money, not anyone else's. I guarantee you that they'll worry more about being on *your* bad side than you need to worry about being on theirs."

"I know you're right. I've just never been in a position like this before. I'm really not a hard person."

"That's one of the things I love about you. But get used to it. You're not a paupered social worker anymore. That's why we're going to Grand Cayman to put the first phase of my plan into action. And don't feel like a sneak. You're not. You're now a prudent businessman making prudent decisions.

"Now, since we still have another six or seven hours on this boat, I want you to read the insurance trust that I printed out when we were at my house and let me answer any questions on anything you don't understand. Then when we get to Grand Cayman you can sign the papers in front of a notary or signature guarantor. I've already taken the liberty of printing out a change of beneficiary form that I found online for your insurance policy. We'll have them FedEx the form and a copy of the trust to the insurance company from Grand Cayman. I still plan on having a tax attorney review it, and if he says it needs replacing, we'll do so."

"Should my insurance policy also be replaced?"

"No, it's a reputable company. The transaction just wasn't handled in a reputable manner by the agent. If you bailed right now, it would be at a loss since their front end costs would be netted out of your cash value. After all, they're a business not a charity, and they have to recover the money they paid Jax as a commission before you can get back to even. And I don't even want to talk about how he padded that commission. And then you'd pay a second time when you bought the new policy. It doesn't make any sense."

"You don't mess around, do you?"

"Oh, I do ... but not with business matters."

She winked. Monte felt his cheeks flush, and he turned red.

NO PUBIC RESTROOMS

CHAPTER 42

When they arrived in Grand Cayman, Monte and Bessie Prince cleared customs and got a taxi to take them to the Meridian Hotel where once again Bessie Prince had reserved a two-bedroom villa on the heart of Seven Mile Beach. The six-story Meridian was a collection of thirty-two totally self-contained luxury villas. Every villa had a clear view of the beach as well as an infinity pool and the rest of the lushly landscaped property.

Monte was awed. He turned to Bessie Prince and said, "I thought the ocean in Jamaica was clear and blue, but I swear, I think the water here is even bluer."

"Very astute observation. Seven Mile Beach has a reputation of being one of the most pristine and sandiest beaches and also having the clearest blue water in the Caribbean."

"That beach is spotless."

"And they keep it that way."

"My eyes are really starting to open up. I'm really starting to appreciate how wonderful the world outside of Detroit really is and what I've been missing. I could stay here for a long time."

"And now you have the money to travel to all these wonderful places, once we get your affairs in order. But right now, it's business before pleasure. You can always come back. It's not going anywhere. What kind of food are you in the mood for tonight?"

"Gee. I don't know. I'll let you decide."

Conclusive, All-Inclusive Confusion

"You like Mexican?'

"I've never had that much of it. I never had the money to eat out much, and mother didn't always do well with certain types of food."

"Then I'm going to introduce you to Mexican cuisine. The Coccoloba Bar and Grill is one of the finest Mexican restaurants in the Caribbean."

"I feel like such a rube up next to you."

"If you'll allow me to, I'm going to change all that."

That evening Bessie Prince began to widen Monte's horizons. They dined at the Coccoloba and had ceviche, charred octopus and pork belly tacos, and shrimp tostadas before retiring early since they had a nine o'clock appointment at the Cayman National Bank in Georgetown the following morning with Ian Whan Tong, a former attorney that Bessie Prince's husband used to deal with. He was now a senior officer at the bank. The following morning she got Monte to repack his luggage and checked them out, taking their overnight bags with them.

They caught a cab to the bank. Monte was immediately impressed with the sleek modern building with an exterior dominated by floor-to-ceiling tinted glass panels that gleamed as they reflected the tropical sunlight.

Before the meeting began, Bessie Prince got permission to use the bank's computer system so she and Monte could go on the internet and print out the most recent statement on his account with Banks. When they showed it to Whan Tong, he was awed by the amount of money involved. He assured Monte that his money would be secure at Cayman National since the bank was publicly owned and the largest bank in Grand Cayman. He explained that Cayman National was a full service bank that dealt with businesses and wealthy individuals worldwide. When he found out what Monte's background was, he told Monte about the bank's community service efforts. Monte was once again awestruck.

Whan Tong told Monte that the bank president, Susan Levy-Elliott and her assistants would personally handle his account and introduced him Ms. Levy-Elliott and her staff. They then walked Monte and Bessie Prince around the building. Monte couldn't get over how courteous everyone was.

Monte was amazed. He had never been given this level of service before. Within an hour, he had signed all the new account and transfer forms and the transfer was underway.

"That was easier than I expected. But Banks is sure going to be pissed."

"Don't let it worry you. If someone needs to take care of Banks ... well, that's why you hired me. My job is to look after you, not Banks Bridges, and I intend to do so. Now that our business is concluded in Grand Cayman, we need to get going to our next stop."

"But it's so beautiful, and we just got here," Monte said frowning. "I'm really starting find out what a wonderful world this is, but I don't have time to enjoy it."

"You will. I promise. We'll come back and let you enjoy the place once our business is concluded. Our plane isn't until this afternoon, and since we're in the middle of downtown Georgetown, why don't we go on a walking tour and then have lunch before we have to go to the airport. When we return the next time, I'll take you to Stingray City and the turtle farm."

This seemed to pacify Monte.

The bank called them a taxi, and Bessie Prince instructed the cabbie to take them to Harbour Drive. Monte found Georgetown to be extremely photogenic. The jeweled-colored wooden buildings lining the waterfront housed a mishmash of venues. They ranged from duty-free stores selling perfume and diamonds to cool cafes serving up Buddha bowls, vegan brownies, and almond-milk lattes. They walked through the Cayman National Museum, where they got a lesson in local history.

"How about some local cuisine for lunch?" Bessie Prince asked.

"Lead on, tour guide."

Monte didn't realize it, but his comment was giving Bessie Prince an idea she would share with him later.

Bessie Prince took Monte to lunch at the U'nique Restaurant. There he ordered the shrimp alfredo over penne and she got the tuna poke, which was made with sushi rice and wasabi mayo.

She let him taste hers, and he immediately reached for his water glass as the wasabi was sucked into his sinuses.

Bessie Prince laughed and said, "I didn't think you were ready for wasabi yet, but just wait, I'm sure I'll be able to refine your palette before it's all over. I'll make an adventurer out of you yet. You've already eaten foods at the hotel and here that you've never tried before."

That afternoon, they caught a flight to their next stop, Miami.

> **ROAD CLOSED HERE
> 29 SEPTEMBER
> FOR THREE NIGHTS**

CHAPTER 43

When Monte and Bessie Prince landed at Miami International, Monte wasn't as overwhelmed as he had been when he and the family had passed through there the first time on the way to Jamaica, but he still didn't feel comfortable there. It was the same menagerie of different cultures with people speaking languages he didn't understand. Everybody seemed impatient or in a hurry to go anywhere else but here, and people ignored him just as they had before. He did cling onto his carry-on bag this time as he thought about what had happened to him on his previous trip down from Detroit. He was thankful to have Bessie Prince as his companion. She seemed unphased by the organized confusion that was occurring around them as she read the signs that would take them out of the terminal and to the ground transportation area.

"I've arranged what I hope is a treat for you," she told Monte once they were in the cab.

"Take us to Kimpton Angler's Hotel in South Beach," she told the hack driver in Spanish. He responded in kind. The only word Monte caught was hotel.

"We're headed for South Beach, Monte. You're in for a treat. Whereas the Vegas strip and New Orleans' French Quarter each have their vibe, South Beach is also one of a kind. "

When they crossed over the bridge to their destination, the narrow nine-mile-long island called Maimi Beach, on the MacArthur Causeway, Monte began to understand why. He gawked at the palatial waterfront mansions. They rode down Collins Avenue where he saw milelong arrays of brand-name stores and independent boutiques mixed in with an array of restaurants and street entertainment. Bessie Prince instructed the driver to detour over to Española Way where he saw Mediterranean Revival architecture evoking quiet French and Spanish villages. He thought to himself that they must be in the people-watching capital of the world until they got to Ocean Drive where the Art Deco buildings presided over the broad palm-fringed beach. The Art Deco candy-colored buildings sparkled in the tropical light.

And then there were the profusion of beautiful people. To Monte, it seemed like a world apart — a city within a city. It appeared to him to be non-stop Hedonism, loose clothes, and he thought probably loose morality. It seemed to not only tolerate difference but to celebrate it. Body fascism seemed to be rife in the throng that ranged from scantily clad, deeply tanned skateboarders and roller skaters to body builders showing off their muscles. Monte couldn't help but think of the movie "The Birdcage."

Bessie Prince had made reservations for them at the Kimpton Angler's Hotel. It was a luxurious 132-room hotel with a touch of chic. By now, the overwhelmed Monte had begun to grow weary from the trip. He was immediately drawn to the lushness of the hotel's outside seating area where the tiles created a repeating, contemporary Escher-like style, and the natural wood seating had been arranged in a unique juxtaposition. When they went up to their suite, tropical was definitely the dominant aura as there was a stress on the unstressed. The soft tones of the décor were only interrupted by the vivid tones of the abundance of green parakeets that seemed to fly everywhere. Since they were scheduled to have a busy day the following morning, the weary travelers stayed at the hotel that night and ate at the hotel's Seawell Fish n' Oyster Restaurant.

The following morning Bessie Prince accompanied Monte to a prearranged appointment back on the mainland with the Rodriguez, Hernandez, Mena, Esteban, and Goldfarb law firm. As they walked into the large, opulent office, Monte felt out of place. The atmosphere just seemed cold and sterile to him. The somber, unsmiling receptionist peered over her half-glasses at them, sizing them up before she checked to make sure they had an appointment. She then pointed them to walk unescorted down a hall to Mr. Mena's office. His secretary seemed equally

Conclusive, All-Inclusive Confusion

dour as she looked them over before she showed them into Mena's office. He was an older man dressed in a custom-made suit. As he reached across the desk to shake hands, Monte noted that his spread-collar white shirt had French-cuffs with gold cufflinks and his wine-colored silk braces had dollar signs on them. The walls were dominated with photos of Mena and various celebrities in golf attire. Monte noted a gold Cartier Roadster watch on Mena's left arm. Monte didn't recognize it, but Bessie Prince did. She also noticed Mena's recently manicured fingernails and his razor-cut hair.

No one offered either of them coffee or tea before the secretary closed the door to leave them alone.

Bessie Prince gave Mr. Mena, as apparently he appeared to wish to be addressed, an overview of Monte's affairs. He then engaged in a long monologue using language that Monte only half understood on why their firm was superior to their competition and suggested that Monte give him a $50,000 retainer that morning to make their relationship official.

When he finished, the distressed look in Monte's eyes told Bessie Prince how unsure he was as to what he was supposed to do. Bessie Prince picked up on his vibes and took charge. She politely thanked Mena for his time and told him that this was premature since she and Monte wished to discuss the matter before they got back to him. Monte looked relieved. Bessie Prince once again picked up Monte's vibes and rose to leave.

Once they got out on the street again, Monte said, "I just didn't feel comfortable in there. Everything seemed so cold. So sterile. And did you feel like he was talking down to me?"

"Yes, I did. Because he was. It seems that he is accustomed to intimidating his clients and then have them blindly follow his directions."

"Would you mind if we keep shopping for an attorney?"

"Not at all. I could tell that you felt that way. And if it's any consolation, so did I. Let's grab some lunch and forget about him."

"Also, I didn't like that big building. There must have been fifty lawyers there."

"Actually, I think it's more like seventy."

"Maybe I'm just a rube, but I'd much rather deal with a smaller firm."

"Chemistry is important. Let me go back to the drawing board. Don't worry. We'll find someone where the chemistry is right for you. Mr. Big Shot isn't the only fish in the sea."

"I don't want to seem too forward, but, Bessie Prince, I'm starting to feel like the chemistry between us seems right."

"Thank you for saying that. The feeling is mutual, you dear sweet man. Yes, the feeling is mutual."

She squeezed his hand to reemphasize her last statement because it was true.

> **PLEASE SATANIZE YOUR HANDS HERE**

CHAPTER 44

Bessie Prince spent much of that afternoon at the hotel on her laptop. She suggested that Monte go down to the outside seating area he had found so attractive when they checked in and read a book or a magazine so she could work undisturbed. She found a U.S. News ranking of recommended law firms, amassed a list of ones that she thought fit Monte's criteria, and made some notes on the ones that interested her. She double-checked those on other websites to boil the list down even further.

When she finished, she went downstairs and found Monte.

"Please, come over here, dear, and let me bounce some things off of you. The team that I would like to see put together for you would consist of an attorney, a CFP, a CPA, and a CIA. And maybe a CPIA. Do you know what all these things are?"

"I know what a CPA and a lawyer is."

"Well, a CFP is a Certified Financial Planner — what your son-in-law, Banks, was pretending to be. You need a real one. A CIA is a Certified Internal Auditor. Remember I told you that I suspected that Banks might have been playing hanky-panky with your money? Well, I want to find out for sure. A CPIA is a Certified Professional Insurance Agent. As I told you before, I suspect strongly that your other son-in-law, Jax, also took advantage of you. Up with me so far?"

Monte nodded.

"I know this sounds like a lot of people so what I've been doing upstairs is to try to simplify the situation. Our first mission is to get you an attorney. I used a rating service to identify candidates. I then went one step farther and narrowed the list down to identify attorneys who were also CFPs. I was also looking for candidates who were either sole practitioners or had small offices instead of a giant office like we were in yesterday. I found four attorneys that could fit the bill. One is in Tampa, one's in Jacksonville, one's in Orlando, and one's in Vero Beach. There was also one in Palm Beach, but he seemed to be part of a big firm kind of like Rodriguez, Hernandez."

"I never heard of Vero Beach."

"Actually, it's the town that's the closest drive to here. It's a small, very upscale community on Florida's east coast with a laidback personality that I think would appeal to you. You just drive up I-95 or the Florida Turnpike for about three hours, and you're there. Do you want to give it a try, or do you want me to tell you about the others first?"

"You know how much I know about that sort of thing. Not much. I'm relying on you."

"Then, as long as we're this close, why don't we rent a car and drive up, assuming I can get us an appointment? The lawyer's name is Merle Connelly."

"I'm Monte Connors, and he's Merle Connelly. That almost sounds like an omen."

"Then let me see if I can get an appointment, and we'll find out."

Bessie Prince was unable to get an appointment for the following day but did secure one for the day after. They headed up the following morning.

"Since we've got all day, why don't we take the scenic route on U.S. 1 or A1A as much as we can?" Bessie Prince suggested. "That way you can see some of Florida."

"A1A?"

"Alternate U.S. 1— the road Jimmy Buffett likes to sing about."

"I love travelling with you. You know so much, and I know so little. You're better than any travel agent."

Conclusive, All-Inclusive Confusion

"And I love travelling with you, Monte. I can't tell you how refreshing your positive attitude is. Your sunshine attitude makes me happy every day."

Monte was mesmerized by the long, palm tree-lined, sandy beaches and the high-rise condos and luxurious resorts that also lined those beaches for miles in South Florida and intermingled with tiki hut-inspired bars and fabulous seafood shacks. He daydreamed as he took in the turquoise waters and the coconut-scented sunscreen, pineapple-kissed pina coladas, and lazy sunny days. He ogled the excessively manicured landscaping in Palm Beach and mentally compared it to weedy yards in Highland Park, Michigan. They passed through Delray, Jupiter, Hobe Sound, Stuart, and finally crossed over the Fort Pierce Inlet onto U.S. 1, then almost immediately back onto A1A and into the low-rise, low-density Indian River County.

Once they crossed over the line from St. Lucie County into Indian River County what they saw was almost entirely single-family residential. As they drove by gated, well-landscaped neighborhoods, he immediately thought that Vero Beach was the most attractive town he had seen on A1A. People casually talked and strolled as they waved at bicycle riders on a sidewalk that ran parallel to the two-lane highway. Vero Beach seemed almost quintessential old Florida. It was a sophisticated little beach town. The pace was just the opposite of what they had seen on Miami's South Beach. It was relaxed with walkers and bicycle riders leisurely going from one place to another. Once they got into town, Monte noted that the east/west cross streets were named in descending alphabetical order for flowers until they got to Beachland Boulevard where they turned back towards the Atlantic and drove south.

And the two-laned, pristine Ocean Drive was no different as it followed the Atlantic a few blocks away to the East. It seemed to have it all — little clutches of one and two story beachside boutiques, gift shops, sweets and ice cream parlors, jewelers, art galleries, small casual as well as fine dining restaurants — offering both sidewalk and interior dining, a park, playgrounds and picnic areas, and, of course, small hotels and motels. People meandered around as they chatted and visited in a friendly manner to each other.

"Different crowd from South Beach," Monte commented. "I don't see any narcissistic young rollerbladers, or hedonistic skateboarders in thong bikinis or sweaty body builders showing off. These folks look like real people."

"Yeah, our kind of people."

Parking was mostly streetside, and there weren't any massive parking garages.

"Bessie Prince, did you notice that there aren't any parking meters on the street?"

Then he saw why. A patrolman in a golf cart was putting chalk marks on cars' back tires so he would know if someone was hogging one of the precious parking spaces. This retro way of doing things tickled both Monte and Bessie Prince and relaxed them. They both felt like they had stepped back into an gentler, kinder time.

There seemed to be shops that filled every budget. They even saw an announcement at the park for the upcoming Saturday's farmer's market. In between and above the retail establishments were law offices, accounting firms, real estate offices, and securities brokerage houses. They were so mesmerized that they drove to Flamevine at the end the commercial part of the continuing through-street before making the block to turn around on Cardinal and retrace their steps.

They arrived back at the five-story Costa d'Este Hotel, where Bessie Prince had made reservations. The building seemed to be a throwback and had the feel of what Monte thought a mellow Florida resort was supposed to be like. But the building's design seemed perfectly current, complete with playful retro flourishes like its Fontainebleau-style porthole windows. When they got up to their room, they saw they had an ocean view from their balcony. She felt their linens. They were of rich Egyptian cotton. Both of their showers were constructed of tumbled limestone.

"You'll never guess who owns this place," Bessie Prince said, and then without waiting for Monte to respond, she added, "Emilio and Gloria Estefan. Let's unpack and go back downstairs."

As they walked around, it seemed to both of them that the restaurants had a pleasant, low-key social energy. Outside, people sat above the unspoiled beach in oversized rattan loungers and were being serviced by poolside concierges serving mojitos, frozen grapes, and spritzes of cool water and also giving people towels and sunscreen.

"Bessie Prince, you really know how to travel. I *never* dreamed I'd ever see a place like this other than on television, but it wouldn't be any fun

Conclusive, All-Inclusive Confusion

without you to share it with. The best thing I ever did was to let you convince me to let you run my affairs."

"I can say with no reservations that the reverse is also true. You are a completely delightful travel companion. Sharing this with you is most of the fun. I asked the desk clerk and she told me that if we don't want to dine in the hotel, one of the most unusual five-star restaurants in Florida is just walking distance a few blocks from here. Wanna go there tonight? It's called the Ocean Grill."

The Ocean Grill turned out to be everything she had hoped it would be and more. After all, she reasoned Monte deserved to enjoy himself. It was an eighty-year-old building constructed by Waldo Sexton, an eccentric entrepreneur, high on a sand dune. It was an wide-ranging mix of pecky cypress, mahogany, wrought iron, and Spanish antiques. Bold red and white striped exterior awnings decorated the many windows. While it looked like at first glance like a ramshackle, unpainted, weathered, one-story building that could easily tumble into the ocean, it was actually now on a solid foundation of concrete and wooden pilings after a nor'easter had once almost washed it away.

As they sat at the bar and looked out of the massive fixed glass windows at the ocean waves breaking on the beach below, the bartender gave them a laminated history of the restaurant to read. When Monte asked for a cocktail recommendation, she suggested a Pusser's Painkiller. Monte looked puzzled, but Bessie Prince reassured him that the suggestion was one she was sure he would like. Both ladies smiled when that turned out to be the case.

They finished their first drink and were about to order a second round when a hostess told them their table was ready. She accompanied them across the well-worn, sometimes uneven plank floor through the dining room filled with Waldo Sexton's eclectic mix of wood, stained glass, wrought iron, and artifacts he had collected from all parts of the globe.

"You really know how to pick 'em," Monte whispered. "I've never seen anything like this in my whole life."

He was even more impressed when he and Bessie Prince shared a bubbling crab dip and baked brie to whet their appetites before they savored their stone crab claws with creamed spinach and a sweet potato on the side.

"This trip just keeps getting better and better. I wish my girls were here with us."

"Excuse me ... Minus those pains who call themselves your sons-in-laws."

Monte smiled and said, "No excuse necessary. You hit that nail right on the head. Mind if I order another Painkiller? That was good."

"Make it two. Salud."

PLEASE SLOW DRIVELY

CHAPTER 45

The following morning Bessie Prince and Monte walked down Vero's Ocean Drive to keep their appointment with the attorney, Merle Connelly. When they walked in, a smiling receptionist immediately rose and held out her hand.

"I'm Debbie Chastain. You must be Mr. Connors and Ms. Blount. Welcome to Vero Beach."

Merle Connelly came out of the open door of his office immediately to greet them as well. The clean-cut, freshly-shaved attorney appeared to be in his forties. Instead of an expensive suit he was dressed in chinos and a blue button-down collared Oxford-cloth shirt.

"Debbie just made a fresh pot of coffee, and I was about to get a cup. Want to join me? Come on in the kitchen. I'll let you make your own since you know how you like it. Cups are in the cabinet; there's some milk in the fridge. Sugar on the table. We're not very formal around here. It's just me and Debbie. There's some doughnuts on the counter is you want one. Some paper plates in the cupboard."

He pointed at a little dinette set in the corner.

"Why don't we just pull up a chair here in the kitchen. We use it a lot of times as a conference room. Debbie, hold my calls, and will you bring me a legal pad and a pen? ... So tell me about yourself."

Monte was already starting to feel relaxed and at home. He reached for a doughnut. This is more like what he was hoping for. Bessie Prince noted his reaction.

She and Monte began to explain Monte's background and the windfall that had befallen him. Merle quietly listened and didn't interrupt as he made notes on his legal pad.

When Monte and Bessie Prince finished, he said, "That's one heck of a story, and if you'll have me, I'd love to have the opportunity to work with you ... if you'll let me. Since I'm both a tax attorney and a CFP, ... that's certified financial planner, in case you don't know ... I believe I can construct a game plan that will work well for you ... and help you put together a team who will work in your behalf."

This time Monte didn't hesitate.

"Bessie Prince, I feel good about this. Do you agree?"

"Yes, I do."

"So what do we do next? Is there a contract that I need to sign?"

"No contracts. If you become dissatisfied, you're free to go elsewhere. I've never been a person who wants to stay where I'm not wanted. And I'm not going to try to be everything. I know my limitations. I'm not a portfolio manager, and I'm not a CPA, and I'm not going to pretend to be either one of them. ... I'm also a lousy plumber and electrician, and if I swung a hammer, I'd probably hit my finger."

Monte laughed. He was really beginning to like this guy.

"The legal framework for you is going to take me some time to put together right. But one thing we can do while you're right here in front of me today, if you have the time, is for me to give you an investment primer. One of the main reasons many people make lousy, emotion-based decisions that they later regret is that they never understood things to begin with and were therefore never comfortable. Also they had false expectations. This is not rocket science. I'm not trying to make a money manager out of you. I just want you to understand what the money manager is doing and to be able comprehend what he's saying when he periodically reports in to you."

"We have nothing but time today. I just don't want to waste your day."

"You won't be wasting my day. In fact, you'll be saving me time in the long run if you understand the basics. Let's get going then. I'm going to explain things in simple terms. I'm not talking down to you. I just want to feel like you understand. A bunch of highfalutin mumbo jumbo that makes you feel dumb doesn't make me feel smart. What makes me feel smart is knowing that we're really communicating with each other. And

Conclusive, All-Inclusive Confusion

ask as many questions as you wish. The only dumb question is the one you don't ask. Now, if I sound like I'm rambling, I probably am. I'm just mentioning stuff in the order I think of it."

Merle then started with the basics, how wealth is built owning assets versus lending money to someone else so they could own assets. He talked about the types of risk. He then went over the legal investment options available. He talked about how billionaires got that way by owning a successful business and explained how the stock market was nothing more than owning a small piece of someone else's business. He then went over cycles and realistic long term return expectations. He discussed the role of dividends in the scheme of things. He talked about value stocks versus growth stocks. He discussed volatility and the difference between global companies and foreign stocks. He talked about the role of a fiduciary. Then he paused.

"Does all this seem overwhelming? If you said no, I wouldn't feel like you'd been truthful with me, and furthermore, that I failed in my mission to convey the rudiments to you. It doesn't have to be overwhelming though. You don't have to try to do it yourself. I wouldn't do that, and I know a hell of a lot more about these things than you do. That's why so many people fail. You hire a team of experts the run things for you."

"I wouldn't know where to begin."

"If you will allow me to, I will make suggestions as to who I think would be appropriate for you to have as part of your team. And also, if you permit me to, I will oversee this team, consolidate their reports into a manageable summary and then report periodically to you in layman's language. And I'll help you interpret what you hear. If I think someone needs to be replaced on the team, I'll recommend that as well. Does this make sense to you?"

"It does to me," Bessie Prince said, "but Monte, it's your money and your decision. I just know this. The so-called team … if you want to call it that … you have right now is not working out."

"Let me go on. Reputable asset managers charge a management fee based on a percentage of the assets they're managing. They do not make their money from commissions. This removes one of the age-old conflicts of interest that the industry has had in memoriam. In other words, as that Fisher guy on TV says, "we do better when our clients do better." He acts like he invented that concept, but believe me, he didn't."

Bessie Prince interrupted at this point and said, "Monte your sons-in-laws were making their money on commissions, not because they were doing you right."

Connelly remained silent and let Bessie Prince's comment soak in before continuing.

"As for me, if you were to choose to hire me to oversee things, I'd work on an hourly basis, not a percentage of assets. That would only be fair. And I'll help you negotiate the asset manager's fees down to a level that I consider to be equitable to everyone. They deserve to make a living, but it doesn't all have to come from you."

"What you're saying makes sense to me. Sounds like you have my best interest at heart."

"I do, but sleep on it. I want you to feel sure because I plan to be working closely with you."

"Well, now we need to find both a CPA and CIA," Bessie Prince said.

"I think I can help you there as well," Merle said. "Just so happens there's a lady a few blocks away who happens to be both, and I've been impressed with both her honesty and her work. I've worked with her for years. Her name's Kathryn Barton. If you wish, I can arrange an introduction.

"By the way, y'all have any plans tonight? We've got one of the best little theaters in Florida right here on the beach. It's called Riverside Theatre. Ever heard of the musical called 'Million Dollar Quartet'? It's about Elvis and all the roster at Sun Records. It's playing right now. If you want, I'll call and have some tickets put aside for you at the box office. And don't worry about money. They'll charge them to my account."

"Sounds like fun, Merle. Thanks."

"Call me after you think things over."

> GRODGE
> SALE
> 9 TO 7 FRI SAT SUN

CHAPTER 46

Monte was sold. He bubbled with enthusiasm all afternoon. This guy was not only knowledgeable, but he was also real. This was so much better than that stuffy law firm in Miami. He could hardly wait to call Merle's office the next morning and tell him it was a go. When he did, Merle asked him if he still wanted an introduction to Mrs. Barton. If so, if Bessie Prince and Monte would come down to his office, they could all take a stroll over there for him to make the introduction in person. He told Monte that he'd already taken the liberty of calling Mrs. Barton, telling her that Monte'd only be in town for a short period of time, and she'd rearranged her appointments in case he did want to come over.

These people are all so accommodating, Monte thought. *Are they typical of Vero Beach? If so, I'm really beginning to take to this place. It's sooo different from South Florida. I hope I'm right.*

Kathryn Barton reaffirmed his hope when they walked into her office on Cardinal Drive, and she greeted them as warmly as Merle Connelly had done the day before.

"I'm glad to meet you, Mrs. Barton. Thanks for taking time out of your day for us."

"It's not Mrs. Barton. Just call me Kathryn or Kathy."

"Which would you prefer? By the way, I go by Monte, and my business manager here goes by Bessie Prince."

"I go by whichever name you're most comfortable with. I'm one to some people and the other to others. Why don't we get a cup of coffee

… or a Coke if you prefer? … And then you can tell me about yourself. Merle told me it's a fascinating story, but that he'd let you tell it to me yourself."

"Oh, it definitely is," Merle said. "God smiled on him, and from what I've seen so far, he picked a really good person to smile on."

Monte smiled and began to turn red.

"Why don't I go back to my office and let you guys talk and get to know each other?"

"Great. Thanks, Merle. I'll call you later. Now, Monte and Bessie Prince, after we get our coffee, why don't we go in my conference room, so we can all sit at the same table and you won't have to look at me over my desk?"

Once they were in the conference room, Monte and Bessie Prince once again went over the same things they had told Merle the day before.

When they finished, Kathryn said, "Wow! What a story! I'd love to have the opportunity to work for you. But now let me tell you a little bit about me. It's only fair that you know my background so you can decide if I'm the person you want to hire."

After she finished, Monte looked at Bessie Prince and said, "What do you think? Have we found who we're looking for?"

"I think we have."

"Just think, two days ago, I'd never even heard of Vero Beach, and now … What can I say? … I've met some of the nicest people I think I've ever met in my whole life here."

"And the most professional," Bessie Prince added.

"So, what do we do next?"

"Not much for me to do right now. Merle needs to get the legal work done first of all. And we all need to talk again about the monthly distributions you say you want to give to each of your daughters. Merle'll be the one who will set things up to give maximum protection to them from their husbands or anybody else for that matter. One thing I can do right now when you give me copies is audit your back statements to see if I can detect any irregularities, and I do have contacts that can examine your insurance policy as well.

"Hey, welcome aboard. I will try my best not to disappoint you. Do you need to go back over to Merle's office? If so, I'll gladly take you."

Conclusive, All-Inclusive Confusion

"It's so pleasant, I think we'll just walk. You really have a lovely town here."

"And lovely, friendly people living here as well," Bessie Prince added.

"Oh, we have some sourpusses too, but they're in the minority."

When they got back over to Merle Connelly's office, Merle said, "There's one more person I want you to meet while I have you here in town. His name is Ken Ligon. He's one of the owners of Professional Advisory Services. They are a very well thought-of money management firm that happens to be local. I planned to recommend that you hire them to be part of your team. I'm not recommending that his firm manage all of your money, only a portion of it.

"As I explained to you yesterday, I want your team to have managers with diverse disciplines. Not every discipline works all the time. If you diversify, however, when one discipline or market segment is out of favor, there's a high possibility that another one will be in favor. And as I told you yesterday, I believe in cycles. Not just in the stock market but life's cycles as well. What is out of favor will cycle back and be in favor again if you just give it time. If you don't remember anything else I've said, remember this. The securities markets are a mechanism for moving money from impatient people to patient ones.

"And if you already have someone managing some of your money with that investment style, when its turn comes up at bat, you won't find yourself chasing the hot dot and missing out when it does make its move. You don't make money by chasing yesterday's winners but being on board with the winners whose turns are coming up.

"I hope you don't mind, but I took the liberty of telling Ken a little about you, and he said he would love to take you to lunch. How's that sound?"

"Yeah! Wow! I don't know what to say. Of course I don't mind."

"Then Ken will pick you up at your hotel at a quarter to twelve. He's got a table reserved for you at the Quail Valley Club, one of the most exclusive private clubs in Vero."

"Do we need to dress up?"

"Just don't wear a t-shirt. They require collared shirts. And turn your cell phone off. That's another one of their rules. Then, just relax and enjoy your meal."

> Lawn
> More
> For
> Sale

CHAPTER 47

Ken Ligon from Professional Advisory Services turned out to be an affable person about Monte's age who made both Monte and Bessie Prince feel at ease since he didn't push them to make an immediate verbal commitment or try to sign them up. He told them how his father and his partner's father had started the firm in 1977 as a alternative to traditional Wall Street marketing firms with a few local clients, how it had established a sound reputation for itself for having both knowledge and integrity and had now subsequently grown into a management firm with clients in thirty states with assets under management of over a billion dollars. He described PASI's investment philosophy of identifying large capitalization companies where they saw consistent earnings growth, dividend growth, and strong balance sheets and then combining them with bonds and small and mid-cap stocks to produce a well-rounded portfolio. He also stressed that each portfolio was customized to meet the needs of that individual client.

Both Monte and Bessie Prince were impressed and relayed that fact back to Merle later that afternoon. Merle then concluded their most recent meeting with some closing comments.

"I think we've accomplished just about everything that I hoped to accomplish for the time being. For the moment, your part of this new venture is concluded. You've met everyone local that I wanted you to meet. The ball's now in my court. I've got to structure some trusts and other legal documents for you. Then I have to finish putting together

Conclusive, All-Inclusive Confusion

what I would consider to be a team of investment professionals that will meet your needs who are within your risk parameters. I will assemble their documents and contracts for you to examine and will explain them to you. I'll negotiate fees. In the meantime, Kathryn will be working on auditing your past statements as soon as you get them to her.

"My friends, ... You're not only clients but friends. ... I think we've accomplished a lot in a short period of time, and I want to thank you for putting your trust in me. I'll do all I can do to keep it."

"I'm flabbergasted. I never dreamed when we drove up from Miami that so many good things were about to happen in only a few days."

"Let me ask you one more thing. Are you totally committed to Cayman National Bank? I.E. If a money manager wished to use a different custodian or if I could get a better deal with a different custodian, would you object?"

"I don't think so," Bessie Prince said. "We were merely parking the money somewhere to get it away and protect it from Monte's son-in-law."

"Good. I'll keep that in mind. Well, I won't get things structured overnight, but I will be diligently working on all aspects. Call me any time you want an update. We could be talking about several weeks before I have all our ducks lined up. I'd rather do it right then fast. Agreed?"

"Agreed."

Later that afternoon as Monte and Bessie Prince sat on the patio behind the iconic, historic Driftwood Resort looking out at the ocean, Monte commented, "I know I should be elated, but I'm feeling depressed that this process is about over and you'll be returning to Jamaica. ... And I may not see you again.

"Uh ... Bessie Prince, I'm going to miss you. I feel at loose ends. And quite frankly, I'm scared to deal with all of this all alone. On top of that, I now don't want to go back to Highland Park. It's like I've been living my life in a cocoon or a coma, and now I'm waking up. You've really made me want to see what a wonderful world this is and make me want to see more of it. You've made me realize just how dull and one dimensional my former life really was."

"Maybe you don't have to, my dear man, I've got another proposition for you. In addition to being your business manager, how'd you like it if I became your personal travel agent? With the money you've got, you can go anywhere on the planet as many times as you want to."

"Uh. That ... would be wonderful!, but it wouldn't be any fun unless you were there."

"Oh, but I will be, dear boy. I don't have anything to go back to. I'm a widow all alone. And Fontana Pharmacy ran me out of business. My husband was disgraced. And on top of that, he's dead. Why do I need to stay there?"

"You mean you'd go with me?"

"That's exactly what I mean. Haven't you enjoyed having me around?"

"You know I have."

"And I love being around you. Then, by golly, why not let the fun continue? If it ain't broke, don't fix it."

"You'd go with me?"

"In a heartbeat. I'll tell you what. Merle said it could be a month or so before you need to be back here to execute any papers. Let's take a trip. Ever been out west?"

"You know that I've never been anywhere except Michigan and now Jamaica."

"Ever wanted to see Yosemite or the Grand Canyon? I have."

"Yes, but I never thought it'd happen."

"Well, which one?"

"I don't know how to choose."

"Why not both? We've got a month more or less until we have to be back in Vero. And we don't have to rush here the moment he gets everything together."

"What about the girls?"

"Simple! Just tell 'em we're going. After all, you're the patriarch who still runs this family, not them."

"OK! Let's do it."

"And after that, I've got an even better idea. How'd you like to sail around the world?"

"I don't know how to sail."

"You don't have to. I've been looking into it. I found a luxury cruise ship that goes around the world in 154 days. And the one I looked into had a two-bedroom owner's suite on the stern of the ship. It goes to forty-one countries on six continents.

"Monte, you only live once. You're going to have Merle and his team in place to run things. You don't need to be there. Just meet with them periodically. And think, no Jax or Banks to foul things up on this trip. And who knows? We may find some place that you'd want to stay permanently. Just imagine."

"I am. I am. Let's do it. I will be the first …

"… And only client …

"… Of Madame Blount's …

"… Prestige …

" …Travel Agency."

"I like the sound of that."

"Monte, this isn't the end of your story. It's only the beginning. Yes, it may the last chapter of one story, but it's the first chapter of one even more exciting."

"Will you help me write it?"

"You betcha, that is, … if you want me to."

"Is the Pope Catholic?"

> JESUS ↘ SAVE
> CAN
> EVEN YOU

EPILOGUE

As bright as the future was for Monte and Bessie Prince, the same couldn't be said about some of their former acquaintances and relatives.

When Niko Caputo, aka Potsy Potter, went to the Montego Bay Airport, he was arrested for drug smuggling thanks to an anonymous tip. Potsy recognized what he thought was Neil's handwriting on the note in the bag of cocaine that said "This should bring you some walking around money. Have a good trip. Tell the old gang hello. N" This forged note plus the amount of cocaine Bessie Prince had put in the bag convinced Jamaican authorities that he was a dealer. He was convicted and sentenced to five years in the General Penitentiary in Kingston known as the Brick Yard.

He vowed revenge. His pent up anger finally triggered a mild stroke. His cellmate, a Rastafarian, convinced him that the stroke had been brought on by his never ending pent-up anger and that if he would adopt the passive Rastafarian philosophy, he could head off future health problems. Before his release, Niko had converted to Rastafarianism, and set up housekeeping with a woman Rasta in the Blue Mountains. He decided to raise ganja and remain in Jamaica.

As for Neil-the-Heel Hackinrider, once Monte and Bessie Prince left for parts unknown, he threw in the towel on what had become a losing scam. He managed to get out of Jamaica before Potsy dropped his name as the author of the anonymous note and fly back to Las Vegas to look for a fresh victim. It was a good thing he did since Potsy finally made the

Conclusive, All-Inclusive Confusion

decision to give up his name to the Jamaican authorities in an effort to save his own hide. Since Jamaican authorities couldn't pin the drugs on Neil for sure and he was now out of their jurisdiction, they let the matter drop. But Neil's name was added to a computer data base of undesirable aliens that they didn't want back in their country in the future.

Neil did not have to wait long for a sucker to come along. Jax Magnus couldn't get Neil's gummy bear presentation out of his head once he got home and went back to the dreary job of prying the collections out of paycheck-to-paycheck clients who owned the debit policies he sold.

When Jax found out that Monte had restructured his affairs to preclude his daughters from being taken advantage of, his distress level ratcheted up even more.

There had to be an easier way. He visualized himself night and day as becoming a multi-millionaire business celebrity whose picture appeared in the *Wall Street Journal*, *Forbes*, and other publications. He saw himself relaxing at resorts like the one in Jamaica far away from Michigan winters. This is the life he deserved — with or without his wife.

I'm better than this.

He used the business card Neil had given him to track Neil down in Vegas. Neil convinced Jax not to just invest the million and half in the profits he had made from Monte's insurance sale but investing as well the half a million he had planned to use to pay taxes. Then Neil changed his name and disappeared to the Bahamas. When the tax bill came due the following April, the now desperate Jax falsified his income and secretly forged Eve's signature on the tax return. When he was subsequently convicted of tax fraud and tax evasion, she decided to get a divorce.

Neil's flirtation with wealth turned out to be short-lived as well. He met a financial cryptocurrency guru named Samuel Bankman-Fried. Bankman-Fried who convinced Neil to invest the entire amount into the stock in his company, FTX Trading Limited.

Unknown to Neil, FTX operated under a veneer of legitimacy. FTX was touted as having the industry's best-in-class controls, including a proprietary risk engine, and that it adhered to specific protection principles and detailed terms of service. Neil didn't know that Bankman-Fried had built a house of cards based up deception. When Bankman-Fried was brought up by the SEC on charges of violating the antifraud provisions of the Securities Act of 1933 and the Securities Exchange Act of 1934, Neil's investment was completely wiped out.

As for Rosa Caputo, aka Foxy-Roxy Savage, chickens from her past came back to roost. Thanks to Bessie Prince, the general manager at Seascape of Runaway Bay anonymously received two DVDs. One was for "Pirates of the Caribbean—XXX." The second one was for "Orgy Pirates of the Caribbean—XXX." A note accompanied the DVD's telling him the reason they had been sent.

A second set was sent to the local chapter of the National League of Decency and the Jamaica Gleaner. When a reporter was dispatched to interview Foxy-Roxy for a human interest article, she was relieved of her duties at the hotel. She chose to return to the U.S., hook up again with the movie company, and convince them to sign her to a deal to star in two pornographic musicals entitled "Deep Throated Anne Bonny—XXX" and "Mary Read, Harlot Queen of the Caribbean—XXX." She was nominated for the Best Actress award at the AVN Awards, the "Oscars" for the adult movie industry, for her role as Anne Bonny and later won it when she played Mary Read. Her male co-star, Ram Rod, won AVN's Best Dick Award for his portrayal of Calico Jack in "Orgy Pirates of the Caribbean—XXX."

When Banks Bridges returned to Detroit and found out that Monte had transferred his entire account to Cayman National Bank, he was devastated. In one short month he had gone from his firm's President's Club to having no book at all. He soon found himself on probation for lack of production. Before going on his Jamaican vacation, he had given all his small accounts away and put his eggs in a single basket, that basket being Beauregard Montgomery Connors. Now a fox had raided his henhouse and stolen all his eggs leaving him left only with an empty basket and a worthless nest. On top of that, he now had no way to recover the money he had lost in the Jamaican jewelry debacle and would have to eat the loss himself at a time he had no income coming in.

Banks' regional manager hounded him for an explanation on what he had done so wrong that he had let a whale like Monte get away, especially since Monte was family. Then Banks found out that a CPA in Vero Beach, Florida, named Kathryn Barton was auditing Monte's back statements.

Monte's hired a CPA and professional auditor? What will she do if she discovers the truth? Will Monte turn me in, or will he overlook my transgressions since I'm

Conclusive, All-Inclusive Confusion

family. Will he tell Viv? Whatever happens, things will never be the same between any of us. My God, what else can go wrong?

His paranoia grew daily, and he began to take out his frustrations on Viv. She began to dread being around him.

Banks became increasingly afraid that his irate regional manager would begin examining Monte's statements closely as well as finding out why Monte had transferred his account and also discover that Banks had been misappropriating some of Monte's money.

The straw that broke the camel's back was when the regional manager of Banks' firm decided to consolidate Detroit's two one-man offices into one and go with the rookie that Banks had given his book to. He told Banks that if he wished to remain with the firm, he'd be an administrative assistant to this now-up-and coming broker. Rather than face this disgrace, Banks simply resigned. All the while, this was what the regional manager was hoping he'd do.

Banks' drinking increased, and he began to smoke pot as well. Every time Viv came home from her job and saw him lounging on the couch drinking a beer, he imagined that she was looking at him and thinking what a loser she had married. So one day while Viv was at work, he took what remained of his Monte stash, along with Viv's jewelry, and simply vanished. The family never saw Banks Bridges again. The abandoned car was found several states away for sale in a used car lot.

Hans and Nan decided with Monte's blessing to continue their honeymoon at the honeymoon capital of Jamaica, Negril. Bessie Prince recommended the exclusive Azul Beach Resort. Monte covered the cost. The two lovebirds took her up on her recommendation and never regretted their choice.

Hans began to have second thoughts about his checkered past and his nefarious motives. For the first time in his life, he found out he had a conscience and was really in love. His deceptions began to bother him and cause him to brood. Nan began to notice his moodiness and questioned him about what was bothering him.

Finally Hans decided to clear the air once and for all and risk alienating his new bride instead of risking the truth about his background coming out later. He confessed all, including the fact that she was not Mrs. Hans Robin Roman but instead Mrs. Billy Don Brown.

He also admitted that the timing of his stay at Seascape at Runaway Bay had not been a complete coincidence. In a settlement move with both the Nevada Attorney General and the IRS because of past tax problems that resulted from his use of aliases and false social security numbers to avoid reporting his own income, he had agreed to secretly work with them as they attempted to build a case against Neil and Potsy. In return, his own infractions had been forgiven. They had also been paying for his stay at the hotel. While he had not been immediately successful, both agencies agreed that the information he provided them did add to their hopes nabbing both con men in the future.

He promised that, because of Nan, he was now a changed man. He told her that if she couldn't live with a former liar and a cheat and wanted a divorce, he would understand and not create any obstacles.

"I wouldn't blame you if you divorced me, but let me say this, I love you with all my heart and always will."

After giving the matter some thought, Nan proposed to him that they take his inglorious past and use it for the framework of a novel. Since she was a creative writing instructor, she would help him write it. The resulting novel was published and became a bestseller. A movie company optioned it and then made it into a feature film starring John Travolta.

Billy Don and Nan then settled down and began to raise a family. Monte and Bessie Prince became doting grandparents.

Kathryn Barton confirmed that what Bessie Prince had told Monte about Banks and Jax was true, but Monte decided to sit on the information since exposing them would not be worth destabilizing the family and possibly alienating his daughters.

And you're probably wondering what happened to Monte and Bessie Prince. When they returned from a trip to Nevada, they returned to Vero Beach and finished getting Monte's business affairs in order. Then, since Monte had discovered what a wonderful place the world truly was and since his worst nightmare was going back to his former dull existence in Highland Park, Michigan, Bessie Prince booked them a two-bedroom suite on a luxury cruise ship circumnavigating the planet and became Monte's exclusive tour guide.

She chose for them to occupy the owner's suite on the 382 passenger Silver Whisper, part of the Silversea Cruises fleet. They felt like they were living the life of Riley and were as happy as a hound dog with two tails

Conclusive, All-Inclusive Confusion

since their suite even came complete with butler service. It was a one hundred and fifty-four-day cruise that left Fort Lauderdale and ended up in Venice, Italy. As she had told him previously, they visited fifty-one ports in thirty-one countries. Midway through the cruise, while in the Greek isles, they got the captain to marry them on the main in a shipboard wedding. They invited all the passengers on the ship to attend. Their well-attended wedding became one of the highlights of the cruise, and the pictures of it became part of the cruise line's marketing brochure.

When they finally returned, Monte and Bessie Prince eventually bought an oceanfront condo in Vero Beach, joined the Quail Valley Club, and hired a golf pro to teach them to play golf and took up tennis as well. They also purchased a home in the exclusive Lyford Cay community on New Providence Island in the Bahamas and hired the golf pro at the Lyford Cay Club to help them further refine their golf playing skills.

Each of their daughters and Monte's grandchildren had an open invitation to visit. All they had to do when they wanted to visit was to charge their airline ticket to Monte's account with Madame Blount's Prestige Travel Agency.

And of course, Monte and Bessie Prince continued to travel.

They are currently down-under in Australia and New Zealand and still as just much in love and just as jubilant as two boardinghouse pups.

YA, MON
YU DUN

Sneak Peek
Excerpt from "SNAKEBIT"
by David Beckwith

CHAPTER 1

FRIDAY A.M.

Normally Matthew "Ace" Booker would be going to work or already be there on a Friday morning, but today was different. He hadn't told his wife, Jo Ann, any differently when he left the house that morning. Jo Ann would find out soon enough about the changes the family would soon be facing when the shit hit the fan. Right now Ace just want some time alone to think things out — as if there were anything to think out.

Ace had volunteered to drop Matthias, who they called Matty, off at the Bowes-Carlson Day School, one of Miami's most prestigious private secondary schools and where he was in the ninth grade and had gotten Jo Ann to agree to pick Matty up that afternoon. He'd prefer to not go back over there to the school once the cat was out of the bag.

Thank goodness it's Friday, and I've got the weekend to maybe sort some things out. After he left the school, he thought about the tuition at Bowes-Carlson — and the family's reputation.

I guess those days are over. ... The public schools were good enough for me.

Matt's head was in the clouds. He was barely aware of the rush hour traffic around him.

Matt got on I95 where he knew he had better get his head out of the cloud unless he wanted to get in an accident. On 95 he had to not only drive for himself but everyone else as well. He had to be alert every second behind the wheel. People wouldn't hesitate to cut him off if they thought they could get in front of him. Everybody was tailgating. And God help you if you're walking in a crosswalk since people would turn right in front of you if they thought they could get away with it. Respect for other people simply did not exist. How different it was from the part of Florida where he was raised! His mind drifted back to earlier days.

Thank the good Lord, he'd be getting off of 95 at Florida Highway 41 headed west.

With a little luck and the creek don't rise in less than three-quarters of an hour I'll be in Coopertown.

Ace was jarred back to the present by the bone-shattering music of a car to the right of his gleaming black Beemer XM SUV.

What a piece of doggy dung!

It was old and had been made dicey by cheap add-ons that probably came from Pep Boys or AutoZone. It had multiple mismatched hub caps and a broken suspension. The windows were down. He guessed that they probably couldn't be rolled up. At least twice the value of the car had been invested in a stereo system, which, while loud, was obviously hacked together and sounded like crap. He recognized the Latin boogaloo sounds of Bobby Valentin's "Use It Before You Lose It" blasting loud enough to be heard all the way to Little Havana.

At least they're not playing that rap crap.

Both men in the car had Miami Heat baseball caps, what they called la viser de béis bols, on, of course, backwards. The driver was only partially visible since his seat was pushed back almost to the car's B-pillar, but Ace could see he was wearing a number thirty-two Heat jersey; his companion wore number thirty-three. He assumed they were probably Cuban, but they could have been Puerto Rican since they were listening to Puerto Rican music. They looked a little too old to be gang members.

At least they have good tastes in jersey numbers — Shaq and Alonzo — two of the all-time greats.

A gap opened in the lane front of him, and the driver veered entirely too dangerously close to Ace in his rush to fill it. Ace hit his brake to prevent a rearend collision, but the car kicked up a rock that cracked his windshield.

Thanks, asshole for hurting my expensive car with that junker ... Oh well, after today it might not make much difference anyway ... The company won't be making the lease payments on it so bye, dye Beemer. It was nice while it lasted. ... Oh, well. ... Screw all of you ... every last one of you.

Finally he reached the highway 836 exit that passed through Little Havana. The ghetto cruiser took that exit as well.

Figures! This ain't my day in any way, shape, or form.

Sneak Peak

He saw a gas station that served Cuban coffee and decided to buy a cup so that the noisy twosome could get well ahead of him. It had some of the flaky guava pastry that Cubans call pastelitos de guayaba that looked good, so he bought one of them as well. Ace's ploy worked, and he was able to drive the rest of the way in peace as he listened with the volume set at a reasonable level to "I Feel A Tequila (Coming On)" on his Gary Roland and the Landsharks CD.

Much better. Actually, a tequila would taste good about right now.

When saw the familiar Coopertown Restaurant, he knew he'd arrived at Coopertown, population eight. The residents were the Kennon family, all of whom were direct descendents of the Coopers. The restaurant was a one-story ramshackle, reverse-board-and-batting building with a gas pump in front of it. A sign on the window said **OPEN**. Another sign beneath the window said **COLD BEER**. A third sign with a bold arrow announced where to go for airboat information.

Originally Coopertown was a Seminole Indian village occupied by Jimmy Osceola and a few Indians until Bob Cooper decided to convert it into Coopertown. The three Cooper brothers were a Missouri family who had migrated to the Everglades from Melbourne, Florida, looking for a better place to go frog hunting.

By 1945, Bob Cooper's small frogging boat became an accidental tourist attraction of sorts when curious tourists began to stop by and offer to pay him to take them out on his airboat. He decided to build a small passenger airboat to accommodate them, and he found himself now to be in the airboat tour business.

After that Bob's brother, Jay, built a fish and tackle shop that was also a gas station, and his other brother, Marion, opened a small stand to sell sodas, sandwiches, and frog legs to the airboat passengers. This led to serving complete meals — fried gator tail nuggets and catfish, and what he called the best (and only) hamburgers in town.

Word spread far beyond Coopertown about his down-home, Everglades-style cooking. The diners' list became almost too numerous to list. It included Doris Day, Dennis Weaver, Burt Reynolds, Dana Andrews, Ron Howard, Ferlin Husky, Slim Whitman, Mickey Mantle, Billy Martin, Jake Scott, Chuck Norris, Kurt Russell, Mariel Hemingway, Raul Julia, and Beverly D'Angelo, just to name a few. The movies "Invasion USA" and "Mean Season" were shot there as well.

Ace parked his clean car next to a dirty pickup and reached into the backseat to get out his sea mist colored Igloo Tag Along Too cooler.

I'll take a leak and get some beer and ice and some Doritos to take out on the boat. Modelo ... might as well get a good beer since this might be my last trip for a long while.

He spoke briefly to Jesse Kennon, the owner. He had phoned ahead to ask Kennon to make sure he had a full tank of gas. Kennon reassured him that the boat was gassed up and ready to go. Ace headed over to the dock where he kept his two-seater airboat, *The Offshore Account*. He smiled since only he knew that the boat's name held more of a meaning for him than anyone else, including his wife, realized. No one was there. Just a well. He wasn't in the mood to make any more small talk anyway. Ace sighed as he untied his airboat.

Soon Ace was shooting across the Glades. He popped his first beer of the day.

To think that this once covered over 11,000 square miles. And there's over ten thousand islands. ... Whoa! ... And also, amazingly enough, it channels 1.7 billion gallons of water a day into the ocean. Man oh man!

He didn't bother to get out the Asset Alliance baseball cap he kept on the boat. As the boat picked up speed, it would only blow off anyway.

Shiiit! With their problems, maybe that'd be for the best.

What looked to a novice like miles of flat land was in fact extensive wetlands perfect for aquatic creatures, and an airboat was the only link to what dry hammocks and tree-covered islands were out there. Whereas the water was shallow, it was no place for swimming. Some days the wonder of it all made Ace's head spin when he thought about how the tides, the salinity, the wind, the moon phase, the depth, the bait, the currents, and the time of day all came into play. But today Ace was preoccupied with other things.

Ace had been around boats since he was knee high to a bullfrog. His daddy and granddaddy both had been Gulf commercial fishermen up the state. They were simple, hard-working, marginally educated people — the backbone of America.

To this day, Crawfordville, the town Ace was born and raised in, remained one of Florida's best-kept secrets. It was still "Old Florida," the way Florida used to be before high rises and condos erased the beaches. To this day, there were still no buildings over three stories high. It had beautiful beaches where both people and pets were welcome to walk its fine, white, sugary sands;

enjoy beautiful clear waters of the Gulf of Mexico; and watch dolphins frolic offshore. Sometimes they seemed almost close enough to touch. Sea turtles still visited its beaches each year. Immense sand dunes lorded over the cape instead of high-rise condos. In the evenings, spectators were treated to spectacular sunsets as the sun went down over the Gulf. At night the sea oats seemed to dance in the moonlight as they were brushed by light ocean breezes.

Alligator Point, a narrow peninsula about twenty miles long, was about an hour east of Panama City and a couple of hours away from Tallahassee, the state capitol. Crawfordville was the home for the St. Joseph Peninsula State Park and the neighbor to both Apalachicola and St. George Island.

Crawfordville's bay was laden with fish, scallops shrimp, oysters, and crabs, which had provided Ace's family with a living for two generations. Apalachicola Bay oysters were considered by aficionados to be the sweetest in the nation. The grouper, flounder, red fish, sea trout, snapper, pompano, and cobia attracted sports fishermen as well, keeping the charter boats busy.

Growing up, when he wasn't in school, Ace helped is dad on the boat, but his parents made it clear that getting an education was always to be their son's number one priority since he had always proven to be a good student. No one in the family had ever gotten a college degree, and they were determined that Ace be the first.

Most local fishermen's children wound up doing what their forebears before them had done, making a living from the Gulf, but times were changing. Overfishing and the high level of bycatch were endangering the oceans' ecosystems. Illegal fishing was raping and pillaging the wild. Foreign competition from loosely regulated parts of the world was on the rise. Bottom trawling was destroying the fishing beds. Pollution was exacerbating fishermen's problems. His parents wanted their son to do better. Jack, his father, continued to do the only thing he knew how to do — fish. Martha, his mother, cleaned motel rooms and took in sewing parttime. They tried to set good examples for Ace morally as well. The family attended the Abundant Life Community Church on a regular basis.

Matthew managed to qualify for the Florida Bright Futures scholarship program that paid his tuition and fees and attended the University of Florida. His parents began to call him Ace after he got an almost perfect score on his SAT. The nickname stuck. His parents covered his remaining costs, and he graduated with an accounting degree and soon afterwards passed his CPA exams on his first attempt.

Matthew Booker became one of the prides of Crawfordville and Wakulla County — the local boy who rose above his humble blue-collar beginnings and made good in the white-collar world. Jolene Maxwell, the longstanding Clerk of Court and Comptroller for Wakulla County, saw his potential as a political asset for her and despite his youth and lack of experience, she gave him a job working in her office. He made sure that she never regretted giving him a chance. He instituted systems and updates that made her office a technological model for other Clerk of Court offices throughout the state. He also became a regular speaker at civic clubs, charity fundraisers, and on other affairs, like local school career days, he made sure to spread goodwill for his boss.

Ace became active with the eight-county Big Bend Chapter of the Florida Government Finance Officers Association and served on the FGFOA's Technical Legislative Resources Committee. It wasn't long before he was invited to speak at their statewide meetings and other conventions for public officials on the technological efficiencies he had brought to Maxwell's office.

Jack and Martha's long term goal had been realized. Ace, the nickname they had given him, seemed to be coming more fitting than ever. Their sacrifices and efforts had not been in vain. Their son was a success. They could hold their head up with anyone in town and say with pride, "That's my son."

They became even prouder yet when Ace married Jo Ann Peeples, the daughter and only child of the owner of Crawfordville's only local bank, the Paradise Financial Savings Bank, and their grandson, Matthias, who they called Matty, was born.

Ace's growing stature did not go unnoticed. It attracted the attention of Alpha Partners, a money management hedge firm in Miami. They made him such a lucrative offer to be their comptroller that he couldn't refuse accept, and the Bookers were off to South Florida. With Ace to help them open doors, Asset Alliance began to manage and invest public funds throughout the state, including those in Wakulla County. Ace was promoted from being only the firm's comptroller to being a partner as well and a member of their investment committee.

Life was good for the Bookers. They lived in a ritzy neighborhood, drove expensive cars, belonged to the right clubs, and enrolled Matty in the exclusive Cushman School. If the people of Crawfordville had been proud

Sneak Peak

of Ace before, then, he was now a rock star in their eyes.

I didn't think anything could possibly go wrong but look at me now. Today my whole world is about to turn to shit.

End Chapter 1 Excerpt

Thank you for reading.
Please review this book. Reviews
help others find Absolutely Amazing eBooks and
inspire us to keep providing these marvelous tales.
If you would like to be put on our email list
to receive updates on new releases,
contests, and promotions, please go to
AbsolutelyAmazingEbooks.com and sign up.

About the Author

David Beckwith is a three-generation native of Greenville, Mississippi, with a BBA and an MBA from Ole Miss. His parents owned an independent cash commodity trading firm which also cleared securities trades through Goodbody & Co. David spent 40 years in the securities business, the first half of his career with Bache & Co. and its successors, the second half with Morgan Stanley. He retired as a Senior Vice President with approximately $500 million in responsibilities. For 25 years he has served as an adjunct professor at five different universities.

His first book was a narrative nonfiction work published by the University of Alabama Press in 2009 entitled *A New Day In The Delta*. The Mississippi Institute of Arts and Letters chose it as the runner-up for nonfiction book of the year. The book is often compared to Pat Conroy's *The Water Is Wide*. David started writing the Will and Betsy Black Adventure Series in 2010.

Moving to Key West, David Beckwith was tapped to write a book review column for the Key West *Citizen*, which David continues to produce on a weekly basis.

For sales, editorial information, subsidiary rights information
or a catalog, please write or phone or e-mail
Absolutely Amazing eBooks
Manhanset House
Shelter Island Hts., New York 11965-0342, US
Tel: 212-427-7139
www.ibooksinc.com
bricktower@aol.com
www.IngramContent.com

For sales in the UK and Europe please contact our distributor,
Gazelle Book Services
White Cross Mills
Lancaster, LA1 4XS, UK
Tel: (01524) 68765 Fax: (01524) 63232
email: jacky@gazellebooks.co.uk